Deadly Keepsakes

Other Books by

Award-Winning Author

Anita Dickason

Tracker Novels

Sentinels of the Night

Going Gone!

Au79

Operation Navajo

Paranormal Suspense

Not Dead

Crime Thriller

Deadly Business

anitadickason.com

Deadly Keepsakes

Anita Dickason

Mystic Circle Books

This is a work of fiction. Names, characters, places, and incidents either are the product of the author's imagination or are used fictitiously, and any resemblance to actual persons living or dead, events, or locales is entirely coincidental.

Publisher: Mystic Circle Books
Dallas, Texas
Cover Design: Mystic Circle Books & Designs, LLC
Editor: Jennie Rosenblum:
https://jenniereads.com

ISBN:
978-1-7340821-8-0 (paperback)
978-1-7340821-9-7 (hardback)
978-1-958464-00-7 (eBook)

Library of Congress Control Number: 2022909416

Acknowledgments

To my daughter,
Christy Kay,
for her innovative ideas and expertise, without which I could not have written this book.

Elizabeth Vansyckle
for sharing her hospice nursing expertise and experiences.

Pat Pratt
Chris Cook
Jennie Rosenblum
for their invaluable suggestions, editing, and critiques.

Vicki King
for sharing her interest in the history of the Top O' Hill Terrace, an infamous Texas gambling casino, and the poker chips. It was the inspiration for the plot.

The

past

becomes

a

deadly

future!

Chapter 1

The dead had no fears, worries, or timetables. Yet, the dead had triggered the cold, spiderlike fingers of anxiety racing up and down Tori Winters' spine. Nothing was as dangerous as a lonely, fog-laden, narrow, winding county road on a pitch-black night in the middle of nowhere. Hidden within the tendrils of swirling mist, the curves and ditches became the enemy.

Her back rigid, Tori leaned forward, her gaze probing the barely visible road. Visions of oncoming traffic flashed in her mind. Was she even in her lane of traffic?

She'd already missed the turn to the Russell farm. Now, she couldn't find a driveway. Muttering under her breath, Tori rolled to a stop. She really was in a pickle. If she couldn't see the edge of the road, how could she possibly turn the car around and not dump it in the ditch?

Tori spun the wheel, inched back and stopped. Then twisted the tires in the opposite direction, this time going forward. Each movement pushed her further into the middle of the road. Her heart pounded at the thought of another vehicle. Would the driver see her in time?

Finally, the car was pointed in the right direction with all four tires on the roadway, leaving Tori hot and sweaty from the hair-raising effort. The glance at the dashboard clock didn't help. Though the dead weren't in a hurry, the delay worried her.

The call from Amelia Russell had caught Tori by surprise. Ravaged by cancer, Amelia's father had been sent home to die. Horace Milburn became her patient. A hospice nurse, the caretaker for the dying, she visited once a week, monitoring his condition and medications. Over the last few weeks, there'd been significant improvement, which was why his death was unexpected.

With a sigh of relief, she turned onto the long dirt road leading to the old, rambling farmhouse. The porch light illuminating the front yard was a welcome sight. She parked near a black pickup and grabbed the large, zippered tote bag packed with her equipment from the front seat.

A dog growled as she slid out of the car, raising her neck's hackles. Surely, they hadn't let the dog loose, a fifty-some pound pit bull with a mean disposition. Tori hesitated, wondering whether to get back in the car and honk the horn. Then she spotted the animal in a pen at the corner of the house. The gate was closed. Reassured, she trotted to the front porch and clamored up the wooden steps.

The front door swung open. Charlie Russell stood in the doorway. His eyes narrowed in anger. "What took you so long?"

The man, tall and overweight, with beefy arms and

shoulders, was belligerent and had an arrogant, know-it-all attitude. From the get-go, Tori had taken a dislike to him. During her numerous visits, his treatment of his wife, falling just short of abuse, at least in her presence, set her nerves on edge.

From her diminutive five-foot-three, one-hundred and ten-pound frame, Tori glowered up at him, refusing to let him intimidate her.

"I got here as soon as I could. Am I coming in, or do I call the sheriff's department and let them handle this?"

He grunted and stepped back.

Tori brushed by him. Amelia rushed out of the hallway leading to the bedrooms. Gaunt with a thin face, she always appeared tired and washed out. The woman habitually wore long-sleeved shirts. Tori had often wondered what they hid.

Tears streamed down her cheeks as her hands fluttered in the air. "Tori. I'm so glad to see you. When I got home, I ... uh, I looked to see if Daddy was awake." A sob erupted. "He ... he was dead."

Behind her, Charlie snorted. "For cripes sake, quit your damn blubbering. The old man's been dying for months."

Amelia gulped. She shot a fearful look at her husband and wiped her face with her sleeve.

Anger surged at Charlie's cruelty, but Tori had to choke it back. It wouldn't help Amelia. "Losing a loved one is never easy, even when it's expected. Let's go see your father."

During her final examination, a family member had to be present. In this case, Amelia had been her father's primary caregiver. From the beginning, her husband made it clear he didn't want any part of taking care of Horace.

Amelia nodded and led the way to the bedroom.

As Tori gloved up, her gaze swept the room. A bed was on one side with a table next to it and a chair. A wheelchair was pushed into a corner. Against the opposite wall was the dresser with bottles of medicine on top and a small TV. The top half of the hospital-style bed was upright, propping Horace up.

A rush of sadness swept over her as she looked at the kindly face. She had liked this old man. Despite the cancer consuming his body and the horrific pain, Horace never lost his lively sense of humor.

Tori pulled the chair closer to the bed. "Amelia, why don't you sit here." She'd learned that getting the family to talk about the deceased helped ease the grief. "Tell me more about your father."

Calmer, Amelia sat and began to speak.

Listening, Tori started the all too familiar routine. She removed a clipboard with an attached form from her bag. After entering the results of her brief examination, Tori turned her attention to the drugs and the chart with the dates and times Amelia gave Horace his medicine. The last entry was at noon.

Before Tori could destroy the remaining drugs, she had to itemize each prescription. Though she hated interrupting Amelia's recollections, the woman had to witness the inventory.

She touched Amelia's shoulder. When she looked up,

Tori said, "I'm going to check the medications. You'll need to initial the count."

Tori wrote down the date of the prescription, then dumped the contents into her hand. While Amelia watched, Tori counted aloud as she dropped each pill back into the bottle. After she wrote the number on the form, Amelia initialed it, and Tori moved to the next drug. The last one was oxycodone, a powerful narcotic for pain. When she finished, alarm stirred inside her. There should have been eighteen tablets, not twelve.

She wrote down the number. While Amelia initialed, Tori's thoughts raced. What happened to them? Several possibilities sprang to mind. Someone stole them or, for some reason, threw them away. Did Horace take them? Or did someone help Horace into the grave? A possibility that sent chills racing through her. Tori recapped the bottle, setting it alongside the others.

Amelia handed her the clipboard. "Is everything okay?"

So much for my poker face, Tori thought. "Oh, yes."

"What now?"

Tori moved the chair away from the bed. "Please, sit back down. I'm almost done."

Her hands tightly gripped the clipboard and pen as she leaned over the body. Her gaze scrutinized every detail of Horace's face. There appeared to be a bluish tint around his lips, a sign of an overdose. Though it was difficult to be certain as the room was poorly lit. In the hallway, she heard a rustling sound. *Charlie? Was he out there listening?* The thought ratcheted the fear roiling inside her.

If there was a question of foul play, procedures were set up to protect the nurse. But there was a distinct difference between reading what to do in a classroom and coming face-to-face with a killer.

In a casual tone, one she hoped would allay any suspicions, she asked, "Amelia, what did Horace eat today?"

A look of surprise flitted across Amelia's face. "His normal breakfast, oatmeal and orange juice. Before I left, I fixed him a bowl of chicken noodle soup." She sniffed. "It was always his favorite."

As Tori wrote, she asked, "What time did you leave?"

"Two or so. I went into town to babysit for my sister. She was late, so it made me late getting home. That's when I found him and called you."

Charlie stepped into the doorway. He growled, "What's with the questions?"

Tori couldn't let him see her fear. Instead, she shrugged as if the question was unimportant and continued to write. "Information for the doctor."

"When is the ambulance getting here?"

"I haven't called them yet."

"Why not? You told us that you could, what was the word you used—pronounce. Yeah, that was it. You could pronounce death, and the doctor signs the death certificate. All we have to do is bury him. It's obvious he's dead. So, what's the hold-up?"

Despite the sick feeling inside her, Tori snapped back. "Mr. Russell, there are certain steps I must follow. I'll tell you when I'm done."

His lips thinned, and his eyes narrowed as he stared at Tori. When he turned, his gaze lingered on the neat row of bottles on the dresser before walking out.

At the expression on his face, she shivered. If Horace had been murdered, help wasn't nearby. Pulling the phone from her pocket, she hurriedly punched the speed dial for the medical examiner. She had already given him a heads-up about Horace before leaving her house.

One of the assistant lab technicians answered.

"Mickey, it's Tori. I'm at the Russell house."

"Hi, Tori. Doc said you'd be calling. Is this the Horace Milburn case?"

"Yes."

From outside the door, she heard a noise. She twisted to look, but the doorway was empty.

"Is everything consistent with his death?"

Tori stared at the body.

"Tori? Did you hear me? Is Mr. Milburn's death natural?"

She took a deep breath. "No," then paused before adding, "I haven't called the ambulance."

"Aw hell! Did I understand *you've* got a code red?"

"Yes. Go ahead and call. I'll finish here, so everything's done when the ambulance arrives." She hoped he understood her double talk.

"Hang on, let me get to another phone, so I can call 911."

While waiting, she continued the conversation as if Mickey still listened.

A few minutes later, he was back. "Sheriff's department

is on the way. ETA, fifteen minutes. Are you safe?"

"No, not yet."

"Get out of there. Can you stay on the phone with me?"

She said, more double talk, "No. I have the form in my car. Once Mrs. Russell signs it, I'm finished." She hoped Mickey understood she was headed outside to her car.

Tori disconnected and stuck the phone in her back pocket. After stripping off the gloves, she shoved them in another pocket. Before slinging the tote bag over her shoulder, she stuffed the clipboard and medication log inside.

"Amelia, why don't you wait in the living room. I need to get a form from my car."

Resigned, Amelia's shoulders slumped as she lightly touched her father's face and walked out.

Tori pulled out her phone. After quickly snapping pictures, she strode toward the living room. *Don't panic,* she kept telling herself.

Seated in a lounge chair with a bottle in his hand, Charlie took a deep swig of beer. Amelia had settled onto the couch.

"Mr. Russell, the ambulance should be here in a few minutes."

From across the room, his unblinking gaze watched her. He smirked. Fear bubbled inside her as Tori forced herself to slowly walk when every instinct screamed—run.

Closing the door behind her, she sucked in a deep breath of relief and pulled the keys from her pocket. She trotted down the steps and headed toward her car. A menacing growl erupted, stopping her in her tracks. Tori slowly twisted, looking toward the sound. Fear streamed through her. The dog stood by the open gate. How did it get open? Then she knew. The reason for the malicious smile on Charlie's face.

During her time in the ER, she'd seen firsthand the horrific results of a dog's attack. She had to move, but where? The dog would be on her before she could get to the front door. Besides, she'd bet Charlie had locked it. The only chance was the car.

Snarling, the animal watched her. Tori slipped the bag from her shoulder. Her movements were cautious as she wrapped the straps around her hand. It wasn't much, but it was heavy. Tori could swing it, maybe deflect the animal. In her other hand, she shifted the keys. Her thumb was poised near the button to unlock the doors.

Despite the overwhelming panic pushing her to run, she took a slow step back, then another. The dog started toward her. The driver's side was too far away. She'd never make it. The only hope was the passenger side. Her hip bumped the front of the car. Her back against it, Tori sidled along the side. The dog was only a few feet away. Its nose pulled back as the animal snarled. Strands of drool dripped from the open jaws.

Tori's elbow struck the side mirror. She eased around it, never taking her eyes off the dog. Uncurling her fist, the bag slid to the ground. She reached out. When she felt the edge of the handle, her thumb jabbed the button to unlock the door. Headlights lit up the yard as Tori jerked the door open. Stumbling around it, she dove inside, frantically reaching to shut it before the dog could follow.

Huddled against the seat, gasping and wheezing, Tori couldn't stop the tremors rocking her body. Horrified, she watched as the dog attacked. Incensed, its body slammed against the car again and again.

In the distance, she heard the sounds of a siren that slowly died away as flashing red and blue lights illuminated the front yard.

Charlie stepped out the front door. He shouted, and the dog trotted up to him. He grabbed the animal by the collar and dragged it to the pen, where he slammed the gate shut.

Tori opened the door and stepped out. Still shaking, she clung to it to keep from collapsing. A deputy sheriff raced toward her.

"Are you okay?"

She nodded.

"We saw the dog when we pulled in. I thought I might have to shoot it. Are you the nurse?"

"Yes. Tori Winters."

"Deputy Hillard. This is my partner, Deputy Jackson."

Tori nodded to the second deputy, who bent over to pick up her bag and hand it to her.

"Tell us what's going on," Deputy Hillard said.

Before Tori could answer, Charlie walked up. He gave the two deputies a hard look. "What are you doing here?"

Deputy Hillard's eyes shifted over him. "We received a call about a death."

"No reason for you to be here. Winters," he nodded toward Tori, "is a hospice nurse and is supposed to take care of all the paperwork. We were told the cops wouldn't be involved."

Hillard said, "Are you Charlie Russell?"

"Yeah."

"Mr. Russell, step back to the porch. We'll talk to you in a few minutes."

Tori didn't miss the flash of anger in Charlie's eyes, tinged with a trace of fear. She edged away from the deputies, giving them room to react.

"You can't tell me what to do on my property."

"Mr. Russell, I will only tell you one more time. Go back to the porch."

Charlie stared at the two men facing him, their legs spread wide, each with a hand resting on the butt of his gun. Muttering curses under his breath, he turned and walked up the steps.

While Jackson watched Charlie, Hillard turned back to Tori. "What happened?"

In a few succinct sentences, she filled him in on her suspicions.

Deputy Jackson spoke up. "You actually believe old man Milburn has been murdered?"

"I believe there is a strong possibility. It's why I'm having the body transported to the morgue."

Jackson looked at Hillard. "I'll notify homicide."

Hillard said, "Let's go inside."

Tori followed him.

When he reached the porch, Deputy Hillard said, "Mr. Russell, we need to examine Mr. Milburn's bedroom."

Charlie roared. "You got no right to come into my house without a warrant. What's that woman been telling you?"

"It's routine when there is an unattended death."

"He's an old man, and he died. If there's anything wrong, it's her fault. She's in charge of the case and his medications."

Red flags sprang up in Tori's mind. No one had mentioned drugs.

Shouting, Charlie waved his hands. "No reason for you to be here."

"Mr. Russell, we're going inside."

His eyes narrowed as he fisted his hands. "Not without a warrant, you're not. If you try, I'll sue you and your entire department."

"Step aside, Mr. Russell."

His shoulders hunched forward. "Lay a hand on me, and I'll charge you with assault."

Hillard took a step, grabbed Charlie's arm, twisted it, and shoved him against the wall. Jackson ran past Tori and up the steps to help. Within seconds, Charlie was handcuffed. Still screaming curses and threats about lawsuits, Jackson hauled him to the squad car.

Tori followed Hillard inside the house. Amelia stood near the door, a frightened look on her face. "What happened?"

The deputy said, "Mrs. Russell, there is a question about Mr. Milburn's death."

Bewildered, Amelia looked at Tori, then back at the

deputy. "I don't understand. What's wrong? What do you mean there's a question?"

"Please have a seat. I'll talk to you in a few minutes."

Her voice rose. "What did you do to my husband?"

"He's outside with my partner. He's fine. Please wait in the living room."

Tori stepped past him. "This way."

Once they were in the bedroom, Deputy Hillard shut the door.

She pulled out her checklist and the medication log from her tote bag. As she handed them to the deputy, Tori explained their purpose and added, "Did you notice Russell's comment about the drugs?"

"Yes, I did."

Tori stepped toward the dresser. "Where is it?" She spun. "There! On the nightstand. Someone moved it. The bottle was on the dresser when I walked out."

She pulled out her phone, tapped the screen and handed it to Hillard. "I took pictures before I left."

From the angle of the shot, Tori had caught the table and what was on top, a box of tissues, a half-filled bottle of water, a book with glasses on top, a remote control, and the lamp. Now, the bottle of oxycodone was next to the book. It wasn't the only change.

"The bed covers."

"What about them?" the deputy asked.

"They aren't in the same position."

"The crime scene officer will download the pictures. I'll make sure you have it before you leave." He laid it on the dresser and stepped toward the bed. "I've known Mr. Milburn since I was a kid. He owned a small grocery store ten miles or so from here. The building's still there. He always had a jar of free candy." He turned toward Tori. "Tell me about the dog?"

"It was locked inside the pen when I got here. But when I walked outside, the gate was open. I barely made it to my car."

"Why were you outside?"

"Under normal circumstances, the body is taken to the mortuary. If the death is suspicious, then it goes to the medical examiner. Procedures are in place to ensure our safety, a code word. The ME asks if the death is consistent with the patient's condition. If a nurse says no, the ME immediately calls 911. We're instructed to leave the house and wait for the police to arrive. I told Mrs. Russell I was going to my car to get a form."

She stopped. A frown crossed her face. "Right before I called, Charlie walked in and saw the bottles I had lined up. I think he was in the hallway listening to the conversation. He would have known I was going to my car."

Deputy Hillard mused, "He opens the pen and lets the dog loose. As big as that one is, it would have torn you apart. He comes in here and moves the bottle." His gaze shifted to the body. "I wonder if we'll find Horace's fingerprints on it. Did the Russells know about the inventory?" He gestured toward the prescription bottles.

"No, it's not something we explain to the family. Still, he could have heard my conversation with Amelia when I verified the inventory. But what did he hope to gain by siccing his dog on me?" A shudder rolled over her at the memory of those nightmarish moments.

Hillard said, "A good way to keep you from talking and get rid of your paperwork. No risk to him, let the dog take care of his problem. If you did survive, it would be his word against yours. Did he know we had been called?"

The color leached from her face. "No," she whispered.

"Could Mr. Milburn have deliberately taken those pills?"

Pulling herself together, she said, "No. Horace hasn't been able to walk by himself for several weeks. When I arrived, the bottles were on the dresser. If Horace tried to get to them, he would have ended up on the floor."

"What was Horace's mental condition?"

"Alert, still mentally sharp."

"Would he knowingly have swallowed that many pills?"

"No. I don't believe he would."

"Is there a way someone could have given Mr. Milburn the pills without him knowing it?"

Realization dawned. "Pudding."

"What?"

"If Horace had trouble swallowing the pills, I told Amelia to crush the pills and mix them into pudding. A temporary method until I could get his prescriptions changed. Oxycodone is water-soluble but has a foul taste. It's why we recommend pudding."

Her gut tightened from the sudden rush of anger at the

image of Horace innocently eating a bowl of pudding laced with a deadly dose of oxycodone.

"We'll check the kitchen, see what we can find. Let's go into the living room. I want to talk to Mrs. Russell."

"What about her husband?"

"We can't hold him. All we have right now are your suspicions, and it's not enough to charge him. If the medical examiner finds something, it's a new ballgame."

"The dog?"

"Again, no proof he intended to harm you. I'll question him about it. That's all I can do at the moment."

As they walked into the living room, the front door opened, and two more officers came in. Hillard led them to the bedroom.

While she waited, Tori sat in a chair across from Amelia. Hunched over in the corner of the sofa, her hands were tightly clasped in her lap. She refused to look at Tori.

The EMTs with a stretcher were the next to arrive. Once Horace had been loaded into the ambulance, Tori told Deputy Hillard she was leaving and asked for her phone. As she strode out, Charlie Russell walked toward the house, followed by Deputy Jackson. As he passed, Russell whispered, "You're a dead woman."

It was the beginning of her descent into a living hell of fear.

Chapter 2

She was running, the dog snapping at her heels. She stumbled. The dog lunged toward her. Her screams turned into musical chimes, breaking through the nightmare.

Who would be calling this early? Tori rolled to look at the clock. "Cripes," she muttered and flopped back against the pillow. She'd forgotten to set the dang alarm. Her boss probably wanted to know why Tori wasn't in her office.

On her way home, she had called Janet Norton. Stunned by what happened, Janet set up the early morning meeting to review the Milburn case file.

Sluggish from the troubled night's sleep, Tori staggered into the bathroom. Once she got her act together, she'd call and explain. Feeling somewhat better after a hot shower, she towel-dried her hair, pulling it into a ponytail before dressing in jeans and a t-shirt.

In the kitchen, she punched the button to start the coffee machine. The aroma wafting in the air boosted her spirits. This time when the phone rang, Tori reached for it. Not bothering to look at the screen, she answered, "Janet, I'm—"

A male voice cut her off. "Ms. Winters, this is assistant district attorney Kermit Layton. I've been trying to reach you to discuss Horace Milburn's death."

Her brief sense of composure plummeted. "He was murdered." It wasn't a question.

"We're not certain, which is why I need to see you in my office. How soon can you be here?"

Tori looked down at her attire. She couldn't go dressed like this. "An hour."

"All right. Please bring your records for the Milburn case with you." He disconnected.

Tori had hoped she'd been wrong, but Layton's call tied her gut in a knot. She shut off the coffee pot and tapped the speed dial.

Janet answered, "Tori, where are you?"

"At home. I forgot to set the alarm. I got a call from Kermit Layton in the district attorney's office. He wants to see the files."

"When?"

"In an hour."

"I'll meet you there."

In the underground parking lot of the Greene County Government building, Tori took the elevator to the second floor.

After giving her name to the secretary, she was ushered into Layton's office. A short, thickset man with thinning brown hair and spectacles rose.

"Ms. Winters, thank you for being so prompt. Please have a seat."

They shook hands, and Tori settled into the chair. "Janet Norton, head of the hospice program, is on her way."

He flipped a switch on his phone and said, "Helen, when Janet Norton arrives, have her come in."

He turned his attention back to Tori. A kindly look settled on his face. "I understand you had quite a time of it last night."

A shudder rippled over Tori before she could stop it. "That's putting it mildly." She handed him the medical records containing her reports and notes for Horace. "These are the files you requested."

The door opened, and Janet walked in. After the introductions, Mr. Layton said, "Please tell me what happened last night. I've read the reports and have the documents and pictures you gave to Deputy Hillard but would like to hear it from you."

Tori began, starting with the phone call from Amelia Russell. The telling took several minutes.

When she finished, Mr. Layton said, "Before you arrived, the medical examiner called. He put a rush on the toxicology report. The cause of death was a narcotic overdose. Is it possible Mr. Milburn committed suicide?"

Janet gasped but didn't say anything.

Tori sucked in a deep breath as anger surged through her. "No, sir. I don't believe he did. Mr. Milburn could not walk without assistance. His medication was kept on a dresser on the opposite side of the room. The first time I went into his bedroom, the bottle of oxycodone was on the dresser."

"Are you absolutely certain Mr. Milburn couldn't have reached the pills?"

"Yes."

Persistent, Layton continued to question Tori about how an overdose ended up in Horace. When she mentioned pudding, his eyebrows shot up. He picked up a stapled document and perused it. "The medical examiner found chocolate pudding in his stomach."

"Dear God," Janet whispered.

Tori's voice trembled. "I asked Mrs. Russell what her father had eaten. I wrote down her answer. She didn't say anything about pudding."

Layton flipped through the documents. Finding the one he wanted, he said, "Deputy Hillard reported that he found a partial bowl of chocolate pudding in the refrigerator." He wrote on the pad in front of him. Then his fingers tapped the form Tori had filled out. "Please explain Mrs. Russell's initials and this inventory."

Janet leaned forward. "I might be able to answer that better than Tori. Prescriptions are inventoried to be sure none of the drugs are missing. This is done with a family member present. Once the medications are accounted for, the drugs are destroyed, again in the presence of a family member. Several months ago, one of my nurses was charged with stealing drugs. While she was ultimately proved innocent, the difficulties of establishing her innocence identified a gap in our procedures."

"I remember the case. Another attorney in our office was assigned to it."

Janet said, "Even though a family member was present, the individual later claimed she didn't really see what the nurse was doing and could have easily slipped the pills into her pocket. As a result, I initiated a new procedure. As the drugs are counted, there is verbal confirmation of the count, then the written verification, which the family member acknowledges with their initials."

"Smart move." Mr. Layton looked at Tori. "Did you say anything to Mrs. Russell about the missing pills?"

"No, I didn't."

"Why not?"

"I was afraid. The Russell's home is in a remote section of the county. I decided to wait until the police arrived and let them question the Russells."

"Did the Russells know about the inventory?"

"I never told them."

Janet said, "We keep the family members informed of our procedures. There are, however, some details, especially those at the time of death, we don't discuss as it can be disconcerting."

"I think that's enough for now. We'll be talking again. A warrant has been issued for Charlie Russell's arrest, charging him with homicide. We've already found a motive. His father-in-law had a very healthy bank account. About six months ago, Milburn sold all his property, home and business. His daughter inherits all the money."

He motioned toward the file folder Tori had provided.

"I may have more questions after I've had an opportunity to review your case files."

Tori said, "You'll find that Horace's condition had improved. I guess Charlie didn't want to wait. There is something else you should know. Charlie said I was a dead woman."

"Considering what happened with the dog, I'll have the police chief assign extra patrol around your house. Be alert to where you are at all times. Make sure you keep your cellphone handy."

As Janet and Tori stood, Mr. Layton said, "One more thing. Despite the attempt on your life, you are to be commended for your head's-up thinking. What you did may make the difference between a killer walking away or paying for his crime."

While they waited for the elevator, Janet said, "Go home. I've already arranged for another nurse to take over your cases for a few days."

Charlie Russell's arrest was headline news that evening. She hoped it would put an end to her fears.

The next day, Tori walked out of her house to find her tires slashed. She was sure the culprit was one of Charlie's brothers, Earl or Farley. She had met them while visiting Horace. Like Charlie, they were crude and borderline abusive with their leering looks and comments. She called the police and Layton's office. An officer showed up. After taking a report, he assured her the police were keeping an eye on the house.

When she moved to Springfield, Tori sold her mother's

home in Joplin. Uncertain about her plans, she rented a small two-bedroom house. Located in an older section of town, it was set back from the road and surrounded by trees. At the time, she liked the seclusion. Now, she didn't. It was too easy for someone to approach the house and not be seen from the road.

Three days later, Charlie bonded out of jail, and the phone calls started. Every call was the same. A muffled voice told her what would happen if she testified. Her face wouldn't be so pretty. The police discovered the calls were coming from a prepaid phone. No way to trace them. She disconnected the landline. Then she started to receive them on her cellphone. In desperation, she changed the number. Only Mr. Layton and Janet had the new one.

The day after she changed her phone number, her tires were slashed a second time. While she waited at the repair shop, she received a call from Layton. He wanted her in his office the next day to be prepped for her testimony in court.

The fear, a living entity inside her, kicked her gut as she thought about walking into the courtroom. The threats and malicious damage had taken a toll. Still, she refused to allow the trepidation to overcome her sense of right and wrong.

The session in Layton's office turned into an all-day event as Layton, and another attorney went over her case records with the proverbial fine-tooth comb. Tori had become the prosecutor's star witness. Charlie Russell's attorney had attempted to have the case thrown out, claiming Horace committed suicide.

After the grueling meeting, she stopped to pick up a

pizza on her way home. When Tori opened the front door, a cry of anguish erupted. The tote bag and pizza box slid from her seemingly lifeless hands.

In stunned disbelief, Tori stared at obscene graffiti spraypainted on the walls. Sofa and chair cushions were ripped apart; the stuffing pulled out. Lamps, her mother's knickknacks, everything that could be broken covered the carpet.

Stunned by the destruction, Tori stumbled into the kitchen. The refrigerator door hung open, the contents dumped on the floor or thrown against the walls and cabinets. Broken dishes littered the floor.

Tori didn't believe it could be worse until she stepped into the bedroom. Dresser drawers hung open. The contents were sliced into ribbons and strewn across the floor. Her clothes in the closet had met the same fate. Nothing had missed the knife, not even the mattress and bed covers. But it wasn't the sight of the sickening damage that triggered a sharp jab of terror. It was the words spraypainted on the wall—YOU TALK YOU DIE.

Amidst the wreckage, she spotted her mother's beloved jewelry box. It had been a wedding present from Tori's father. She fell to her knees. Tori's hands scrabbled through pieces of clothing, stuffing from the mattress and broken glass and ceramics, searching for her jewelry. It was all gone. While the simple earrings and bracelets weren't valuable, losing her mother's cameo brooch necklace was the final blow. Inside was a picture of her parents.

Sobs racked her body while she gently picked up the

broken pieces of the box, clasping them to her chest. She cried until there were no tears left. For a long time, Tori sat in the debris. Her heart felt as shredded as the clothes around her. Finally, she picked herself up and walked out to retrieve the phone from the tote bag lying next to the pizza box.

It didn't take long for police officers to fill her house, taking pictures and dusting for fingerprints. Tucked into a corner in the living room, Tori tried to stay out of their way. Just when she believed everyone who could show up had arrived, Mr. Layton walked in.

An officer escorted him through the house before he walked over to her. He dropped to one knee. A look of sympathy filled his eyes. "Tori, I am so sorry. I can arrange to have one of the officers take you to a hotel for the night, then pick you up in the morning."

Tori shook her head. "Thank you, but I'm staying here."

"All right. An officer will be parked outside all night. I'll see you in the morning."

After the police left, the thought of eating pizza made her physically ill. Tori stuck the box in the refrigerator. At least, it still worked. The Russells hadn't thought to look in the washer or dryer. So she had a few clothes, jeans, sweatpants, and t-shirts. But the only outfit suitable to appear in court was what she had worn to the meeting with Layton.

Once they were washed, dried and ready for the next day, Tori collapsed on what remained of the bed. Even in the dark, it seemed she could see the words spraypainted on the bedroom wall—you talk you die.

Scared, the crying jag she'd held at bay erupted. Curled in a ball, Tori pulled a tattered blanket over her as sobs shook her body. Would she ever feel safe again? At least for tonight, she had an officer in her front yard. Still, it wasn't enough to stop her from tossing and turning, waiting for the alarm to buzz.

The next morning, a police car followed her to the courthouse. Inside, she was escorted to a barebones witness room with nothing but a table, chairs and outdated magazines. Unable to sit, she paced. Tori couldn't rid her thoughts of the frightening words on her bedroom wall. Fear paralyzed her when the door opened, and the bailiff called her name. Tori's legs wouldn't move. It was the image of Horace, flashing in her mind, that propelled her forward.

As Tori entered the courtroom, all eyes turned toward her. Charlie shifted in his chair to stare at her. His face had the look of a man who believed he would get away with murder. Refusing to be cowed, a grim determination settled over her. It was up to her to see that he didn't. Tori squared her shoulders and marched to the witness stand.

She answered Layton's questions with a calm, assertive tone. When the defense attorney went on the attack, deriding her experience and knowledge, Tori never faltered. She repudiated every attempt to prove Horace committed suicide. After all, the attorney argued, his fingerprint was on the bottle. All the while, her gaze never wavered as she stared at Charlie Russell.

Once the trial was finished, it took the jury less than an hour to find Charlie guilty of murder. Seated in the courtroom, she had the satisfaction of seeing his smug look vanish when the judge read the verdict. He would be in prison for a long time.

Her body limp with relief, she walked out of the courthouse. There shouldn't be any more threats. The terror was over. Now, she had to get her life back together. On her way home, Tori stopped at the store and bought several boxes of large trash bags.

The cleanup was a daunting task. Most everything in the house had to be hauled to the dump. An officer who had responded to her call gave her the names of two fellow officers. They did odd jobs. She'd already called them, and they would be at her house bright and early the next morning with a trailer.

Despite her resolve, Tori couldn't stop the sense of desolation that swept over her when she walked into the house. Much of what was maliciously destroyed was all she had left of her mother. It was like losing her all over again.

Swiping at the tears with her hand, Tori headed to the bedroom and changed into jeans and a sweatshirt. She started in the living room, sweeping the debris onto a dustpan. Once a bag was full, she set it by the front door. Tori leaned over to grab another bag from the box. A gunshot cracked. The front window exploded, spewing glass across the room.

Tori belly-flopped, scrambling to get behind the remains of the sofa. The Russells! They'd just tried to kill her. Frantic at the thought they would break into the house, she scooted along the floor, keeping her head down. Believing the threat was over, she'd left the phone in the bedroom.

Once she reached the hallway, she stood and raced into the room, slamming the door behind her, then locking it. She upended the tote bag on the bed and grabbed the phone. Huddled in a corner, she waited for the police to arrive.

An officer took another report, and another crime scene unit showed up. The only evidence was the bullet, and it wasn't to be found. Missing its intended target, it went across the room and through the window facing the backyard. Though officers tromped around the woods, they couldn't find it. And again, there was no evidence to connect the Russells.

This time, she wasn't staying in the house. One of the officers followed her to a hotel. Ensconced in a room, Tori lay on the bed and thought.

She didn't have a doubt it was either Earl or Farley who fired the shot. Just as she was certain, they would try again. The cops couldn't protect her. From now on, it was up to her.

As long as she was in Springfield, she wasn't safe. As the old saying went, she needed to get out of Dodge, pronto. Thankfully, she had some savings and the money from her mother's estate. Not much, but she could pay the bills and not starve.

On the way to the house the next morning, she called

Janet and resigned. A task she could tick off her to-do list. Next was to find an apartment, though it would have to wait until she dealt with the cleaning crew.

When Tori arrived, the officers had backed a large flat-bed trailer up to the front door. She told them to start hauling everything out of the living room, then left. She found a furnished one-bedroom apartment in a gated community available on a monthly lease. While pricey, it would keep her away from the Russell's prying eyes. And it gave her time to figure out where to go. Somewhere far away from Springfield.

On the way back to the house, she called the owner. When the woman showed up, she examined the damage with dismay. When Tori said she was moving, the owner didn't bother to hide her relief.

After the woman left, Tori filled trash bags and tossed them on the trailer. Twice a black pickup drove by and honked as she stood outside. The driver, Earl Russell, waved.

Feeling like a hunted animal, Tori called the police and Mr. Layton. She was told they couldn't stop someone from driving past her house. She asked about a restraining order. Mr. Layton said the judge would deny the order until they had proof the Russells were involved.

It took several days to clean out the house. The day she finished, she met with the owner and handed over the keys. The new clothes, personal items she salvaged, and boxes belonging to her mother she had stored in the attic were already in the new apartment. When Tori drove onto the parking lot, the satisfying clang of the gate as it shut gave her a sense of security.

Seated at the small kitchen table with a glass of wine, crackers and chunks of cheese, she opened her new laptop. Thankfully, the Russells missed seeing the auxiliary hard drive in one of the desk drawers. She uploaded her records and files, including her nursing and training certificates. Those she would need in her hunt for a new job. Tori was thinking of Denver, a safe distance from Springfield.

The mail was next. For days, she had shoved it into a box. Bills were laid aside to pay, and advertising in another pile to throw out. Near the bottom, she picked up an envelope from an attorney in Granbury, Texas, a town she'd never heard of. The short letter only added to the mystery, simply asking she call at her earliest convenience.

Tori pulled Granbury up on the computer. Why would an attorney in a small town southwest of Fort Worth with a population of just over 10,000 want to talk to her? Satisfying her curiosity would have to wait.

The next morning, she called. Tori was immediately transferred when she identified herself to the woman who answered.

"Ms. Winters, this is Jonah Greer. Thank you for calling. I was beginning to wonder if you received my letter."

"There was an unfortunate delay." She wasn't about to explain why.

"I would like to meet with you as soon as possible to

discuss a legal issue. I can be in Springfield tomorrow."

Surprised, it took a moment for her to respond. "A legal issue?"

"It involves an inheritance. I don't want to discuss the details over the phone."

When he said inheritance, she began to suspect the call was a scam. Her parents and her grandparents on both sides of her family were dead. She didn't have any other relatives.

"Mr. Greer, are you sure you have the right person?"

"Yes, I am. What time and where can I meet you tomorrow?"

"I'm sorry, but a meeting isn't possible right now. Would you please tell me what this is about?"

"As I said, I don't want to go over the details on the phone."

"Then it will have to wait. I'll call back."

Persistent, the man said, "Ms. Winters, I would like to resolve this matter as soon as possible. Surely there is a way I can have a few minutes of your time."

"No, there isn't. I will contact you." She disconnected, laying the phone aside.

How odd. Despite the man's assurance that she was the right person, Tori didn't believe it. Even if it were true, it had to be some remote connection, which meant it couldn't be a big deal, especially since he wanted to meet her in Springfield. Wouldn't it have been the other way around if there was anything to it?

Pushing the thoughts aside, Tori turned her attention

back to finding a job. Everything had to wait until she got out of Springfield, including some attorney who didn't want to explain.

Online, she searched various databases. Several hospitals in the Denver area had openings. Tori spent the rest of the day filling out applications.

It wasn't until she snuggled into bed that the strange call began to niggle at her. While she still didn't believe it would amount to a hill of beans, it did open the door to other possibilities. Nothing said she had to go to Denver. What if she went to Texas?

The next morning, Tori shifted her search to the Fort Worth area. New hospitals were popping up, all advertising for nurses. It certainly appeared more lucrative than Denver. The more she thought, the more she was convinced heading to Texas made sense. Granbury was close to Fort Worth. Even if the deal with Greer turned out to be a dud, who would think of looking for her in a small town?

It wasn't until later that day that fear sparked a new sense of urgency. A black pickup was parked near the entrance as she drove out the gate. Farley gave her a smug smile as she drove past his truck.

Frightened, Tori turned around. As she waited for the gate to open, Farley honked his horn, waving to her as he drove off.

Forget finding a job. She had to get out of town. She couldn't hole up in the apartment forever. But how could she keep Earl and Farley from finding her?

Janet's phone call about a farewell party sparked an

idea. She took a chance leaving the apartment, but it was worth the risk.

By the time Tori left, everyone believed she was headed to Colorado. When she contacted the apartment complex manager, Tori casually mentioned moving to Colorado. She lied to Kermit Layton when she called to let him know she was leaving town.

Hoping she'd laid a false trail, her next step was to get another car. It had taken two trips to haul her belongings to the apartment. While she didn't have much left, Tori wasn't leaving any of it behind. Though it put a major dent in her savings, she traded her car for an SUV.

The sun had barely crested the horizon when she snuck out of town. It wasn't until Tori was on the freeway that she finally relaxed, breathing a heavy sigh of relief. The sparse traffic made it easy to see any black pickups behind her. The road was clear, and Tori was on her way to Texas. She had escaped.

Chapter 3

Granbury, Texas

Late in the afternoon, Tori shifted to relieve the strain on her back. It had been a long drive, and her only stops were for gas. Each time, she scrutinized the parking lot before pulling out. The closer she got to Texas, the less she worried, though Tori still kept an eye on the traffic behind her.

About mid-morning, she had called the attorney's office. When Jonah Greer came on the line, Tori told him she was on her way to Granbury. Though he stammered in surprise, he quickly recovered and made an appointment for the following morning.

At the sight of the LaQuinta sign, she breathed a sigh of relief. She was over five hundred miles from the Russells, and they didn't know where to find her.

Parked under the hotel canopy, Tori crawled out and stretched. Check-in was a mere formality since she had the foresight to call ahead for a reservation. She moved the car and retrieved the small bag she'd bought, hoping the contents would tide her over until she knew where she'd be living.

In a ground-floor room, fading sunlight streamed through the window facing the rear of the hotel. Drawn by the view, Tori dumped the tote bag and carry-all on a chair and walked to the window. With a wistful look, she stared at the pool, wishing for a swimsuit. If she stayed here for a few days, she might shop for one. Then berated herself. No matter how enticing the pool looked, she couldn't waste money on something as impractical as a swimsuit.

After setting the alarm on her phone, she stacked the pillows on the bed, kicked off her shoes and collapsed. For the first time since Horace Milburn died, she felt safe. Odd, until her life was threatened, Tori never knew what a precious feeling it was.

Still, she couldn't stop the memories. Physically she'd escaped, but emotionally she was still in Springfield, reliving the horrific events. It had to stop. She couldn't spend the rest of her life dragging around what had happened.

A trickle of excitement coursed through Tori as her resolve built, raising her spirits. No matter what happened at the meeting, she was in Texas, and limitless possibilities were ahead.

A good night's sleep and she'd be ready to face whatever the next day brought.

Too restless to stay at the hotel, she was early. Parked

near the Granbury Historic Square, she stared at a western-style building. Across the front, broad-brush letters proclaimed *Greer Law Firm,* with a painted herd of cattle and horses above the name. Seeing the attractive building eased some of her initial suspicions. It would seem the law firm was on the up and up. Intrigued, she wondered if there might be something to Greer's mysterious phone call.

Impatient, Tori fidgeted. Fingers drummed the steering wheel. A foot tapped the floorboard. She dithered, stay in the car or go inside.

Unable to sit any longer, she jumped out of the car. Walking might work off the excess energy bubbling inside her. For a moment, she admired the Hood County courthouse, topped by an impressive clock tower, before strolling along the sidewalk. The charm of the quaint stores captivated her. If this was her new home, which was a big if, the shops would be fun to explore.

By the time she circled the square, even stopping to gaze at the window displays, she still had time to kill. *Might as well wait inside,* she thought. A bell tinkled as she entered. A tastefully decorated waiting room contained several chairs and tables.

Seated behind an elegant desk, an older woman with distinguished grey hair looked up. A momentary expression of shock crossed her face before she said, "May I help you?"

How odd. It was as if the woman knew her, but that was impossible. "I'm Tori Winters. I have an appointment, but I know I'm early. I thought I could wait here."

The woman stared at her with a keen look of interest. "Ms. Winters, I'm Linda Keaton. I'm so happy to meet you. Please have a seat." She motioned toward a small table in the corner of the room. "There is fresh coffee. Soda and bottles of water are in the refrigerator under the table. Please help yourself. I'll let Mr. Greer know you are here."

Desperately wanting a cup, Tori eyed the coffee bar. Not a good idea, though. As nervous as she was, she'd probably spill it. The white dress trimmed with yellow daisies was the only dress she had. She'd purchased it after the Russells trashed her clothes and couldn't afford to buy another.

She perched on the edge of the chair and glanced at the magazines on the table before turning her attention to the paintings on the wall. Bluebonnets, cattle, and horses were the predominant themes. Tori wondered if local artists painted them. Before she could examine them further, the woman returned.

"Ms. Winters, please follow me."

Tori took a deep breath and stood, hoping this wouldn't turn into a waste of her time.

The secretary directed her toward an office at the end of the short hall. An older man, late fifties, rose to greet her when Tori entered. Thick, deep-brown hair sprinkled with strands of grey was brushed back from a broad brow. Bright blue eyes twinkled in a lined, tanned face.

He extended his hand across the desk. "Ms. Winters, I'm Jonah Greer. So glad to meet you." *Linda warned me, but I didn't believe her. My god, she's the spitting image of Elly,* he thought. Russet hair tinged with red hung over her shoulders and framed an oval face with deep-set, grey eyes topped by long, sharp eyebrows. She was even the same size, small framed and about five-foot-three. He already knew she was twenty-seven. Catching himself staring, he quickly said, "Please have a seat."

She'd caught the shock that flashed in his eyes. *What's with the strange looks?* As Tori settled into a chair, she surreptitiously glanced down to make sure something wasn't wrong with her attire.

"How was your trip?"

"Uneventful and long."

"I'm surprised you decided to travel to Texas. As I explained, I was happy to fly to Springfield."

"Um, yes. I appreciate the thought."

"Is this your first trip to Texas?"

"Yes. I haven't done much traveling, Mr. Greer."

"Please, it's Jonah. May I call you Tori? We're pretty informal here."

"Yes," she murmured.

"Would you like a cup of coffee, water or soda?"

"No thanks." The small talk was becoming an irritation. Tori wanted him to get on with it. Tell her why she was here.

"I'm sure you have questions, so let me start by explaining … " he shuffled the papers on his desk.

Thank god, she thought, *finally.*

"I am the executor for Elly Leichter's estate."

"Who?" Tori asked, straightening in the chair. Elly was her middle name. It had to be a coincidence.

"Your grandmother."

Hope plummeted. "Mr. Greer ... Jonah. There must be some mistake. You have the wrong woman. My mother, who passed away a few months ago, was the last relative I had. I've never heard of Elly Leichter."

Taken aback, Jonah said, "Oh, my. This does make things a bit more difficult."

"I'm sorry to have taken up your time." She rose, struggling to hide the disappointment.

"Tori, I have a copy of your birth certificate."

She fell back into the chair. "What! How did you—"

He interrupted. "Before I contacted you, I thoroughly investigated your background. I can assure you that you are indeed Elly Leichter's granddaughter."

"I don't understand."

"Your father, Michael, was Elly's son."

"His name was Winters, not Leichter. He died when I was a small child."

"After your grandfather, Henry Winters was killed in a hunting accident, Elly resumed her maiden name. Your mother never said anything about Michael's family?"

"Mother never wanted to talk about it. All she'd say was they were dead."

"Your grandmother died about a month ago. I can't explain why you didn't know, but Elly knew about you. She had a copy of your birth certificate. It took me some time to track you down. The last address I had was Joplin."

"After my mother died, I moved. I took a nursing job in Springfield." Dazed, Tori shook her head.

"I know all this is overwhelming, but there is time later for more details."

A tap sounded.

Jonah looked toward the door. "Linc, come in. I want you to meet Tori Winters."

Tori twisted in her chair to look up.

A slim man about thirty or so, six-foot and attired in a tailored suit that bespoke money, walked in. He was a younger version of Jonah, though his hair curled over his ears and touched his collar. The look of interest in his blue eyes turned to shock as he glanced down at her. "Good lord! You look just like Miss Elly."

"Tori, this is my son, Lincoln Greer. He's also an attorney. You'll have to forgive him, though I was also struck by the resemblance."

A brash smile popped out as Lincoln extended his hand. "Call me Linc. Everyone does." After shaking hands, he propped his hip on the corner of the desk.

"How far did you get, Dad?"

"I just found out Tori doesn't know anything about Elly."

"I'm not surprised. You know how tight-lipped she was."

"Humph … well, yes. But we're straying from the reason Tori is here. You are the sole heir of Elly's estate."

Tori gulped. "What does that mean?"

"Bottom line, a house, and several million in stocks, bonds, and cash. You, young lady, are a wealthy woman."

Her mouth gaped open. Tori looked from one to the

other. They had to be joking. Stuff like this only happened in the movies. When she tried to speak, she choked.

Linc hopped off the desk to thump her back.

Her hand flew upward to stop him as she wheezed, "I'm okay." Clearing her throat, she said, "Would you please repeat that?"

With a smile, Jonah told her again.

She said, "I think I'd like that cup of coffee now."

"I'll get it," Linc said. "Cream, sugar?"

"Black." She needed a full-strength punch.

"Dad?"

"Why not. Doesn't hurt to have an extra jolt of caffeine now and then."

Dumbfounded, questions buzzed in her head. Where to start? "Why didn't you tell me this when you called?"

"The estate is too complicated to discuss over the phone. I thought it better to break the news face-to-face."

Though Tori disagreed, she let it go. "You said you are the executor."

"I've been Elly's attorney since my father died."

"Then you knew my parents."

"Only your dad. I never met your mother." He didn't think it was necessary to inform her that he didn't know about her existence until Elly died.

Linc walked in with a cup in each hand. "Linda told me this is your absolute last cup for the day. She wanted me to remind you about Doc's orders."

"I figured I'd get some flack."

Tori steadied the cup with both hands and swallowed

a large mouthful. It didn't calm the ball of nerves roiling inside her. She took another swig. Still didn't help.

Jonah took a sip and set the cup aside. "I have papers for you to sign and need a copy of your driver's license. After your call yesterday, I set up a bank account in your name."

With her nerves still atwitter, she carefully set the cup on the corner of the desk. Rummaging inside the tote bag, she pulled out the license.

Linc took it, saying, "I'll make a copy."

Jonah slid a form toward her. "Sign this. I'll get it back to the bank." Once she signed, he handed her a checkbook and a slip of paper. "Temporary checks and instructions."

Tori opened the checkbook. A gasp erupted. Wide-eyed, she looked at Jonah, then back at the balance, fifty thousand dollars. An irrelevant, almost hysterical thought occurred. Yesterday, she couldn't afford a swimsuit.

Linc, who had returned with her license, saw her reaction. "That's the good part. Before you get too excited, wait until you see the house."

Reluctantly, Tori pulled her gaze from the checkbook. Her head tilted to look up at him. "Is there something wrong with it?"

"It's old, a white elephant."

A frown creased her forehead. His comment wasn't reassuring as she dropped the checkbook, paper, and license in her tote bag.

"Linc, don't go scaring her. Though, he does have a point. I recommend you sell it. As a matter of fact, I have a buyer already lined up." He pushed another form toward her. "This will be filed with the court transferring the estate into your name."

She carefully perused the document though it seemed straightforward. She signed, handing it back.

Jonah said, "I want to get this filed with the Court. In the meantime, Linc can show you the house."

He flipped open his calendar. "Let's meet at three this afternoon to discuss the offer. I'll have the sales contract ready for your signature. When do you have to be back in Springfield?"

"I'm not going back."

Jonah's eyebrows shot up, and he flashed a quick look at Linc. "You're moving here?"

"Yes. Is there a problem?"

"No. Not at all." He removed a set of keys from a desk drawer and handed them to Linc.

A warm fatherly expression crossed his face. "What's important is that there is nothing you have to do about the estate. Enjoy yourself. There is a lot to see in Granbury. Go shopping and have some fun. Let yourself get acclimated. Consider it a vacation. If you decide you want to live in Granbury, I'll set you up with a realtor. Texas is a big state. You have the money to live wherever you want."

The idea of doing nothing was as foreign to her as the notion she would suddenly be rich. "I still can't believe this."

"That's why you need to take your time. Take a few weeks; then we'll talk." He handed her the thick file folder lying on the corner of the desk. "Your copies of estate documents."

Still in a daze, she slung her tote bag over her shoulder. With her arms wrapped around the folder, she followed Linc out of Jonah's office. Linda looked at him as he passed. "Don't forget you have an appointment with Carly."

A grimace crossed Linc's face. "How can I? She hasn't let me forget," he muttered. He looked at Tori. "We can go in my truck, or you can follow me. It's not far."

"I'll follow, so you won't have to bring me back."

He nodded. "I'm parked across the street."

After placing the file folder and tote bag on the passenger seat, Tori walked around the car and slid behind the wheel. She stared at the office in front of her. Just a small-town lawyer. Nothing to have forewarned her. Her gaze shifted to the folder stuffed with documents. Yet, there was the proof.

She felt as if she had stepped into never-never land, but here she sat, the owner of a house and millions of dollars. Slowly, jubilation overtook the disbelief. Tori let out a whoop of joy, loud enough that a couple walking by stared at her. She wiggled her fingers at them. A horn honked. Linc had stopped his truck in the street, waiting for her to back out. Time to go look at her house.

Chapter 4

Several blocks past the railroad crossing, Linc turned onto a narrow street shaded by thick trees. Brake lights flashed as he pulled to the curb, his arm extending out the window to signal Tori to pass him.

When she drove by, Linc pointed to the driveway in front of him. Tori turned and slowly stopped. She couldn't believe her eyes. She slipped out of the car and stared in disbelief.

A three-story blue and white Victorian-style house sat on a large, wooded, almost park-like piece of ground. Despite the faded and slightly dilapidated appearance, the grandiose façade proclaimed durability and permanence.

The house was a mish-mash of arched windows, plain and stained glass, and gingerbread trim. Dual columns separated the lattice railing on the expansive wrap-around porch. A turret extended from the first floor to the rooftop on one corner.

No words could describe the sudden rush of emotion Tori felt or the instant bond to the house. There was an odd sense it had been waiting for her. The click of footsteps approached. She turned toward Linc with a wide-eyed look of wonder on her face.

Her hands made a sweeping motion. "All this is mine?"

"Yes."

She turned back to stare at the house. "It's magnificent. And it's mine. Oh, my, god!"

He groaned. "Good lord, are you going to be another Miss Elly? This place was her whole existence."

The hint of cynicism sparked her anger. Annoyed, she said, "That's the second snide comment about the house. What is it *you* don't like?"

"Like I said, a white elephant."

"Why?"

He ticked them off on his fingers. "High maintenance. Something always goes wrong, old wiring, old plumbing, old woodwork, old fixtures. Need I go on?" He stopped to draw in a breath. "It's why you should sell it. If you want to move here, there are many new homes in the area. I'm sure you won't have any difficulty finding one you like."

Tori glowered at him. "You've got to be kidding! I'm not selling." She turned to stare at the house with a worshipful gaze and didn't see his look of annoyance.

"Don't get too hasty. Wait until you hear the offer. When the house was built, it was on the outskirts of Granbury. Now the town has grown around it. This is ten acres of prime land in the middle of the city."

Tori didn't bother to answer, just shook her head as she continued to study the house.

Linc took off, heading to the rear of the driveway.

Tori trotted to keep up with his long stride. Why did he seem irritated, she wondered.

He motioned toward the four-car detached garage. "Miss Elly's car is still inside."

Another car. What was she going to do with two cars?

He stopped. "That's the guesthouse, though it's been shut up for years. It needs to be torn down. Near the back of the property is the old well house. Be careful. It's dangerous, even though there hasn't been water in the well for years."

Tori looked at the run-down building, offset behind the large house. "Uh, how big is it?"

"Small. Three bedrooms, kitchen, living area, about eighteen hundred square feet."

Small? She thought. *That's about the size of the house where I grew up.* Tori looked over her shoulder. "Then just how big is the main house?"

"I don't know for sure. Six bedrooms, two rooms in the attic, four bathrooms, two up and two down, a library, living room, dining room, music room, study, kitchen, and the servant's quarters. Come on. I'll give you the grand tour." He turned to walk back to the front of the house.

Staggered by the enormity of his description, all she could think to ask was when it was built.

"Somewhere around 1937 or 38."

Was that another snide tone? She looked up at him.

His lips twitched upward in a smirk. "I told you it was old."

Was he always this annoying? "Who built it?"

"Your great-grandfather, Frankie Leichter, a notorious crime lord in Dallas and Fort Worth in the thirties and forties."

The spark of interest wiped out the irritation. "Really!"

"Oh, yes. The house has quite a history." He ran up the steps. From his jacket pocket, he pulled out the keys and unlocked the front door.

"Are you coming?" he said from inside the doorway.

Still musing over the arched, stained glass windows, Tori walked past him to come to another abrupt stop. Despite the dirt and stains, she stared at the large entryway in awe. Blue and white cream-colored wallpaper accented mahogany walls. Stairs rose to a landing where sunlight gleamed through a stained glass portal, casting a mellow glow before sweeping upward. Base and crown moldings were carved in an intricate pattern, and the parquet floor extended into a long hallway. But it was the etched glass chandelier that held her gaze. All she could do was gawk.

Linc tugged her hand. "At this rate, we'll be here all day."

Large sliding doors on one side opened into a library with floor-to-ceiling bookcases, though there wasn't an abundance of books on the shelves. In a nook formed by the curve of the turret, windows framed a built-in bench covered with cushions. Drapes covered another set of windows. Ample-sized chairs, a sofa, and small marble-topped tables with lamps were scattered around the room. In one corner was a delicate writing desk and chair.

"Oh, my gosh, there's a sliding ladder. I've only seen those in movies."

Linc stepped to the windows and opened the drapes, setting off clouds of dust in the hazy light.

"The upstairs is even worse," he commented.

Under the stairs was a small half-bath. On the other side of the entryway, an arched doorway led to the living room with dark, old-style furniture. Embossed gold wallpaper covered the walls. Next to the double glass doors opening onto the veranda was the fireplace. A large oil painting of a woman seated in a chair, and a man who stood slightly to the side with his hand on her shoulder, hung over the mantel.

"Who are they?"

"Your great-grandparents, Frankie and Irene Leichter."

She studied the couple for a few seconds before following Linc to the doors at one end.

He slid them open with a flourish, announcing, "The music room."

Enthralled by what she saw, she slowly moved across the room. Her hand reached to stroke the dark wood of a baby grand piano. "It's beautiful."

Behind her, Linc said, "Miss Elly loved it and would sit for hours playing."

Tori moved around and slid onto the bench. Her fingers lightly touched the keys. The notes, crystal clear, seemed perfectly tuned. Sensing her emotions were about to spill over at the thought of not only owning another piano but a baby grand, she rose. "I can see why."

Another set of doors in the music room opened into the dining room. Each had doors that opened into the hallway, extending from the entryway to the back of the house.

Red floral wallpaper accentuated the cherrywood furniture in the dining room, albeit with a heavy layer of dust. With Linc prodding her to move on, she only caught a glimpse of the dishes and glassware displayed in the hutch.

Before they headed to the kitchen, she peeked into the study. The smallest of the rooms so far was obviously Elly's office.

The kitchen with a center island and breakfast nook with a large table that could easily seat eight people had a more modern look. A short hallway led to the walk-in pantry and utility room.

Linc turned the corner and opened a door. "Originally, these were the living quarters for the housekeeper." He stepped into a nice-sized room. On one side was a bed, and on the opposite wall, an armoire and dresser. There was also a small desk, chair, nightstand, and large easy chair.

"When she began to have trouble navigating the stairs, Miss Elly closed the upstairs and moved in here."

"Who was helping her, a nurse?" Tori asked as she opened the door to the bathroom, looking inside.

"No, not Miss Elly. She wasn't the type to rely on someone else. Besides, she wasn't ill. It was some type of rheumatism."

"How did she die?"

"Fell down the stairs."

"If she moved down here, what was she doing upstairs?"

Linc shrugged, turning to walk out. "No one knows."

On the second floor, even the built-up grime, dust, and dirty windows couldn't disguise the beauty of the woodwork, carved motifs and etched ceilings. In one bedroom was a multitude of boxes.

In response to her questioning look, Linc said, "Her clothes."

At the end of the hallway, a second set of stairs led to the attic. A jumble of boxes, furniture, and suitcases filled the two rooms. When Linc kept glancing at his watch, Tori didn't linger.

Downstairs, she stood in the middle of the entryway and spun, arms extended as she gazed up at the ceiling. "I can't believe it. This doesn't seem possible. But I'm here." She stopped to pinch herself. "No, I'm definitely not dreaming."

"It takes a bit of getting used to," Linc told her. "Are you ready to leave?"

She gazed around, looking past the deterioration, seeing only the beauty. "Are all the utilities working?"

"Yes, except for the phone line."

"I'm staying."

"Just because the utilities are working doesn't mean it's ready for someone to live here. You would be more comfortable in a hotel."

Her eyes narrowed. "If Elly was living here up to the

time of her death, I'm certain I can too. Please tell your father there is no reason to have another meeting. I don't plan to sell."

"As one of your lawyers, I recommend not making any decisions just yet. You should hear the offer. It might change your mind. You should keep the appointment."

"No. There is no point."

With a shrug of his shoulders, Linc handed her the keys. "In addition to the house keys, there is one for the guesthouse and garage. Once you get settled, I'll take you around town and introduce you."

"It's nice of you to offer, but first, I'd like to explore on my own. A little less formal."

He frowned. "Okay, but once people know you are here, be prepared to have visitors. Are you sure you want to stay here?"

The unexpected resistance to her staying in the house seemed odd. Maybe he was only worried about her. She smiled. "Thank you for your concern. I'll be okay."

Tori stood on the porch and watched him drive away while she thought about her meager belongings. All the boxes wouldn't fill a single room in this place. With a wry smile, she remembered thinking they were the pitiful total of her worldly possessions when she loaded the car. She wondered if it was possible for her to feel any more incredulous than she already did.

Slowly closing the door, she turned to look down the hallway. Where to start? Her mother's advice came to mind. When faced with an overpowering situation, take it one step at a time. Right now, that was deciding where to sleep. Since the downstairs bedroom was more appealing than the grime-encrusted master bedroom upstairs, she opted to use it.

Thankful she hadn't left her suitcase at the hotel, she called and canceled her reservation. She'd already left the card key at the front desk, planning on picking it up when she returned.

After dumping everything from the car in the entryway, Tori picked up the carry-all and headed to the bedroom. Though the room was in better shape than the rest of the house, it still needed a good cleaning.

From the small bag, she pulled out an old pair of jeans and a t-shirt and quickly changed. After sliding into tennis shoes, she stripped the bed. The washing machine and dryer were in the utility room. While they looked somewhat new, she held her breath. The flow of water was a satisfying sound. Armed with an assortment of cleaning materials and dragging a vacuum cleaner she found in a closet, she went back to the bedroom.

Once she finished, the carpet was relatively clean, and the furniture gleamed. A lemony scent filled the air. All she needed was the clean bedding. Next, she tackled the bathroom with its old-fashioned claw bathtub and pedestal sink.

As Tori gazed at the tub, she envisioned a candle on the counter, a glass of wine, and slipping into warm water filled with soothing bath salts. She chuckled at her musings. The enticing bath would have to wait since she didn't have the time, a candle, wine or even the bath salts. Instead, Tori dropped to her knees to scrub the floor, then scoured the fixtures and cleaned out the cabinet over the sink. Satisfied with the two rooms, she hauled the boxes from the entryway into the bedroom, stacking them against the wall.

Though the hotel had a buffet breakfast, she'd been too nervous to eat. Hungry, she wondered if there was even any food in the place.

She opened the refrigerator, only to stare at empty shelves. It was running, though someone had cleaned it out. In the walk-in pantry, she found several cans of soup, vegetables and numerous boxes of tea. She wouldn't starve until she could get to the store, though she didn't relish soup for breakfast.

Coffee? Now that was a priority. A search didn't turn up a coffee pot or the makings. *Okay,* she thought. *Forget cleaning the kitchen or eating. I'm not facing the morning without coffee.*

Tori retrieved the tote bag from the bedroom. Seated at the table in the breakfast nook, she pulled out a pad of paper and pen and started a list.

Not only did she need food but also additional cleaning supplies. Did she have enough money? Then, feeling like an idiot, Tori remembered the checkbook. Of course, she did. A surreal feeling buzzed through her at the thought of fifty-thousand dollars in the bank. How crazy was that, and from a woman, she'd never heard of. She wondered if she would ever know why her mother didn't tell her about Elly.

Her mind filled with thoughts of her mother, Tori locked the front door and strolled to her car. She had already backed out when it dawned on her that she didn't know where to go. Tori groaned and pulled to the curb. After a quick search on her phone, she picked the nearest grocery store and tapped the address into the GPS. Following the woman's voice, she soon pulled into the parking lot.

Tori grabbed a cart and slowly worked her way through the store. Before she had half the items on her list, the cart was near overflowing. Leaving it in the aisle, she dashed to the front to grab another one. While she finished shopping, Tori pushed one and pulled the second.

Heavy and unwieldy, the carts were difficult to steer around the end of the aisles. After a near collision with another cart and the angry retort from the woman behind it, she decided to quit and come back another time. Even then, Tori almost collided with another cart before she reached the checkout line.

Once the last item, a coffee machine, was on the conveyor belt, she pulled out the checkbook Jonah gave her. The checks didn't have an address, so Tori wrote her new address at the top. Seeing the total, she thought in amazement that she'd never spent so much money in a grocery store or any other store.

As she dug in the bag for the license, behind her, a man loudly huffed. Finding it buried at the bottom, she handed it and the check to the teenager and gave the man an apologetic look.

The checker perused them before saying, "I'm sorry. I can't accept this." He waved the check in the air. "You have a Missouri driver's license. This has a Granbury address."

"I just moved here. As a matter of fact, today. The account is new, and it's a temporary check."

"I still can't accept it."

"The check is good. You can call the bank or my attorney, Jonah Greer. He'll verify it's good."

"Let me get a manager."

The man behind her growled again. This wasn't a good start in a new town. How many people had she already pissed off?

A woman, wearing a vest with the store name emblazed on it, walked up. The clerk handed the check and driver's license to her. She examined it. "This address is the Leichter house." She lifted her head. Her stern look turned to one of shock.

Tori looked at her name badge, M. O'Brien. "Yes, Ms. O'Brien. I'm Elly Leichter's granddaughter. I just moved in."

"I'll be danged. You sure do look like her," she said. "A rumor's been floating about a new relative." She scribbled her initials on the check and handed it to the clerk. "Welcome to Granbury."

"Thank you." She grabbed the receipt.

The manager signaled to a teenager sacking at the next counter. "Help Ms. Winters out to her car."

As Tori pushed one of the carts toward the door, voices swelled behind her. In a booming tone, a man said, "If she inherited the Leichter place, she's worth millions."

Ms. O'Brien said, "It *is* odd since everyone thought David Tucker would inherit."

Who was David Tucker? Tori thought. As she and the teenager stuffed sacks into the back of the SUV, she made a mental note to call Jonah the next day.

She pulled into the driveway and drove to the end, where it curved behind the house. Easier to take the groceries through the utility room than the front door. It took several trips. When she finished, sacks covered the counters, breakfast table, and even the floor.

The cold stuff was easy. All she had to do was wipe out the inside of the refrigerator. But after looking at the pantry, it was a waste of time to unpack the groceries. She'd have to move it all back out to clean. With a sigh, she retrieved the vacuum from the bedroom to get the worst of the dirt and dust bunnies.

Filling a pail with hot water and cleaner, she grabbed an old towel and scrubbed the shelves and floor. Rocking back on her knees, her arms weary, she swiped at the sweat on her face. Though exhausted, she stared at a clean floor, or at least as clean as she could get it. It needed to be replaced.

It was after midnight by the time she filled the shelves, made the bed, and folded towels. Sweaty and dirty, her mind flipped between a bath or food. Since she still hadn't eaten, the bath could wait. While a bowl of soup heated in the microwave, she slapped two pieces of bread together filled with peanut butter.

Seated at the table in the breakfast nook, the aroma of chicken noodle soup tantalized her senses. Interspersing bites of the sandwich with a spoonful of soup, she pondered the day's events. It was the stuff movies were made of. A young woman, her life threatened, escapes, only to find she has become rich. Fiction had become fact.

With the last bite of the sandwich, she settled back in the chair. Tomorrow, she'd start on the kitchen and work her way to the other rooms. It was going to take time. The entire house needed a major overhaul. A thought suddenly occurred to her. *What an idiot I am. I can afford to hire someone.* As she reached for the notepad to start a new list, she heard the front door open.

Oh, god, did she forget to lock it? Tori couldn't remember, and the phone was in the bedroom. So much for being safety conscious. A faint click of a footstep echoed. Fear clogged her throat.

Tori eased out of the chair. Could she get to the phone? No, better to get out through the back door in the utility room. Outside, she could run to a neighbor to get help. The footsteps grew louder. On the counter, a knife block held a variety of knives. She grabbed the biggest one. It wasn't much but better than nothing. Tiptoeing, she pushed open the door to the utility room and slipped inside.

She rushed across the room, reaching to grab the doorknob. An arm wrapped around her neck, hauling her backward. Unable to swing the knife, she kicked and twisted. Terrified, she screamed.

"What the … a woman!"

The abrupt release propelled her into the door. She pivoted. Backlit by the hallway light, a man stood, his long legs encased in faded blue jeans, braced and slightly apart. The canvas jacket couldn't disguise the broad shoulders. Eyes, as dark as his short hair, glittered in a hard face. A scruff of beard lined the tight square jaw. His full lips thinned as he focused on the knife she tightly gripped. Tori sensed he could disarm her in a flash despite his empty hands.

"What are you doing here?" He reached inside a pocket.

She tensed, raising the knife.

He pulled out a cell phone. "I'm calling the cops."

"Good. I'll have you arrested for breaking and entering."

He snorted. "This house belongs to the Leichter estate."

"I inherited it."

His hand shot out to flip the light switch. The man's face went slack with disbelief. "Good lord, you look just like her. You must be Tori Winters." He pocketed the phone.

She nodded.

"I've been out of town. When I left, Jonah still hadn't located you."

"Who are you?"

"David Tucker. Elly's step-grandson."

Tori lowered the knife. "Jonah never mentioned you."

"We need to talk." He turned and walked out.

In the kitchen, Tori slid the knife back into place. "I'm guessing you have a key?"

"Yeah, I do."

She held out her hand.

After removing one from his key ring, he handed it to her and settled in a chair.

"I really don't go around attacking women. I drove by

and saw the light. I thought you were a burglar. I don't suppose you have any coffee. Elly never liked the stuff. She drank tea."

"I noticed. More tea than food in the pantry."

Tori retrieved the box with the new coffee machine. The heady aroma of coffee soon filled the kitchen.

"What do you do?" she asked, reaching for cups in the cupboard.

"I own an engineering company."

"Why wouldn't Jonah have mentioned you?"

"You'll have to ask him. Though, I'm not surprised. Jonah Greer and I don't always see eye to eye."

Not what she'd call a recommendation. There was nothing reassuring about his appearance as he watched her with a guarded look. She handed him a cup of coffee.

He took a sip. "So, what's your story?"

"I lived in Missouri and got a letter from Jonah. I came down and found out I had inherited the estate. I moved in today."

"I take it you plan to stay."

Over the brim of the cup, she eyed him. She swallowed a sip. "Yep."

He gulped down the rest of the coffee and rose. "Thanks."

Tori stepped back.

His lips twitched with a wry look as he set the cup in the sink. "It's late. I've had a long day. I'll be around if you need any help." He strode out of the kitchen.

Tori set her cup on the counter and followed.

Standing in the doorway, a cocky grin crossed his face. "You *should* lock the door. I didn't need a key to get in." He closed the door behind him.

Really! she thought, irritated by his smug attitude.

Tori locked the door, turned off the lights, and headed to the bedroom. A hot bath eased the aches in her body. She wasn't used to crawling around on her knees.

In bed, she punched the pillow into place under her head and let her thoughts drift back to the encounter with Tucker. While he hadn't gone out of his way to garner her goodwill, the look on his face when she said she planned to stay disturbed her. He didn't like it. Why? she wondered.

Chapter 5

Up early and eager to start, Tori sat at the kitchen table. Between sips of coffee, she worked on a new to-do list. By the time she polished off the rest of the pot, she had fifteen entries. First up was the call to Jonah. As soon as she identified herself to Linda, she was transferred.

"Good morning, Tori. Are you getting settled in?" Jonah asked.

"Yes, thank you. If you have time, I have a couple of questions?"

"I do."

"Who is David Tucker?"

"How did you learn about him?"

"He showed up at the house last night."

"Did he cause a problem?"

What a strange comment. Why would Jonah immediately think there was a problem? Not wanting to stir up unwanted trouble, she didn't mention the initial encounter. "Just surprised to find me in the house."

"David's been out of town. I didn't expect him back so soon. I planned to tell you about him after you had a chance to get your feet on the ground, as they say. It's pretty simple. David isn't kin to Elly. Elly had a daughter, Lea, who married Victor Tucker. David is Victor's son by a previous marriage."

Another astonishing revelation. Her father had a sister. Why didn't Jonah mention David or Lea yesterday if it was so simple? Why would he wait? For some reason, Tori found his explanation less than satisfactory.

"What happened to Lea?"

"She and Victor were killed in a plane crash years ago."

"He had a key to the house."

"I'd forgotten. Do you want me to call him and get it back?"

"No, I've got it."

"Good. I don't expect David will make any trouble. What else?"

This wasn't a reassuring conversation. Still troubled, Tori let it go and turned to the other reason for the call. "Can you recommend a cleaning company?"

"Absolutely. Try Summer Clean. They are the largest cleaning service in town. Anything else?"

"No. That's it. Thank you."

"Don't hesitate to call if you have any more questions."

Was that a note of relief in his voice, she wondered as she disconnected.

Several cleaning services popped up when Tori searched for Summer Clean. One was O'Brien's Home

Cleaning. The encounter with the store manager came to mind, and she clicked on the site. The owner was Mia O'Brien. She'd bet it was the same woman. On a hunch, she called.

A bubbly voice answered, "O'Brien's Home Cleaning. How may I help you?"

"This is Tori Winters. I'd like to get an estimate to clean a house." There was no mistaking the gasp that echoed in her ear.

"Ms. Winters, this is Mia O'Brien. We met yesterday at the grocery store. When can I come by and talk with you?"

"Whenever it is convenient."

"I can be there in about fifteen minutes."

"That would be great. Thank you." *Nothing like a small town*, she thought.

Two entries were crossed off the list. The next one, a trip to the bank, would have to wait. Tori started a new pot of coffee. There wasn't much choice other than the kitchen as a place to talk. It was better than any of the other rooms.

She set out a package of cookies along with plates and cups. When the doorbell rang, Tori rushed to open it. The woman she'd met yesterday faced her.

With a cheerful smile, she stepped inside. "Ms. Winters, you can't imagine how excited I am about your phone call. I've always had an itch to see the inside of this house." She stopped and gazed up at the chandelier. "Wow!"

"Please, it's Tori. If you don't mind, let's go into the kitchen. I'm still trying to get settled in, and right now, it's the most comfortable place in the house."

"Not at all, and I'm Mia." Following Tori, she said, "Ever since your trip to the store, you've been the center of the gossip. If you know anything about small towns, it doesn't take much to set off the rumor mill. Everyone is buzzing about the new owner."

Tori motioned toward a chair. "Coffee?"

Mia sat, her sharp gaze taking in every corner of the room. "Thank you, but I'll pass for right now."

As Tori settled into a chair, she studied her. The attractive woman, maybe twenty-seven or twenty-eight, tall with a curvaceous build, was attired in blue jeans and a white T-shirt. Long blond hair was pulled into a ponytail. A fringe of bangs clung to her forehead. Dark blue eyes in a round face sparkled with excitement.

Mia turned her attention back to Tori. "What do you need done?"

"The entire house."

Mia gasped, "Everything?"

"Yep. Is it something you can handle?"

"Absolutely. Even though I'm a manager at the grocery store, I have three employees, all bonded. We clean several homes in and around Granbury. This is a resort town. Many people from the Dallas and Fort Worth area own weekend homes here."

"What do you charge?"

"I'd need to take a tour and see what needs to be done. I'll send you a proposal."

Tori liked her answer, professional and organized.

From the large bag, Mia had set on the floor, she pulled

out a notebook and pen. "Where do we begin?"

They started with the living room. Seated on the couch, Tori watched as Mia strolled around the room making notes, examining every piece of furniture, the carpet and the walls. She'd stop, tap a lamp with the pen, and make a notation in her notebook. After the third tapping, Tori's curiosity got the better of her.

"Why are you tapping lamps?"

"To find out if they are genuine Tiffany. An original lamp had a layer of beeswax between the metal and glass. Over time, the wax disintegrates, causing the glass panels to rattle. These are the real deal and quite valuable."

Fascinated, Tori followed Mia from room to room, listening to comments about the different pieces of furniture. When she stopped in the bedroom doorway, Mia glanced over her shoulder at Tori. "This room is clean."

"I needed a place to sleep. Cleaned the bathroom too. You'll see why when we get upstairs."

By the time they finished, Mia had copious notes and still gushed over Queen Anne chairs, Hepplewhite furniture, and antique colonial beds. All of which Tori had heard of but couldn't have identified if her life depended on it.

As she poured out the hours-old coffee and made a fresh pot, Tori said, "You are quite knowledgeable about antique furniture."

"It's been one of my passions for years. My next-door neighbor owns an antique restoration shop. As a kid, I loved to watch him. As I got older, I worked in the shop on weekends. I've also taken a couple of courses through the

Appraisers Association of America. It's why I started the home cleaning business. Some of the homes I clean have beautiful antiques. It's a way to hone my knowledge."

While she waited for the coffee to brew, Tori leaned against the counter. "Is there a big demand for restored furniture?"

"The prices would boggle your mind."

A beep sounded. Tori reached for the pot and filled two cups. One she set in front of Mia before dropping into a chair across from her.

As she sipped, Mia looked out the window. "That's one huge backyard. You're going to need a landscaper."

Grimacing, Tori nodded in agreement.

"How long have you been here?"

"Two days."

"Really! You sure hit the ground running."

"I got here the day before yesterday and met with Jonah Greer yesterday morning."

"You did all this cleaning, plus shopping, yesterday?"

"I did."

"Dang. I could use you." She chuckled. "Where did you live?"

"Missouri. I'm a nurse."

"That accounts for the cleanliness. Are you planning on selling the house?"

"No. Why do you ask?"

She waved a hand in the air. "It's a big place for one person, or do you have family that will be arriving?"

Tori suppressed a grin. Mia was very good at getting information. "Nope. Just me. But I'm not selling." Time to turn the tables. "Did you know Elly?"

"Oh, yes. I don't think there's any long-term resident of Granbury who didn't know her or at least know her name. Miss Elly was the grand dame here for many years. She headed many civic and charity organizations, part of the political scene. You might say, the power behind the movers and shakers."

"What about David Tucker? Do you know him?"

"Sure do. The last I heard, David was somewhere up north, working on a project."

"He stopped by last night. Introduced himself."

"I didn't know he was back, though I might as well warn you. Everyone thought David would inherit. It was a shocker to find out he didn't."

"What's his story? I don't know much about the family dynamics." That was putting a good spin on it since she didn't know anything and didn't want to admit it.

"David was Lea's stepson. Lea and David's father were killed in a plane crash. I'm not sure when. Miss Elly raised David. He was ahead of me in school. David liked to walk on the wild side, brash, arrogant, and always ready for a fight. He was the class hunk."

Based on what she had seen last night, Tori couldn't disagree with Mia's description.

"Miss Elly was super conservative, a perfectionist. For some reason, they always seemed to rub each other the wrong way. David went out of his way to push her buttons." She swallowed the last of the coffee. "I'll work up an estimate and have it to you by tomorrow. Do you want me to drop it by or email it?"

"You can email." Tori wrote the address on her notepad, tore off the sheet and handed it to Mia. "If I decide to go ahead, when can you start?"

"It's a project that will take several weeks to finish. I'll work out a schedule and add it to the estimate. Then you can decide when you want to start."

"Good enough. Thank you for coming."

"Oh, the pleasure is all mine. I finally got to see the inside of this house. It's a crying shame it's in the state it is."

As Mia backed out, Tori stood in the open doorway. She liked the woman, and though she didn't want to commit until she saw the estimate, she fully expected to hire her.

With another task checked off her list, she activated her new bank account using the password Jonah gave her. She stared at the balance on the screen. Used to working with figures in the low hundreds, it was a shocker to see the large amount. A few quick taps and she had new checks on order.

After a wistful look at the backyard she wanted to explore, Tori reluctantly decided it would have to wait for another day. The file folder from the attorney awaited.

Enticed by the thought of a cup of hot tea, Tori perused the tea boxes in the pantry. While the teabag brewed in a mug of hot water, she retrieved the file folder from the bedroom. Until the study was cleaned, she'd use the breakfast nook for an office.

Pushing her laptop to one side, Tori opened the folder

jammed with papers and dividers and removed a document from the section labeled will. Taking a sip of tea, she began to read. Much was legal jargon dealing with the intricacies of probate. She skimmed over pages until she reached the section on the estate's dispersal.

No surprises until she reached the last page. The will had been prepared by Atkins, Foote, and Smart law firm in Fort Worth and signed by Daniel Foote. She leaned back with the cup cradled in her hands. As she sipped, she pondered the signature. Jonah said he was the family attorney. Why didn't he prepare the will? Then she spotted the date. Elly signed it only a few months before her death. Did she change the will and not want Jonah to know? A troubling question. There must be a logical reason. Only one way to find out.

She picked up the phone and tapped the number printed on the last page. When a voice answered, she said, "This is Tori Winters. I'd like to speak to Mr. Foote, please."

The woman said, "Mr. Foote is out of the office and won't be back until next week. May I take a message."

Tori gave her the number and added, "Please tell him I'm calling about Elly Leichter's will."

Disappointed, she disconnected. She stuffed the will back into the folder and pulled out another set of documents, more court filings for the estate. As she began to browse through them, the doorbell rang.

When she opened the door, dismayed, she stared at two women attired in three-inch high heels, suits that probably cost more than she made in a year, makeup and perfectly styled hair. Incredulous, their gaze swept over her.

Tori suppressed a groan. She had on the ratty old jeans and t-shirt.

The older woman in her late forties recovered first. "Are you … Tori Winters?"

"Yes."

"Ms. Winters. I'm Myra Swanson. This is my daughter Carly."

Carly, a tall woman with short blond hair that cupped her chin line, nodded as she stared at Tori with a cold look in her light blue eyes.

Since she didn't seem to have a choice, Tori took a step back. "Please come in."

The women minced inside and avidly scanned the entry.

Panic fluttered inside her. She couldn't invite them into the dust-laden living room, not in those clothes. That left the kitchen, which was even worse. Still, it was all she could offer. "The house isn't ready for company yet, but if you would like to come into the kitchen, I'd be happy to make a pot of coffee."

Myra Swanson quickly said, "We can't stay, Ms. Winters. We're on the way to a Chamber of Commerce luncheon. We are here to extend an invitation to a dinner and party tomorrow night. It's at the Landmark Lake Country Club. It would allow us to introduce you to members of the Granbury community."

In as gracious of a voice as possible, she said, "It's Tori. Might I have a rain check? Right now, I expect most of my time will be spent getting settled in this house."

"Well, yes, of course. The club party is a weekly event, so we can easily arrange it for another time. Also, we know you aren't familiar with the area. If you need any recommendations on businesses or shopping, I'll be glad to help. Jonah mentioned you called about a cleaning service. My husband and I own Summer Cleaning. We'd be happy to give you an estimate." She pulled a business card from the minuscule handbag slung over her shoulder and handed it to Tori.

"I haven't decided what I want to do."

"Of course, dear. That's understandable since you just arrived. I'll expect to hear from you."

"Thank you for coming."

As the women reached their car, in a shrill voice, Carly said, "Can you imagine? *She* inherited everything instead of David. My god, what was the old woman thinking?"

Clearly, Carly meant Tori to hear since she still stood in the open doorway. Resisting the urge to slam the door, she'd make sure dinner at the country club wasn't on her agenda anytime soon. Still seething over the condescending comment, she marched to the kitchen.

After stuffing the papers into the file folder, Tori started toward the bedroom and stopped. A disturbing thought popped into her mind. Was it wise to keep the documents in the house? Jonah surely had copies, but did she want to rely on that? After what happened in Missouri, she decided not to chance it. A quick call to the bank confirmed they had safety deposit boxes available. If she was going to town, she might as well pick up a few other items on her list. After changing clothes, she headed out. On the way, she stopped by an office supply store where she copied all the documents.

At the bank, Tori got a feel of her new status in life. Within minutes of identifying herself, the bank president rushed out of his office to greet her. After introducing himself, he ushered her into his office.

As she settled into a chair, he said, "Ms. Winters, how may I help you?"

"Mr. Reynolds, I'd like to rent a safety deposit box."

"Please call me Malcolm. At Liberty Bank, we pride ourselves on being a family bank." He tapped a button on his phone. "Ms. Granger, bring in a form for a safety deposit box." He turned back to Tori. "Of course, there won't be a charge. It comes with your account. What else can we do?"

"I'd like to make a withdrawal."

"How much?"

Tori took a deep breath. "A thousand dollars."

Malcolm didn't even blink. "Certainly. How would you like it?"

A few minutes later, the file folder safely stashed, she walked out the door with more cash than she'd ever had. Okay, she had money. Now what? Odd, but shopping didn't hold much appeal. Tori's conservative upbringing was rearing its ugly head. She couldn't bring herself to spend money just because she could. Besides, she had a house that was a heck of a lot more interesting than spending time in shops. Instead, she stopped at the grocery store on the way back to the house to pick up a few items she didn't get the day before.

The rest of the day Tori spent cleaning the kitchen. By the time she finished, the room gleamed, or as much as it could with old flooring and wood cabinets that also needed to be replaced.

The only interruption was the email from Mia. Room by room, the lengthy proposal detailed the steps she recommended. Impressed, Tori opened the attached schedule, which outlined the length of the project. The only item missing was the start date. Tori shot back a reply telling Mia she had been hired and asking when she could start. The answer was immediate. The team would be on-site at eight the next day.

After another quick supper of soup and a peanut butter sandwich, Tori was ready to call it a night. Before heading to bed, she checked the front door. On a whim, Tori turned on the living room lights and stepped toward the mantel. For several minutes, she stared up at the painting. Formally dressed in the era's attire, Frankie Leichter's hawkish face had a predatory look. Tori sensed he was a man who knew what he wanted and would do anything to get it. By contrast, a slight smile lightened Irene's face. Tori had to wonder what her life was like married to a crime lord.

Curious, she picked up her computer on the way to the bedroom. With the pillows piled behind her, Tori propped it on her lap. A ream of articles popped up when she typed in Frankie Leichter. Picking one titled *Dallas Gambling Lord,* she began to read.

He was born in 1902 on a farm outside Anna, Texas, a small town near the Oklahoma border. In 1947, he was gunned down outside his Dallas gambling casino, the Red Door.

A creak echoed, followed by a muffled scraping sound. Startled, she closed the computer, pushing it to the side. Tori slid out of bed, padding to the doorway, where she stopped to listen. Not hearing anything unusual, she went back to bed.

It was an old house, and old houses creaked. She'd get used to it, she told herself.

Chapter 6

The doorbell rang, heralding the arrival of Mia and her crew. Tori eagerly rushed to the door, swinging it open.

Mia marched in with her arms loaded with cleaning materials, followed by three similarly laden women.

"Good morning," Mia sang out in a cheerful tone. "Where do you want me to put this stuff?"

With a smile of delight, Tori said, "Hello to you, and wherever it's easiest."

"Okay, probably the dining room. Ladies, follow me."

Bundles of rags went on the table. Bottles of cleaning material, boxes of trash bags and other items were grouped on the floor.

Her arms free, Mia turned to Tori, who stood in the doorway. "Everyone, this is Tori Winters," before pointing to the women. "Tina Lopez, Heidi Grant, and Cammie Dodd."

Tori figured they were all about her age. Tina was petite, with long brown hair and dark eyes. Slightly taller and on the heavy side, Heidi's near-black hair hung in one long braid. Her broad face with high cheekbones hinted at a Native American heritage. About the same size as Tina, redheaded with a dusting of freckles across her nose, Cammie nodded to her.

"It's nice to meet everyone, and it's Tori. I have fresh coffee in the kitchen."

Mia said, "I'd like to get started. We can take a break later this morning."

"I'll be in the kitchen if you need me," Tori said.

As Mia walked out, she issued orders over her shoulder. "After a quick tour, we'll start with the drapes on the lower floor. Stack them in a pile near the front door. We'll load my car before we leave, and I'll drop them at the cleaners."

Tori filled a cup before plopping into a chair and booting up her computer. The article from the night before was still on the screen when it opened. She picked up where she left off. Fascinated by what she was reading, she lost track of time.

When Mia walked in, Tori reluctantly looked up.

"Am I disturbing you?" Mia asked with a concerned tone in her voice.

"Not at all. I've been reading up on Frankie Leichter. Since I didn't even know he existed, it's hard to imagine he's my great-grandfather."

"Really!"

"Yeah, long story for another time. Coffee? Donuts?"

"You bet. Sit still. I can get a cup, though, I'll pass on

the donuts." Mia filled a cup before dropping into a chair. She took a sip. "Oh, this is good. I was so busy getting organized this morning that I didn't have time for coffee."

"I didn't expect three women."

"It's a big job, though at times, there may only be one or two of us. In about an hour, another group will show up. The windows need to be washed. I hired off-duty firemen. They've got the ladders to reach the upper windows."

"Wow, good thinking. Getting to the windows never occurred to me."

With a smug look, Mia said, "Hey, that's why you're paying me the big bucks. Oh, by the way, the kitchen looks good. I'll scratch it off my list and give you credit."

"If I was going to eat in here, I had to clean it."

From her bag, Mia pulled out a large folder. After selecting a stapled document, she made a couple of notes before sliding it to Tori. "To make sure we're on the same page, I typed up a contract. I didn't know about the payment arrangement, so I left it blank. Usually, I bill once a month, but this is different."

Tori set her cup down and picked up the contract. For several minutes, silence reigned as she studied it. "Looks good to me. How about half now and the balance when you finish?"

"It's okay with me."

She picked up Mia's pen and signed. "I'll give you a check before you leave today. It's still a temporary one."

Mia flashed a hand as if to wave off any concerns. "Hey, I know it's good." She signed it and stuck it back into the folder. "I'll email you a copy when I get home." Settled back in the chair, she studied Tori over the cup's rim as she sipped. "You look tired."

Tori sighed. "The last few weeks have been hectic."

"Have you changed your mind about selling?"

"No."

"There's a rumor floating you are. Don't be surprised if you start getting calls from realtors. They'll be chomping at the bit if they think there's a chance to sell this place."

"Thanks for warning me. I wonder how it got started."

Mia shrugged. "I'm sure you know how the gossip mill goes. Someone makes a comment, it doesn't matter if it's true, and it's off to the races."

"I certainly haven't told anyone. In fact, I've only talked to a few people. A welcoming committee did show up yesterday, but the topic never came up. Besides, they were only here for a few minutes."

Mia held up her cup. "Okay to refill?"

"My gosh, yes. Feel free to help yourself to any food or drinks. Make sure your crew also knows."

"Thank you for the offer, but we don't raid a client's pantry."

"I'm sure you don't, but this is a special circumstance. It's not a quick in-and-out cleaning job. You'll be here for extended periods of time."

"In that case, thank you. I'll let my team know." She refilled the cup and grabbed a cookie. "Seen these before, the store's bakery. I sure got a kick out of you dragging two carts around. It was a first. So, who showed up yesterday?"

She bit into the cookie and munched.

When Tori told her, Mia grinned. "I bet that was fun."

"Why? Do you know them?"

"Oh, yeah. We have a lot of people in this town, super nice people. But a few believe the 'haves' should be separated from the 'have nots.' Myra and Carly are at the top of that list."

Tori realized Mia was a treasure trove of information and wasn't shy about sharing it.

"They were only here for a few minutes. I was invited to a dinner tonight at some country club."

Laughter erupted. "I bet you were. They sure didn't waste any time. Are you going?"

"Good lord, no. Not interested, though I did politely decline."

"I bet they weren't happy. Myra likes to be at the forefront. Having you in tow at the country club is right up her alley."

Tori said, "I don't think it bothered them. As they were leaving, Carly made sure I heard a snide remark about my inheriting instead of David."

Mia swallowed the last of the cookie. "Par for the course."

"You don't pull any punches, do you?"

"Not me. I call it like I see it. By the way, why *did* you call me?"

"By chance. I called Jonah, and he recommended another service."

"Summer Cleaning?"

"Yes. How did you know?"

"Jonah and Judd Swanson are tight, have been for a long time, both born and raised here. Jonah is Judd's lawyer. The Swansons have a finger in a lot of pies in Granbury. One is Summer Cleaning. I bet Myra hit you up."

"She did. Jonah told her about my call."

With a cynical tone, Mia said, "She didn't waste any time rushing over here. So, how did I get the job?"

"When I looked up cleaning services on the computer to get the number for Summer Cleaning, I saw your name. I wondered if you were the person who helped me at the store. I appreciated what you did and decided to call."

Mia laughed. "I'll be danged. Isn't there some saying about no good deed goes unnoticed."

"I think the actual quote is unpunished, but in this case, your version is better."

Another laugh rolled out of Mia. "I do like you."

Tori refilled her cup and grabbed a couple of the cookies before settling back in the chair. "Okay, give me the skinny on Carly. She was decidedly unfriendly."

"I'm not surprised. She'd see you as competition. I went to school with her, cheerleader, prom queen, president. If there was an award, she got it. Her father is a big land developer. Myra is one of the Wainwrights, old money in Granbury. Carly hasn't just had a silver spoon in her mouth, it's been a gold one."

Tori's phone rang. She glanced at the screen. "I need to take this."

"I'll go check on the crew. We can finish this later."

Tori nodded as she answered, "Hi, Jonah."

"I'm calling to see if you need anything. Myra Swanson mentioned she stopped by to say hello."

"Yes. It was very kind of her."

"I'm sorry you won't be joining us for dinner at the club. Maybe next time. Tori, I'd like to talk to you about selling the house. I do have an excellent offer. And, I've had two realtors in town contact me."

"Jonah, I am not selling. If you get any more calls, please tell them."

"Tori, it's something you need to consider. It's a lot of house for one person. Over the last few years, Elly certainly had difficulty with it."

"I'm sure she did, but remember, I'm a lot younger. There really isn't any reason I need to sell."

"We can talk more about it later. Do you need any help with the cleaning service? Though they are usually straightforward, I'd be glad to examine Myra's contract. I've known the Swansons for many years."

"Thank you, but I've already hired a service. As a matter of fact, I just signed the contract."

"You did! Myra didn't tell me."

"I hired O'Brien's Home Cleaning. They've already started."

"I wish you had spoken with me before you signed the contract. I know Mia O'Brien, a very nice young woman, but she certainly doesn't have the expertise for this type of job. There are a lot of valuable antiques in the house that could be damaged. I'll come over and work out an arrangement with Mia to cancel the contract."

"Jonah, I appreciate your concern, but there is no reason for you to come over here. I'm not canceling the contract. Mia is far more knowledgeable than you may realize. I was impressed with her knowledge and experience in furniture restoration and antique appraisals."

"I see. Well, if you are satisfied, that's all that counts."

"Thank you for calling. I'll be in touch." She hit the disconnect button.

Standing in the doorway, Mia said, "I take it that he didn't react well to my getting the contract."

"No. He was pushing Summer Cleaning."

Mia picked up her cup, filled it and sat down. "Thank you for standing up for me."

"I was serious. I don't like it when someone is underrated and doesn't get the credit they deserve."

Mia shrugged. "Not the first time I've run into the problem and lost business to Summer Cleaning."

"With this house on your resume, maybe it will change. I'd better make another pot of coffee."

While she washed the glass container, she said, "Finish your story about Carly."

"Where was I? Oh yes, high school. Even back then, she was trying to get her hooks in David Tucker. Still is. Not surprising since everyone thought he was the heir apparent to Miss Elly's fortune. I wonder if it will change."

Outside, voices rang out.

Mia jumped up. "That's probably the firemen. I'll get

them started. Then I need to leave to pick up more supplies."

After washing her cup, Tori ambled around the house. Still bewildered by what she owned, she spent time in each room, though she steered clear of the library where the crew was working. It was late in the afternoon when Mia returned. Tori helped her haul the sacks into the house. At the sound of a vehicle, she turned. Her hand shaded her eyes, blocking the bright sunlight.

A truck parked on the street. Linc exited and strolled toward the porch, eyeing the men on the ladders. One hollered down at him and joked, "We can use an extra hand."

Linc flashed him a grin. "Doug, it looks like you're doing a fine job on your own. You don't need my help."

"You just don't want to get that fancy suit dirty."

"I'm much better at supervising. You missed a spot in the corner."

"If a lady wasn't present, I'd tell you what you could do with your advice."

Linc just laughed.

"Hi, Linc. Didn't expect to see you today," Tori said, suppressing a grin.

Linc followed her into the house. At the sight of the stack of drapes, he said, "I heard a major cleaning project was underway. Smart to get the firemen to help."

"It wasn't my idea. Mia gets the credit."

"Hey, Linc," Mia said as she walked out of the living room.

"How's it going?" Linc asked.

"Just getting started. Tori, as I spot issues, I'm making a list. Wallpaper is one. It's separating from the wall. I can patch it, but it's really not worth the time and cost. It should be replaced."

Tori and Linc followed Mia into the living room. Mia pointed to the damaged areas.

"All right. Once you finish the house, we'll talk about new wallpaper."

Linc spoke up. "Tori, you can't be serious. Are you really going to throw good money after bad on this place? Once you're done, you still have an old house. You should sell it."

"Linc, your father and I have already had this conversation. I'm not selling. That's final. I don't know how to make it any clearer."

He tossed his hands in the air. "Okay, don't shoot the messenger. But as your attorney, I think you are making a mistake." He looked at Mia. "How do you know about wallpaper?"

She sniffed. "I know lots about a lot of stuff."

Heidi stepped into the doorway. "Tori, we found something in the library. We didn't know if you knew."

Intrigued, Tori rushed into the library with Mia and Linc close behind. A section of the wood paneling was open, revealing a safe.

Tori stopped in front for a closer look before turning toward Linc. "Did you know about this?"

"No, I didn't. I'll call Dad. He might have the combination." He stepped into the entryway.

Cammie spoke up. "I was wiping the wall, and it suddenly swung open."

Mia said, "A lot of old houses have a safe. Show me where you were."

Cammie pointed to a raised oak leaf cluster. Mia lightly fingered it and twisted, setting off a click.

Linc stepped back into the room. "Dad didn't know about it either." He walked to the safe. "If you can't find the combination, you'll have to get a locksmith to open it."

Mia glanced at her watch. "Time for us to go. Is it all right to leave everything?"

"Certainly. It will save time if you don't have to drag it in and out."

"I need to leave as well." Linc looked at Tori with a wry smile. "I couldn't get out of the dinner as easily as you did. I should warn you, Myra won't give up. Do you want me to get a locksmith out here?"

"Thanks, but I'll take care of it."

Linc nodded and headed to the front door. Mia's crew gathered up their belongings and were close on his heels.

Mia turned. "I need to get my bag. It's in the kitchen."

Walking alongside her, Tori asked, "Do you have any plans for tonight?"

"Nope. My usual is fix supper, work on the books, maybe watch a Hallmark movie."

"Interested in a glass of wine before you go?"

"Sounds darn good to me."

Tori stopped in the dining room and pulled two wine glasses from the large hutch.

"Do you realize what you are carrying?" Mia laughed.

"I may not know much about old houses or antiques, but I can recognize quality glassware. I suspect these are Waterford."

"That they are. Not just any Waterford, but vintage Waterford. Makes them even more valuable."

Tori rinsed the glasses in the sink and carefully dried them. "White or red. I have a bottle of chardonnay open, but I also bought a bottle of red."

Mia settled in the chair. "White's good for me."

As Tori poured, Mia looked at the label. She started to laugh. It built until her eyes watered.

"Okay, what's the joke?" Tori handed her a glass.

Mia wiped her eyes as she held the glass up to the light. "We're drinking a six-dollar bottle of wine from glasses that could easily sell for hundreds of dollars."

Tori said, "Bet they're not doing this at the country club," sending Mia into another laughing fit.

When she finally got herself under control, Mia said, "I haven't laughed this hard for a long time. It sure felt good." She took a sip. "Ah, yes, the nectar of the gods or some such stuff."

"Why are we sitting in the kitchen when I have a perfectly good, albeit still dusty, living room to sit in?"

"I have no idea, but lead on, and I'll follow."

"Grab the bottle. I've got a plate of crackers and cheese I forgot to set out."

"What about the crumbs?"

"Hey, I've got a super good cleaning lady. Not worried."

They settled in two wing-backed chairs with the plate of food on a small table between them.

Mia kicked off her shoes and curled her legs under her. "You know, this isn't bad for a horsehair chair."

Tori choked. "Horsehair!"

Mia swallowed. "Most vintage furniture was made with horsehair. It's in the stuffing. Oh, by the way, your chandeliers are Waterford, probably fifteen to twenty thousand each."

Tori choked again, followed by a spate of coughing.

"You keep doing that, and I'll be taking you to the ER."

"No. Don't forget I'm a nurse. I'm just having a hard time adjusting to all this."

"I can't imagine why." Mia picked up a cracker topped with a chunk of cheese.

"Is there a Mrs. Greer?"

She swallowed. "No, to both Jonah and son. The last I knew, Jonah's ex-wife, Linc's mother, was somewhere in California."

"You said Carly was hot after David. What about Linc? He's certainly not hard to look at either."

"I've often wondered myself. Since David didn't inherit, Linc's probably moved up on her list. Any interest there?"

Tori's eyes widened. "Me! Not a chance. He may be good-looking, but I'm not interested. How about you?"

"No. Known him for too long. Besides, I don't have much time to date. I've been too busy with my full-time job at the grocery store and my business."

"How do you manage to juggle both?"

"It's not easy. Thankfully, I have some flexibility with my hours at the store. It helps."

Tori filled their glasses with the last of the wine. After taking a sip, she popped another cracker into her mouth.

Mia looked around the room. "This house is fabulous. Everything I expected and more."

Tori took another sip of wine, washing down the cracker. "What I don't understand is why Elly let it go. She had the money. Do you know if she had a housekeeper?"

"Yes, she did. For as long as I remember, Ethel Morris worked here, even living in the house. Miss Elly would hire extra help when needed."

"What happened?"

"I'm not sure. One story is that Ethel was fired, which I highly doubt. The other is she quit, which is more likely. She's getting up in years, and this place is a lot to keep up. Ethel doesn't talk about it. She still lives in Granbury, out at the senior citizen center."

"When did she leave?"

"A few months before Miss Elly died. Maybe, seven or eight."

Odd, that was about the time when Elly changed her will, Tori thought.

"So, what are you planning on doing with this place?"

"I'm going to live here, but beyond that, I don't know. When I headed to Texas, I expected to go back into nursing, but of course, that's all changed."

A thoughtful look settled on Mia's face as she gazed

around the room. "This house would be perfect for a bed and breakfast inn."

Struck by the idea, Tori stared at Mia. "Really!"

Mia shrugged. "The way the rooms open up, there is a nice flow between the dining room, music room, and living room. Easy access from the kitchen to the dining room, then add in the library across the way. A great place for guests to cluster and relax. Something to think about." She uncurled from the chair. "Time for me to go."

When she reached for her glass, Tori stopped her. "I'll take care of all of this."

"My bag is still in the kitchen, so I might as well help."

After Mia left, Tori finished cleaning the kitchen, setting out what she needed for the next day. As she checked her list, she remembered the combination and added it. This would be a good time to search Elly's office.

The glass doors opened into a carpeted, wood-paneled room. A large mahogany desk and executive-style chair sat in front of two narrow floor-to-ceiling windows. In between the windows were two wooden file cabinets. Positioned in front of the desk were small, easy chairs. One entire wall was a built-in bookcase, though most of the shelves were bare, and against the other wall was a small sofa flanked by tables and lamps.

A heavier accumulation of dust covered the shelves and tables than the desk. Tori figured Elly had still used it. As she stepped behind the desk, she stared at smudged dust. While Tori didn't consider herself an investigator by any means, she did pride herself on her observation skills.

Something she'd developed during her years as a nurse, needing to detect any change in her patients.

Puzzled by the location of the smears, it looked like the contents of the drawers had been laid on top of the desk. It appeared to be recent. Who searched it? Tori didn't believe it was Mia or her crew. The only possibilities that came to mind were Jonah, Linc, or David. But why?

For cripes sake, she thought when she realized what she was doing. Gun-shy after her experience with the Russells, now she was turning something unimportant into nefarious signs. It probably had to do with the probate.

Pushing the concerns aside as nothing but paranoia, she searched the drawers on each side. The few file folders contained correspondence but no combination. In the center drawer, she found a business-style checkbook and a calendar. She quickly flipped through both of them.

Next were the file cabinets. One cabinet held file folders, and the other was filled with office supplies. Frustrated, Tori sighed. While she doubted she'd find anything in the master bedroom, she headed upstairs.

Standing in the doorway, she studied the room. In the curve of the turret was a window seat similar to the one in the library. On the opposite wall was a door to the closet. Two sets of windows overlooked the front of the house with a dresser between them. Next to the windows facing the driveway was a large, canopied bed with a nightstand on each side. An elegantly carved rosewood armoire was in each corner.

A flicker of disquiet stirred when Tori stopped in front

of the nightstand. Like the desk in Elly's office, the heavy dust on top was smeared. Same for the second nightstand and dresser. Maybe she wasn't so paranoid after all. She gave the other bedrooms a cursory look. Large sheets swathed most of the furniture. If someone had searched, she wouldn't know it.

Downstairs, she settled in a chair in the breakfast nook with her to-do list. Next to the entry for the combination, she idly added several question marks. Tori tapped the pen as she thought. Linc had said there were people in the house. It was probably one of them. Surely, there wasn't any reason to be concerned.

Before heading to bed, she walked the lower floor, marveling at the workmanship and detail in the woodwork. In the music room, she perched on the piano bench and flexed her fingers. Familiar notes of old favorites rose as she lost herself in the music. Her mother loved listening to Tori play, always claiming she had a natural gift. Even in those last days, her mother seemed at peace as she listened. Tears flowed as the final notes faded away.

It wasn't until she was in bed that her thoughts strayed to Mia's comment, a bed and breakfast. Surely it wasn't feasible. Still, she couldn't stop thinking about it.

On the edge of sleep, a muffled sound brought her upright. Moonlight streamed through the window, casting deep shadows in the room. Her heart raced as she listened. A shutter rattled. A sense of relief flowed through her. It was just the wind.

Chapter 7

Cars pulling into the driveway the next morning alerted Tori that Mia and her team had arrived. Walking outside, she relished the early morning fresh air as she waited for them to grab their gear.

Her arms loaded, Mia swung her hip to close the car door.

Chattering and laughing, the women surged toward the house, cheerfully greeting Tori as they passed. Inside, they headed to the dining room with Tori following.

Once the new cleaning items were unloaded, Mia said, "Start where you left off yesterday. If you finish, we'll decide what's next."

"What time are the firemen arriving?" Tori asked.

"In about an hour. They should finish today."

The women grabbed cleaning materials and walked out. Mia and Tori headed into the kitchen.

After filling a mug with coffee, Mia dropped onto a chair. "I have to leave for a few hours. One of the managers at the store called in sick. I'll be back later this afternoon. I do have a couple of items I didn't ask about. When will your moving van arrive?"

"Nothing is coming."

Mia gawked at her. "I guess, I … you mean all you have is what's in the bedroom?"

"I disposed of most everything before I left." *No point in saying it went to the dump,* she thought.

"Wow! You may have given new meaning to traveling light. Okay. Moving on. What about the garage and the guesthouse?"

Tori hadn't had a chance to even look at them. "I don't know. Do you have time to go look?"

"Yes. Lead the way."

"Let me grab the keys," Tori said.

A path led from the back door in the utility room to the guesthouse and the garage. Stale air tainted by a putrid odor assailed their noses as Tori opened the front door.

"Oh, this is bad. Something's died. I wonder how long it's been since anyone was in here." Mia stepped inside.

Leaving the door open, Tori followed. "Linc said it hasn't been used for a long time."

Closed drapes shut off most of the light. Tori flipped a switch by the door. Though it didn't work, even in the dim light, it was easy to see the accumulation of mice droppings across the shabby carpet. A low counter separated the large family room from the kitchen. A hallway led to the bedrooms. Not wanting to linger, they hurriedly looked around before rushing outside.

Mia said, "This place needs a major overhaul, even

gutted. Cleaning isn't going to make a dent."

"Let's see how bad the garage is."

Tori unlocked the side door and opened it. This time the light switch worked.

"Oh, my gosh," Tori exclaimed.

An old, very large, maroon and white Lincoln Town car was parked inside.

Tori walked toward it. "How old is it?"

"I remember David talking about it one time. I think he said 1990 or thereabouts. He always called it the Tank. Miss Elly refused to get rid of it."

"What am I going to do with it?"

Mia laughed. "You can always sell it."

"I guess so."

Tori looked around. Boxes, tools, and even some discarded furniture were piled across the rest of the floor.

"When I get a chance, I'll look through the boxes. See if there is anything worth keeping."

They headed back to the kitchen.

"What about moving you into the upstairs bedroom?"

"Let's wait. I'm comfortable where I'm at now."

"Okay." Mia glanced at her watch. "I'd better get moving." She picked up her bag. "The crew has their instructions, so there shouldn't be a problem."

Tori laughed. "I don't expect any. In another life, you'd have made a great general."

After Mia left, Tori filled a mug and strolled out the back door. She lifted her face, enjoying the light breeze and warm sun before ambling around the house. The firemen looked down from their perch on the ladders and gave her a wave or a cheery hello.

One of them climbed down. "I'm Doug Coleman, Ms. Winters. What do you plan on doing with the yard?"

"It's Tori, and I haven't decided."

He pulled a card from his shirt pocket. "When you do, I'd appreciate it if you'd give me a call. A group of us have a landscaping business."

She looked at the card, A-Z Yard Work, and the names of three men. "Thank you, Doug. I will."

Tori spent the rest of the day in her bedroom, unpacking and tossing boxes.

It wasn't until late afternoon that the doorbell rang. It was Mia. After checking with her crew, she walked into the kitchen.

"Everyone is headed home. Your office is ready. Heidi and Cammie finished up there. It was the easiest room in the house. Don't forget, we won't be here tomorrow."

After Mia left, Tori turned her attention to the laundry. Since she'd couldn't afford to replace all her clothing before she left Springfield, Tori had only bought a few pieces. It meant washing clothes was a daily event.

A chuckle erupted. How ironic. She had the money, but now she didn't want to waste time shopping.

While she waited for the clothes to wash, she made a sandwich and opened a bottle of wine. Her phone, lying on the counter, rang. Tori glanced at it and froze. A sense of foreboding raced through her. She picked it up.

"Hello."

"Tori, this is Kermit Layton. Are you enjoying Colorado?"

Since she still didn't want anyone to know she was in Texas, she didn't bother to correct him. "Yes, I am."

"That's good to hear. I know it's a bit late, but I'm calling to give you an update on your jewelry. We located the cameo necklace in a pawn shop."

She dropped onto a chair, her knees weak with relief. He'd found her mother's necklace. "How?"

"Since you had a unique necklace, I sent an alert to pawn shops in the area with a description. Two days ago, a woman walked into one and sold it and several other pieces that match the list you gave us. The investigation is still ongoing, so I can't comment on the details."

"Then the Russells weren't involved?"

"No. I didn't say that. I believe they are."

"Did you get all of the jewelry?"

"No, only a few pieces."

"What about the pictures inside?"

"Surprisingly, still there. I suspect the person who sold it didn't know pictures were inside the brooch. You did say it has an unusual fastener."

Tears formed at his words. She gulped them back. "When can I get them?"

"Until the case is complete, I can't return them. Once I have more information, I'll contact you."

"Thank you, Mr. Layton."

Tori laid the phone on the table. Layton's call had stirred up the fears which never seemed to go away. Would she have to look over her shoulder for the rest of her life? But if Layton didn't know where she was, how could the Russells? The thought strengthened her resolve not to let them destroy any more of her life. The Russells were in her past. And that's where they needed to stay.

While she ate, Tori pondered the unexpected changes in her life, ones beyond her wildest imagination. A wry smile crossed her face. The seed Mia planted, about a B&B, was fast taking root in her mind. Tori couldn't stop thinking about it.

Setting her plate on the counter, she refilled her glass. As she meandered her way through the lower floor, she paused to examine a piece of furniture, a vase on the fireplace mantel, and the Tiffany lamps, wondering at their history. That's what this house was all about—history. Tori stood in front of the painting of her great-grandparents. A gangster, a criminal, had built it. If only these walls could talk, what secrets would they reveal?

In the music room, Tori positioned herself on the bench, wishing for her sheets of music. All she could play were pieces she'd committed to memory. As the notes soared, a warm feeling encompassed her, a strange sense that she was home and no longer alone. As the final note died away, any lingering doubts were laid to rest. This was her destiny, where she was meant to be.

Upstairs, she flipped on lights until the entire house was lit up. She wandered in and out of the bedrooms. So much work still to be done. So much for her to still discover. At the back staircase, she swallowed the last of the wine.

Before starting up the narrow stairs, she set the glass on the floor.

She poked around the attic, with barely enough space to maneuver amidst the boxes, old trunks, and castoff furniture, relics from the past. Fascinated, she found old clothes, books, and more. Tori realized they were a treasure trove. Tomorrow, she'd spend a few hours up here, sorting and sifting. Her own treasure hunt.

Reluctantly, she trotted downstairs, turning off the lights as she went. After a quick bath, she collapsed in bed, too tired to read more about Frankie.

Her chest heaved as she ran, but she couldn't escape. She fell to the ground as the dog charged toward her.

Tori jerked awake and pushed herself up. Her hand trembled as she swiped at the damp hair clinging to her face. She hadn't had the dream since she left Springfield. Layton's call had been even more disturbing than she realized. She glanced at the clock. It would soon be daylight. Then she heard the odd scraping noise. She waited, but it wasn't repeated.

Tori slid out of bed, flipping on lights as she strode through the rooms. All the windows and doors were locked. With a sigh of frustration, she went back to the bedroom. The wind had to be rattling something on the side of the house.

Wide awake, it was a waste of time to go back to bed.

Since she planned to rummage through the dust-laden and dirty attic, Tori dressed in sweats and a t-shirt.

While waiting for the coffee to brew, she cracked two eggs, adding milk and a small chunk of cheese into a skillet. After setting the plate of scrambled eggs and a steaming cup of coffee on the table, Tori settled into a chair.

As she forked up bites of the eggs, she watched the rising sun cast a golden hue across the sky. Nearby, a mockingbird sang. A soothing calm flowed through her, the tension of the nightmare fading. After all, it was just a dream. She had a new life and home where she was safe.

After the last swallow, Tori washed the dishes. Leaving them to dry on the counter, she picked up her notepad and pen and headed upstairs. As she neared the back staircase, something crunched under her shoe. Tori looked down. Uneasy, her gaze flicked around the hallway. A new fear stirred as she looked back at her foot.

Chapter 8

Her hands clenched the notepad against her chest as she stared at pieces of glass. It was the wineglass she'd left on the floor. Was this what woke her? But how could she hear glass breaking up here from inside her bedroom? Tori spun, dashing from room to room to check the windows. An inconceivable notion since the firemen had to have ladders. But she had to be sure. Nothing had disturbed the heavy dust on the sills.

Thoughts and questions jumbled in her mind as she went back, only to stare at the broken glass in consternation. How did it get broken? If someone was in the house, how and why? She reached for the attic light switch and started up the stairs.

At the top, sunlight filtered through the stained glass portals, adding to the dim illumination of two light bulbs dangling from the ceiling. Then Tori spotted the trunk she'd opened. Had it been moved? At this point, she wasn't sure what was real and what wasn't.

Before she did anything else, she had to clean up the

mess. Since most were large pieces, Tori found a small box in the attic she could use. On her knees, she gathered them up while her mind raced with thoughts. It didn't make sense. What would a burglar be doing prowling around up here? Should she call the police? They'd think she was crazy.

Maybe a mouse knocked it over. Tori chuckled, then muttered, "Cripes, it would have to be a really big mouse." She didn't even want to think about that image. But could there be rats in the house? It was a scary idea.

Engrossed in her thoughts, Tori flinched at the sound of the doorbell. She stood, picking up the box and notepad. By the time she reached the bottom of the stairs, the bell had rung twice. "I'm coming. Hold your horses."

With the box tucked under her arm, she flung open the door. David lounged against a porch column. In a pair of jeans that hugged his narrow hips and long legs and a t-shirt under a light weight-jacket, the hard-edged aura he exuded did nothing to improve Tori's mood. "You do realize it's a bit early to come calling?"

He glanced at his watch. "Why, you're absolutely right. So it is."

"Ha, ha. It's also too early for witticisms."

"I thought you might take pity on me. Got any coffee? Besides, I wondered how the cleanup was going. I heard Mia had her bevy of women here."

Tori eyed him with suspicion. What did he want? While she was tempted to shut the door in his smug face, it might be to her benefit to let him in. She'd have a chance to learn more about Elly. She stepped back.

Another self-satisfied look crossed David's face as he walked past her. He whistled as he gazed at the spotless entry. "If the rest of the house looks this good, I guess Mia's doing okay. What's in the box?"

"A broken glass. Coffee's in the kitchen."

"Lead on, beautiful."

She glared at him. "Tori. My name is Tori."

"Prickly too. Any other traits I should know about? After all, we are practically relatives."

Ignoring his comment, she set the box in the utility room. When she walked out, David studied her to-do list on the notepad she dropped on the table.

"What's all this?"

"None of your business." She snatched it from his hand and laid it on the counter.

His eyes gleamed with humor as he sat in a chair, tilting it back on its legs. "The old place is certainly getting a facelift. Getting it ready to sell?"

"Not you too. Why does everyone think I want to sell?"

"It seems to be the general consensus." He waved a hand at the kitchen. "Why would you, a single and very attractive young woman, I might add, want to live in this old mausoleum? Sell, take the money and run. Do whatever you want."

"Well, I'm not selling. The house is fascinating. It has history. I want to learn more about it. Besides, I'm thinking about turning it into a bed and breakfast."

The chair thumped the floor as he straightened. "You

can't be serious. Do you have any idea what would be involved, the cost? And why? It's not like you have to earn a living."

"I haven't decided, but I like the idea. I'm not the type to sit around doing nothing. Besides, it is my house. I can do whatever I want."

A bitter tone surfaced. "You don't have to remind me." Then David laughed as if to erase a wrong impression. "But, I was never interested in it. The damn place is nothing but a major headache. If I had inherited it, I would have dumped it on the market as is."

The machine beeped. She poured two cups, handing one to him. Leaning against the center island, she asked, "How long did you live here?"

He drank, then set the cup on the table. "About fifteen or sixteen years. I was three when my dad married Lea. My mother died when I was born. When I left for college, I moved out and didn't move back."

"Were you and Elly close?"

"I don't think anyone was ever close to Elly. She wasn't what you would call an amiable person. How come you never visited?"

"The first time I heard about Elly was in Jonah's office."

Astounded, David stared at her. "I don't know why I should be surprised. How typical of her."

Tori shrugged. "This is all new. Did you know about me?"

"Not until her new will showed up. I knew Michael had been killed, but Elly never mentioned you."

A sudden ache crashed over her. Not wanting him to see, she picked up the pot and topped off her cup.

Startled by the distress on Tori's face, David leaned back, watching her quick movements. Did she really care about the old lady? Prepared to dislike Tori Winters, she wasn't what he expected. Despite their disastrous first meeting, Tori seemed to be an antithesis of her grandmother, with a quick smile and air of friendliness. A sudden thought crossed his mind. Maybe Elly had been the same when she was younger.

When she turned, he lifted his cup.

As she refilled it, she switched subjects. "Where did you go to college?"

"Texas A&M, got a degree in engineering. Linc mentioned you're a nurse."

"Yes. I had planned to apply to several hospitals in the area."

"If all you want is something to do, your nursing career might be easier than turning this place into a profitable business."

Tori shot him a look of irritation. "I happen to believe I can."

David felt a glimmer of respect. She was a feisty little thing. "I really am sorry about what happened the other night. I'd like to make it up to you."

At her sudden look of distrust, David laughed and said, "Honest, no hidden agenda. It's a beautiful day. What do you say to a tour of the town and countryside?"

Her look of delight took his breath away. Be careful, he

reminded himself. He couldn't afford any more problems. He had enough already.

"I'd love it," Tori exclaimed. "I need to change out of these clothes. I'd planned on working in the attic today. It won't take but a few minutes." The mention of the attic reminded her of the wine glass. For now, she shoved aside her disquiet. Her fears weren't going to ruin the day.

She rushed out the door, leaving him to wonder whether he had just made the biggest mistake of his life.

When she tripped back into the kitchen, he was certain of it. At the sight of her, an unwanted emotion sparked inside him.

The scruffy jeans and t-shirt were gone, and so was the ponytail. Instead, her long russet hair curled down her back. The white dress, trimmed at the neckline and hem with daisies, stopped at the top of her knees. Strappy high-heeled sandals accentuated long, toned legs.

While she was the spitting image of Elly, the warm look in her eyes wasn't anything she had acquired from her grandmother. Good lord, he didn't want to like her, but he did.

"Ready when you are." A smile lit up her face.

After helping her climb into his pickup, Tori asked, "Does everyone in Texas drive a truck?"

With a chuckle, he replied, "Not really, but trucks are big here."

While she had reservations about spending the day with David, surprisingly, from the start, she had fun. As a tour guide, he excelled. As they strolled around the square, she learned about the history of Granbury, its unique culture and fun events. When he mentioned a tour about ghosts and legends, she made a mental note to add it to her list. Seeing a poster in a store window about the hike and bike trail was another interest she planned to explore, also a visit to the Hood County Jail Museum.

But it was the Granbury Opera House that held her enthralled as she stood in the lobby, staring at the magnificent twin chandeliers and elegant curved staircases. Older than her house, it was built in 1886 and now housed the Granbury Theatre Company.

By the time David pulled into a quaint restaurant overlooking Lake Granbury, Tori was thoroughly enchanted by the town.

When handed the menu, David asked, "Wine?"

"Yes, whatever you recommend."

They ordered. When the waiter opened the bottle, she glanced at the label.

David said, "It's from a local winery."

She took a sip of the deep red liquid and exclaimed, "It's delicious. I'll have to get a couple of bottles."

She turned to watch the boats on the lake. Two sailboats gracefully glided along the water. A look of excitement crossed her face. "Kayaks," pointing to a group. "Can you rent one?"

"Yes. Are you interested?"

"One of many things on my to-do list."

"That sounds interesting. What else is on your list?"

"I've added a few today." She ticked them off on her finger. "Jail, ghost tour, winery, opera house, shops—"

David's hand flew up to stop her. "Okay, I get the idea. So, did you work in a hospital?"

"Um … no, more of a private nurse, hospice."

"Tough way to make a living. What prompted you to go that route?"

"My mother died of cancer. I was impressed with the hospice nurse assigned to her case. After Mom died, I switched from the ER to the hospice program. There was an opening in Springfield, and I applied for it."

She didn't want to spoil the day by talking about Missouri. "Did you know my father?"

The waiter walked up, setting their plates in front of them. David had ordered the rib-eye, the house specialty, while Tori had gone for shrimp scampi. Once the waiter walked away, David answered her question. "No, I didn't. But growing up, I heard a lot about him."

"What was he like?"

He speared a chunk of meat with his fork. "Michael was always up to some devilment. No one was surprised he joined the Army. I always heard it was what caused the rift with Elly."

"Why?" She cut a shrimp in half and slid a piece into her mouth. A look of pure pleasure crossed her face as she chewed.

With a shrug, David said, "I guess it wasn't what she wanted him to do. He left and never came back."

"How sad. She must have been miserable." Tori swirled the pasta with her fork.

"Elly! If she was, she certainly never let it show."

"It's still sad. What a waste."

Hoping to cheer her up, David said, "There is another event you might want to add to your to-do list."

When she looked up with a questioning expression, he said, "Bulls on the beach."

Laughter tinkled. "Whatever is that?"

"During the Founder's Day Celebration, a bull riding event is held on the beach."

Her eyes gleamed. "Fascinating." She popped a piece of shrimp in her mouth. She'd add it to her to-do list.

As David pulled into the driveway, her opinion of him had improved. "I can offer a cup of coffee if you like before you leave."

"I'll take you up on it. I'd like to see what else Mia has done to the place."

"So far, it's the office and working on the living room and library," Tori told him.

She unlocked the front door and flipped on the light. David followed her to the kitchen. She poured water into the machine, added coffee, and hit brew.

"Excuse me for a minute." She headed to her bedroom.

David wandered into the living room. When Tori reappeared, she carried two mugs of coffee. She'd also changed into jeans and a t-shirt.

"Are you sleeping in that old bedroom behind the kitchen?" he asked as he took the cup she handed him.

"Yes. The upstairs isn't anywhere close to livable. But Elly had moved downstairs. Didn't you know?"

"No, I didn't. I haven't been in the house that much, so I wouldn't have known. Elly never mentioned it." His tone casual, he said, "I wonder why she moved."

"From what I was told, she had difficulty going up and down the stairs." She waved her hand around the room. "So, what do you think?"

"Mia's doing an amazing job. I didn't realize she was this good."

He settled into a chair. Tori curled up on the sofa, tucking her bare feet underneath her.

"David, do you know why Elly let it go? Mia said she didn't even have a housekeeper for the last few months."

"I'm not sure. Over the last couple of years, I've been out of town a lot. Besides, what difference does it make?"

"It's a puzzle, and I have a thing about puzzles. I keep gnawing at them until I get them figured out. The condition of this house doesn't seem to fit what I've learned about Elly's character."

He drank a swig of coffee. How could he steer her away from pursuing this line of thinking? "Elly ... well, she wasn't herself in those last few months. Some thought she'd become senile."

"Do you think so?"

"A possibility, though I didn't see it. From what I've heard, it's not unusual for elderly people to experience a change in their character."

She sighed. "That's true. But still, it's bothersome. Do you know anything about the safe?"

Shock rippled through him. Elly never told anyone about it. "Safe?"

"Yes, the one in the library?"

"How did you find it?"

"I didn't. Cammie was cleaning the paneling and twisted one of those raised scrolls. A door swung open. I'll show you."

She hopped up and strolled into the library. On the wall, she twisted a piece of wood. The small wood panel popped open.

David stepped up to look at it.

"Did you know it was here?"

He didn't see any reason to deny it. "Yes. Do you have the combination?"

She said, with a worried look, "No, I don't. It seems no one does. I checked with Jonah. According to him, he didn't even know there was a safe."

The look on her face caught him by surprise. Why would she be bothered by a question about the combination? "I'm not surprised. Elly never told me. It was just by accident that I saw her close it one day."

"Why keep it a secret?"

"Elly was a secretive type of person. It's how she ran her life and controlled the people around her. What do you plan on doing about the safe?"

"I guess I'll have to get a locksmith to open it, but it's not high on my priority list right now."

He glanced at his watch. "I'd better get going. I've got

an early meeting tomorrow. I'll put my cup in the kitchen."

"No, I'll take care of it. David, thank you for today. I had a great time."

"I did too."

As she followed him to the front door, Tori wondered if he was one of the persons Elly had controlled with her manipulations.

After resetting the coffee machine for the next day, she picked up her computer and notepad. In the office, she set them on the gleaming surface of the desk before dropping into the oversized executive-style chair. Her body sunk onto a thick cushion that was surprisingly comfortable. Her feet actually touched the floor. As short as she was, chairs could be a problem.

Since she'd only taken a cursory look at the desk's contents when searching for the combination, she went through the drawers again. Most of the files dealt with Elly's numerous charity events. Eyeing the large business checkbook in the center drawer, she pulled it out and flipped through the check stubs. How odd. Elly seldom wrote a check. When she did, it was a donation. Who was paying the bills? Where were they?

A search of the file cabinets didn't turn up any bills, or bank statements, though she did find the CPA firm that prepared the tax returns. Who should she ask, Jonah or the CPA? Since it was bills for the estate, it seemed logical to contact the accountant. Below the entry on her to-do list, check on rats, she wrote the man's name, Sam Cantrell.

Before heading to bed, she strolled through the lower floor, turning off the lights as the sense of wonder built from room to room. Would there ever come a time when it would all be commonplace? The idea of an inn—no, it was more than an idea. A vision for the house, the epitome of grace and excellence, floated in her mind. A thought she pondered as she snuggled under the covers.

Chapter 9

A sound night's sleep turned into a late start for Tori. Rushed by the imminent arrival of the cleaning crew, she dropped a frozen waffle into the old-style toaster. Not having used it before, she made the mistake of turning her back. The toaster pinged. The waffle shot upward and landed on the floor. Laughing, she tried again but this time was prepared for the launch. She'd just finished eating when the doorbell chimed. With a jaunty kick to her stride, Tori headed to the front door.

Mia strode inside, her arms laden with more cleaning products, followed by Heidi, Tina, and Cammie.

"Good morning. It's going to be a beautiful day," Mia exclaimed. The others greeted her with a sunny smile and a cheery hello as they passed.

Tori followed them along the hallway, and when they stopped in the dining room, she kept going to the kitchen. After filling two mugs, she set one on the table. Mia breezed in like a breath of fresh air and collapsed in a chair. Tori wondered if the woman ever just sat. Her boundless energy seemed to keep her in high gear.

"What a dreadful day I had yesterday. I had to pull a double shift at the store." Her eyes twinkled with merriment. "How was your day?" She picked up the cup and took a deep swig.

Tori casually said, " Good. It was good."

Mia chuckled. "I bet it was. I heard you were out and about with David. Okay, give me the skinny."

Tori exclaimed, "Where did you hear about it?"

"A main topic of gossip yesterday at the store. A customer saw the two of you walking around downtown."

"Good lord. I wouldn't expect something so trivial to set off a round of rumors."

Mia rolled her eyeballs. "Girl, news flash." She held up both hands, fingers wiggled. "Let me explain the nature of the beast to you. You are now *big* news. Everybody is watching and wondering about you. Who is Tori Winters? What is she going to do? Inquiring minds want to know—and the know—is *you*."

"For cripes sake, how silly. David took me on a tour of the town, nothing more."

"Yes ... well, you got the tongues wagging. One customer said the two of you looked mighty cozy."

"For goodness sake, your customer needs their eyes examined. I barely know David, and I'm not the type to cozy up to any man."

"Hey, you don't need to convince me. So, where'd he take you?"

"Downtown, as you already know, and around the

lake. We had dinner at the Lazy Owl Restaurant."

"Ritzy, ritzy."

"You're right about that. I was a little concerned at the prices and whether David could really afford it."

"Why ever not?"

"I got the impression he doesn't have much money."

Wide-eyed with surprise, Mia said, "Where'd you come up with that notion?"

"I'm not sure." The faded blue jeans and scruffy canvas jacket came to mind.

"Another news flash. When his dad was killed, David inherited a considerable fortune, though it was in some kind of trust fund until he turned twenty-one."

Stunned, Tori plunked into the chair. "You're kidding."

"Nope, scouts honor." She mimicked a broad Yankee accent. "His family were *the* Tuckers of upstate New York, old money, steel and railroads."

Tori burst out laughing. "Hey, that's pretty good."

"I was a whiz in the school plays. Bottom line, he's loaded. Rumor has it that it ticked Miss Elly off big time. She couldn't control him with threats of money."

"Now, isn't that interesting."

"How so?"

"He mentioned something about Elly's manipulation of people."

"From what I heard, she was dang good at it."

"If he had family in New York, why did Elly raise him?"

"He was an orphan. His mother died when he was a

baby. Some law firm back east controlled the trust fund."

"Says something for Elly that she took on raising a child."

Mia shrugged. "Miss Elly was an odd woman. I'm not sure if anyone understood her unless it was Ethel, her housekeeper."

"Refill?"

"Lordy be yes. I need all the caffeine I can get today. I plan on spending most of the day upstairs pulling down the drapes."

The broken wine glass, she thought. Should she mention it? No. Her fears would sound crazy. Though, she did have to ask, "Mia, have you seen any signs of mice or rats?"

Mia's eyebrows raised. "Where did you come up with that? Did you see one?"

"No, I was just wondering."

"I'll check, but so far, I haven't seen any signs of mice. A few spiders, yes. Mice, no."

"Okay. If you need me, I'll be in the office. I've moved out of the kitchen."

Mia headed toward the library, and Tori strolled into the office. Settling into the chair, she pulled her cellphone from her pocket. First on the agenda was the call to the CPA. Before she could make the call, her phone chimed. It was the attorney's office in Fort Worth.

"Ms. Winters, if it's convenient, Mr. Foote would like to meet with you the day after tomorrow."

"Yes. I can be there."

"Is one o'clock a good time?"

"Absolutely. I'll see him then."

Next was the call to Cantrell.

When a woman answered, Tori said, "I'd like to speak to Mr. Cantrell."

"Who is calling?"

"Tori Winters."

"If you will wait a moment, I'll check to see whether he can take your call."

After a short silence, a man's voice came on the line.

"Ms. Winters, this is Sam Cantrell. I planned to call you this week. I had waited, wanting to allow you time to get settled."

"Thank you. That was very thoughtful. I would like to meet with you. I have several questions regarding Elly's finances. When is a good time?"

"This afternoon. I'd be happy to stop by the house."

"No. I'd like to meet in your office."

"All right. How about two o'clock?"

"I'll see you then. Thank you."

Tori pulled out the calendar she'd bought at the grocery store, noting the two appointments. On the to-do list, she crossed off two items.

The doorbell chimed. When Tori opened the door, Myra Swanson sailed inside.

"Hello, my dear." Her eyes swept over Tori before she looked around the entry. "It's somewhat better." She pulled off the white gloves she wore.

Tori stared in amazement. Who wears gloves anymore?

"I hope you have a few minutes."

She abruptly remembered her manners. "Yes, I do. Why don't we go into the living room?"

"Have you already made the house presentable?" she asked.

Slightly annoyed, Tori replied, "It's getting there."

"I can't imagine you received a quality cleaning this fast."

Tori decided to take the high road and ignored the remark. "Would you like coffee or tea?"

"No, thank you. I can't stay long."

As they walked through the doorway, Tori bit back a sigh of relief.

Myra avidly studied the room. "Still needs work." She wandered over to the table with a Tiffany lamp. "I never could get Elly to part with these." She fingered the glass. "I'm surprised you let Mia's crew even touch these lamps. But then, you probably don't know how valuable they are."

"I didn't until Mia told me they were Tiffany and very expensive."

"Mia?"

"Yes, she's quite the expert on antiques. She even discovered an original Sevres porcelain box. It's on the mantel."

Astonished, Myra turned to look. "I had no idea."

Feeling better at the one-upmanship, Tori asked, "Would you like to sit down?"

"No. I'm here to invite you to a small dinner party tomorrow night at my home. Jonah talked to my husband, Judd, and suggested it since you *didn't* join us at the country club. I absolutely insist on your attending. Linc volunteered to pick you up. He'll be here at six-thirty. I know it's early, but you'll need time to meet the other guests. My little get-togethers are formal. Would you like me to take you shopping tomorrow?"

Her jaw tightened. "I appreciate the offer, but I won't be able to attend."

"I'm not taking no for an answer. You are Elly's heir, and people are quite anxious to meet you. Now, I really must leave, or I'll be late for a meeting at the Mayor's office. Let me know if you change your mind about the shopping. I know Carly would love to give you a few pointers." She strolled toward the front door.

As the door shut, Tori panicked. She raced upstairs and burst into the bedroom, where Mia was folding drapes. "I need to talk to you. In the kitchen."

Mia followed, trying to keep up with Tori as she ran down the stairs. She couldn't imagine what happened to put Tori in such a tizzy.

In the kitchen, Mia said, "Okay. What's wrong?"

"Myra just left."

"Ah, that explains the panic. What did she do?"

"Invited me to a dinner party tomorrow night at her house. I couldn't get out of it."

A roar of laughter erupted.

"Mia, this isn't funny. She said it's formal. Even offered, along with Carly, to help me shop for a dress. She wouldn't take no for an answer." Her voice rose. "I don't know anything about fancy dinner parties. I've got to get out of this."

Still laughing, Mia swiped at the tears in her eyes. "I guess you could call and say you're sick, but it will only put off the inevitable. Face up to it, you're stuck."

Agitated, Tori fluttered her hands in the air. "I won't know what to do or say. And that's not all. Other people are going to be there. She's having Linc pick me up early, so I can meet the other guests."

"Hey, it could be worse."

Skeptical, Tori stared at Mia. "How can this be any worse?"

"It could be one of her fancy parties at the country club. Lots more people."

"Oh, god! What am I going to do?"

Mia plunked into the chair. "First, stop panicking. You got this. Second, when you show up, we'll make sure you kick some serious butt."

With a look of disgust, Tori exclaimed, "And how do *we* plan to make this miracle happen?"

"We're going shopping." Mia stood. "Here's the game plan. Tomorrow morning, we'll head to a mall on the northside of Dallas. It's a long drive but worth it. Heidi used to work for a beauty salon. She can do your hair and makeup when we get back. What time is Linc going to be here?"

"Uh … six-thirty."

"That gives us plenty of time. Do you have a credit card?"

"Yes."

"What bank are you using?"

After Tori told her, Mia added, "Call Malcolm and tell him you need the credit limit on your card raised. I don't think you want to carry a lot of cash. I bet he'll take care of it for you."

With a sinking feeling, she wondered how expensive the stores were. "You know the bank president?"

"Girl, I know most everybody in this town."

Tori grabbed Mia, giving her a big hug. "I'm so glad I walked into your grocery store."

"You know what? So am I."

Tori headed to the office, and Mia trotted up the stairs.

Feeling somewhat reassured, she called the bank. As Mia had predicted, when Tori explained what she needed, Malcolm said he'd take care of it. After giving him her credit card information, he said he'd call back once the change was effective.

To get ready for the appointment with Cantrell, she noted the questions she wanted to ask on a new notepad. She pulled out the last two years' filings from the file cabinet, thinking it would be helpful to review them. *Good lord,* she thought. Her tax return was usually three or four pages. These were fifty to sixty pages. Absorbed by the complicated forms, she almost ignored the incoming phone call until she quickly glanced at the caller ID.

"Ms. Winters, it's Malcolm Reynolds."

"Please, it's Tori."

"Thank you. I've taken care of the credit card. Your limit has been raised to one-hundred thousand dollars."

Tori managed to stop the gasp.

"I hope it is sufficient."

Her voice weak, she said, "Uh, yes. That should be more than enough."

"Is there anything else I can do?"

"Yes. Elly had an account with you. I haven't found any bank statements—"

He interrupted. "The statements are sent to Sam Cantrell. He's the CPA that handled Miss Elly's finances for years. He even paid the bills."

"I see. What is the balance in the account?"

"Hold on for a moment."

Malcolm came back on the line and said, "Two-hundred and fifty-four thousand dollars, and sixty-five cents."

Would she ever get used to, or get comfortable with, such large amounts of money? "I'd like to close it and transfer the balance to my account."

"I'll make the arrangements. After Miss Elly's death, Jonah said to keep the account open."

Of course, Jonah would have known about the account. She had to wonder why he didn't mention it. After all, he had set up a new account for her. "Is it possible to obtain a duplicate set of bank statements for this year and last year?"

"Certainly. It will take about an hour. I can have them delivered."

"Thank you. But it won't be necessary. I'll stop by later today. Did Elly have other accounts or credit cards with your bank?"

"Just the one account. I'd suggest you ask Jonah or Sam about the credit cards."

"I'll see you later today. Thank you for your help."

She added a note about the credit cards to the list of questions for the CPA.

From the doorway, Mia's voice broke into her musings. "Take a break. Time for lunch."

Grateful for the reminder, Tori followed her to the kitchen. The plate of sandwiches she made earlier was on the counter, along with a large container of potato salad she had bought. Heidi, Tina, and Cammie were already seated at the table.

Mia and Tori each grabbed a plate, adding a sandwich and scoop of potato salad.

Tori set her plate on the table. "Mia, what would you like to drink?"

"Whatever's in the fridge." Mia pulled out the chair and plopped.

Tori grabbed two cans of diet soda, handing one to Mia. Then she popped the top and took a deep swig of the icy liquid as she tuned into the chatter. Cammie was talking about a problem with her landlord, but once Tori was seated, the conversation turned.

Evidently, Mia had spoken to Heidi about the hair and makeup; of course, the other two also knew. Why should she have been surprised? In the short time she had known them, she discovered the four women were also close friends.

Tina eyed Tori. "Heidi, I think her hair should be piled

on top of her head, maybe a few curls alongside the face. It will make her seem taller."

Cammie chimed in. "What about a braid coiled on top?"

With a shake of her head, Heidi studied Tori as she chewed on a bite of the sandwich. "Hmm ... depends on what she's wearing. Maybe pull her hair back with clips, letting it flow down her back."

Mia's head swiveled to look at Tori. "I like that idea. What about makeup?"

"I'll bring some with me. With her skin tone, she won't need much."

Feeling like a bug under a microscope, Tori waved her hands as she swallowed. "Hello, remember I'm here."

Mia asked, "Do you have any makeup?"

"Uh ... no. Lipstick is about it."

With a smug look, Mia said, "I thought so. Heidi, bring everything you can. What about her nails?"

"Good thought," Heidi said. "Maybe a pedicure as well. You might end up getting sandals. How much time do I have tomorrow?"

Tori groaned.

Mia said, "Linc is supposed to pick her up at six-thirty. We're headed to Dallas in the morning to find a dress."

"That's cutting it close. We need to do the nails and pedicure tonight. Tomorrow, it's just the hair and makeup."

"That okay with you, Tori?" Mia asked.

"I guess so. Are you sure this is absolutely necessary?"

As if one voice, the four women said, "Yes!"

"Okay, okay. I'm convinced. Tonight it is."

While Mia told Heidi to go home and get her equipment, Tori picked up the plates. When Tina tried to help, Tori waved her off. "Thanks, but I've got this."

After the team left, Mia said, "You might as well know this has become one of our hen parties. Cammie and Tina won't be leaving. Before I forget, all the covers we pulled off the furniture have rotted. There's no point in washing them. They'd probably come apart in the process. It means several bags of trash, and we'll have more by the time we finish. You'll need to arrange for a special pickup."

"I'll add it to my list. I will be gone this afternoon. I have an appointment with Sam Cantrell."

"That should be interesting."

Curiosity sparked in Tori's eyes. "What do you know about him?"

"Sam fancies himself as quite the ladies' man. Never married. One of Myra's clique. He's tight with Jonah and Judd Swanson. The three of them grew up together. Sam probably does their taxes since he handles the taxes for a lot of folks, mostly on the high end of the scale. I've never heard any complaints about how he handles his business."

"That's good to know. If I turn this place into a B&B, I'll need to learn more about the finances."

Mia's plate clanged against the counter. "What!"

Tori grinned as she grabbed a dishcloth to wipe the table. "I've given your idea a lot of thought, and the more I think about it, the more it makes sense."

"Well, dang!"

"It will be a long process, but I like the idea. It's a great way to make use of this house." She glanced at her watch. "I need to get going. You okay here? Do you need me to pick up anything?"

Mia, a stunned expression on her face, said, "No. I can't think of anything." Still dazed, she walked out shaking her head.

When Tori stepped outside, she found she had a problem. Four cars blocked the driveway. She couldn't get out.

Stepping back inside, she shouted, "Mia."

When Mia stuck her head around the door to the music room, Tori said, "I need cars moved."

Mia stepped into the hallway, tossing her a set of keys. "Take my car."

Tori snagged them midair and gave Mia a quick salute before heading back out.

Chapter 10

Located on a wide street with large trees, Cantrell's office was in a renovated house. A discreet sign next to the door read—*Cantrell's Management Services*. A bell tinkled when Tori walked in.

At the back of the room, a woman stood behind a desk. A keen expression crossed her face. "You must be Tori Winters. I've heard about how much you look like Miss Elly. Please have a seat. I'll let Sam know you are here."

Tori sat, looking around. The green and white carpet complimented dark green walls with white trim. The room exuded expense.

A tall, slim man, dressed in a dark blue suit, blue and white pinstriped shirt, and red tie, stepped through an arched doorway. The brown hair gelled in waves to expensive-looking leather shoes fit Mia's description to a T, even the long ogling look he gave her. From Mia's comments, the man was the same age as Jonah.

"Tori, I'm Sam Cantrell. Nice to meet you."

She stood, feeling like a ragamuffin in her jeans, blue t-shirt and vest.

He extended his hand. In a low, almost sensual voice, he said, "I must say, you *are* a pretty little thing and certainly the spitting image of your grandmother." He held onto her hand while his thumb stroked the back. "She was such a dear friend, a painful loss."

Uncomfortable by the intimate gesture, she pulled her hand back.

"Let's go to my office. Would you like something to drink?"

"No, thank you."

Tori followed him into a richly appointed room with a carpet similar to the reception area. Wood-paneled walls and a large executive desk with two leather chairs in front enhanced the ambiance of elegance. Tori felt it was overblown for an accountant's office, but what did she know? She'd always done her own tax return.

With a wave of his hand, he said, "Please have a seat." He walked behind the desk and sat down.

Before dropping the tote bag on the floor, she removed the file folder and pen, balancing the folder in her lap.

He frowned. "Would you prefer to go into the conference room?"

"No, Mr. Cantrell. This is fine. I don't expect to take up much of your time."

He leaned back, elbows resting on the arms of the chair. "It's Sam. There's nothing for you to worry about. We'll take whatever time you need. How do you like Texas?"

"What little I've seen, it's an interesting change from Missouri."

"I understand you plan on staying."

"Yes, I do."

"A most interesting turn of events. Everyone believed David would inherit. When I read Elly's new will, I was shocked to learn some unknown person inherited everything."

His tone made it sound like it was her fault. "Why did you read the will?"

"I'm responsible for the estate's final tax return. Jonah and I have had numerous conversations. As a matter of fact, he called to tell me you were in town and had moved into Elly's house. I was quite surprised you would take such a step, considering the condition of the place. Jonah also mentioned you didn't want to sell, though I find it difficult to believe."

She smiled. "It's true. I'm not selling."

His close-set eyes narrowed. "Tori, that's not a wise move. After all, you've only been here for a few days and have no idea what is involved. As your financial advisor, I strongly recommend you sell the property. Jonah has a very generous offer for the place. You should consider it before making such a rash decision."

She stiffened. "I don't believe it is rash. But that's not why I am here."

"Then what can I do for you?"

"As I said on the phone, I have a number of questions about the finances. I found the tax returns when I went through Elly's files, though I was unaware you were doing the estate's return."

He gave her a patronizing smile. "Tax returns are only one of my many responsibilities for the estate."

She opened her file, removing her list. "That's the problem. Mr. Reynolds at the bank told me the bank statements are sent to you. He also mentioned you pay the bills."

He leaned forward. In a tone not nearly as friendly, he said, "I fail to understand why it should be a problem or a reason for *you* to make unnecessary inquiries at the bank."

In disbelief, she said, "I'm the new owner. That's why. I've already requested a copy of the bank statements. I need a list of the accounts you pay and an itemization of the monthly expenses for the last two years." She glanced at her list before adding, "You mentioned other responsibilities. What else?"

His jaw tightened. "One of the services I provide is asset management. I oversee the financial investments of many individuals in this area. You must be aware that Elly had substantial funds invested in different companies. It's a varied portfolio I handle, along with financial advice."

"Then I'll need a list of the companies and financial reports for the last two years. After reviewing them, I will probably have additional questions." She wrote on her pad. When he didn't answer, she looked up.

He scowled. "Tori, none of this is necessary. There isn't anything you need to worry yourself about. I have successfully handled Elly's financial affairs for years and will continue to do the same for you. I'm sure there are many other things a young and pretty girl like you would rather be doing than keeping track of boring expenses and investments."

Annoyed by his condescending attitude, Tori leaned forward. "Evidently, I have not made myself clear. I am assuming control of the estate."

A red flush stained his face. "Surely, you are joking."

"I assure you I'm not."

"I would be remiss in my duties if I didn't tell you this is an ill-advised and highly irresponsible act. The estate is a complicated consortium that requires considerable financial knowledge and expertise to manage."

Tori's irritation built. "In other words, you don't think I can handle my own affairs."

"Quite frankly, you don't have the background or education. It will take time. Jonah and I have already discussed this. We believe there shouldn't be any changes to the administration of the estate until you are, how should I say, up to snuff? We also believe it is in your best interest to sell the house. It's a liability. The land, though, is quite valuable. The profit from the sale would certainly add to your financial assets."

"First, there is no *we* here. I am not selling. I am taking over the administration. This isn't open for debate. I've already closed Elly's checking account."

His body tensed. Not bothering to hide his anger, he said, "Have you discussed this with Jonah?"

"Let me remind you that Jonah Greer no longer makes the decisions. I do."

His lips thinned. "Then, I don't believe we have anything further to discuss."

"I'm not done." She looked at her list. "I assume you have a checkbook. Please let me have it."

His finger jabbed a button on his phone. Over the speakerphone, a woman answered, "Yes, Mr. Cantrell."

"Please give Ms. Winters the Leichter checkbook when she leaves." Then he looked at her. "What else?"

"What is the status of Elly's credit cards?"

"She had three. Jonah closed the accounts."

"Were those billing statements sent to you?"

"Yes."

"Add a copy for the last two years to the other documents I've requested." She glanced at her notepad again. "How soon will you have the documents ready?"

"It will take a day or so."

"I'll pick them up the day after tomorrow at ten a.m. If there are any outstanding fees, please include an invoice."

"Are you firing me?" He started to rise, then sat back down. "Do you have any idea how long I've worked for your grandmother? Not once," he thumped the table with his hand, "did she *ever* complain about my services."

"It's not my intention to fire you, though I will let you know which of your services I will continue to use."

She slid her checklist into the folder and picked up the tote bag. "Thank you for your time." Her back rigid and her head held high, Tori marched out of his office.

On the way out, the secretary handed her the

checkbook. From the strange look on her face, Tori had to wonder how much she'd overheard.

Well, that certainly didn't go as planned, she thought, settling behind the wheel. The meeting wasn't what Tori expected. The up-to-snuff comment still rankled. She'd be the first to admit she was in over her head. But the only way to learn was to take control. Cantrell's idea was to push her aside while he made all the decisions. Once she had a copy of the records, she'd send him a letter terminating his services. There wasn't any way she could work with the man. She made a mental note for the list—hire a new CPA.

Before driving home, she swung by the bank and picked up the statements. It was a start. When she passed a pizza place, an idea sparked. Tori stopped and ordered four large pies of varying kinds to be delivered. At the grocery store, she dashed inside and bought an assortment of wine.

Though still troubled by the confrontation, her nerves had somewhat calmed when she reached the house. How was she expected to be responsible for the estate when at every turn, she was handicapped? If Cantrell could be believed, he and Jonah had already decided to keep her in the dark.

As she thought back, Jonah had said much the same during that first meeting. Don't worry about the estate, take a vacation, shop, enjoy yourself. At the time, she didn't fully comprehend what he meant. Tori was beginning to wonder who she could trust.

She parked behind Heidi's car and grabbed the box

from the bank. As she plodded her way to the front door, Mia opened it.

Beaming, she said, "You're not going to believe what we found upstairs."

Her excitement gave Tori's spirits a much-needed lift. "Let me drop this stuff in my office. Where is everyone?"

"In the music room. I'll be in the room next to the master bedroom," Mia shouted as she raced up the stairs.

When Tori walked in, Mia stood next to a piece of furniture that had to be at least eight feet tall and five feet wide. Even to her untrained eye, Tori knew she was looking at a unique antique. The top was ornately carved with scrolls, flowers, latticework and a vase. The center was a large oval mirror that extended to a bottom shelf that looked like one-half of a figure eight with carved wooden feet. On each side of the center glass were rounded shelves banded by a lattice frame. The mirror extended behind the shelves.

Mia's voice vibrated with enthusiasm. "It's an Alexander Roux rosewood etagere. He was a French cabinet maker who settled in New York City. I'd date it to around 1850 to 1860. It's in mint condition. Isn't it gorgeous?"

Awe-struck, Tori's hand gently touched the wood frame. "It is. What is an etagere?"

"It's made to display ornaments." She pointed to each of the shelves. "The lattice, which looks like a fence, keeps the object from getting knocked off. I'm not sure what the value is. I'd have to look it up."

Her tone turned serious. "Tori, if you turn this place into a B&B, you need to consider what to do with the antiques. I had no idea the extent of what you have. You don't want people coming in and possibly damaging them."

With a sense of dismay, Tori said, "Something to consider." What would she do with them?

"Okay, that's it for today. How did your meeting go?"

"It was okay. I got my answers, but you're right. Cantrell's definitely a ladies' man," she said as they walked down the stairs.

"Don't tell me he hit on you."

Thinking back over the confrontation, Tori had to grin. It was probably the last thought in Cantrell's mind. "No, just his attitude. We've got about thirty minutes before the pizzas I ordered get here. In the car are several bottles of wine."

"Dang, this is going to be fun. I'll grab the wine."

From the dining room hutch, Tori carefully picked up five glasses, liking the Waterford touch of elegance. In her vest pocket, the phone vibrated. Cripes, it was still on mute from her meeting with Cantrell. After setting the glasses on the kitchen counter, she pulled out the phone. A missed call from Jonah. She'd bet Cantrell called him.

Holding the phone to her ear, Tori waited for Jonah to answer as she set plates on the table.

When he did, in a terse tone, he said, "Tori, I received an alarming call from Sam Cantrell. He said you asked for an unwarranted number of records for the estate that was a total waste of his time and terminated his management of the estate. I have to agree with his assessment. First, there is no need for you to deal with the estate's financial documents. You need time to get acclimated, then down the line, we'll ease you into the process if you want to get involved. As your attorney, I don't recommend that you take over. Such an action would be disastrous, and it's certainly not necessary."

Though resentment stirred deep inside her, she kept the emotion out of her voice. Instead, she calmly stated, "I disagree. I'm not going to sit back and let someone manage my affairs. The administration of my property and assets are my responsibility. Not yours or Sam Cantrell's. I am entitled to a copy of all the records. He has been paid for his services. I expect to receive his full cooperation."

"I strongly object. Sam said you even canceled Elly's bank account. He's quite concerned about any outstanding checks that haven't cleared and insists the account needs to be reinstated."

"No. If he's that concerned, give me a list of outstanding checks. If necessary, I will reissue one. Shall I call him, or do you want to tell him?"

"I'll take care of it. Tori, he is preparing the final tax return for the estate. I wish you had consulted with me before you canceled the account. Ensuring the accuracy of the return is critical."

"While I don't know much about estate taxes, I can't believe terminating a checking account would affect the process."

"In my opinion, this is not how it should be handled, but it is your decision."

"Yes, it is."

"Since you are moving in this direction, we should set up an appointment to discuss the estate records and status later this week."

"I'll call tomorrow and make an appointment."

"Be that as it may, I look forward to seeing you tomorrow night."

Her face scrunched in a scowl as she jabbed the disconnect button. She turned. Mia stood in the doorway, holding the cardboard box with six bottles of wine.

"I didn't want to interrupt by walking in. It doesn't sound as if the meeting with Sam went well."

"No, it didn't."

"I don't know what was behind the call, but I will say this. What you did was right. If you don't take a stand, they'll run right over you. Some people didn't like Miss Elly because she didn't take BS from anyone. I can see a lot of her in you."

Tears clouded Tori's eyes. Oddly, Mia's words comforted her.

"Enough of the small stuff. We have an important decision, white or red?" Mia said.

Tori laughed. "Open both. Let everyone have a choice. If someone doesn't want wine, there is plenty of soda in the fridge."

When the doorbell rang, the crew was clustered in the kitchen, sipping wine.

A teenager stood on the porch holding a large red bag. Barely able to see over it, he said, "Order for Tori Winters."

She stepped back to let him enter.

Wide-eyed, he looked around. "Wow! I never thought I'd get an order for this place." The kid unzipped the bag, sliding the boxes out. He handed them to Heidi and Mia, who had followed her.

After Tori paid him and added a healthy tip, his lips curved upward in a big grin. "Ask for Jack if you want any more deliveries."

She locked the door and followed the aroma of pepperoni, garlic and onions. Boxes were already open on the counter, and everyone was piling pieces on their plate.

Over the next hour, as they stuffed themselves with pizza, they talked about everything from men to work. Tori couldn't remember when she had felt so relaxed and comfortable.

It was hard to imagine that she'd been looking over her shoulder just days before as she drove out of Springfield with no job, no home, and a small savings account.

Mia leaned back as she patted her stomach. "I wish I could eat another piece, but I'll be sicker than a dog if I do."

Tori laughed. "I don't know where you put all the slices you did eat."

Heidi spoke up. "You ought to see her at the all-you-can-eat shrimp buffet. It's downright embarrassing to be at the same table with her. She piles boiled shrimp on one plate, has a second plate for the hulls, bowls of shrimp sauce, a bowl of water with a slice of lemon, and mounds of napkins. All this is arranged in a precise order in front of her before she attacks the shrimp."

Laughter filled the room.

"All right, you've had your fun. But remember the saying about payback," Mia growled.

They whooped even louder.

Tori asked, "How long have you known each other?"

Cammie said, waving a slice with cheese dangling from the edge, "Forever," setting off another round of laughter.

"She's not kidding." Mia eyed another piece. "We've known each other since grade school. Except for Tina, who was a year behind, we were all in the same grade. Ah, heck, what's another piece?"

Heidi groaned. "She never gains a single pound. Just looking, it's another five pounds for me."

"Genetics, superior genetics," Mia proclaimed, setting off another round of laughter.

Heidi wiped her hands on a napkin. "I'll get my equipment. Tori, do you want to stay in the kitchen?"

She shrugged. "This is as good a place as any." Over the next hour, Tori wallowed in enjoyment from Heidi's hand and foot massage that went along with painting her nails. The rest of the crew scrutinized and critiqued as they watched.

Once Heidi finished, she asked, "Anyone else?"

Everyone murmured no.

Seeing the questioning look on Tori's face, Mia spoke up. "Occasionally, we have our equivalent of girl's night out. Except we get together for a pizza party. We provide food and drink. Heidi gives us manicures and pedicures."

Tori had wondered whether to offer to pay Heidi. Now, she was glad she didn't. Somehow, Tori felt she might have insulted her.

When they were ready to leave, barefoot, Tori padded to the door with them, where she gave Heidi a big hug, thanking her.

Mia said, "We'll be here early in the morning."

"I'll be ready with the coffee."

It was dark when they tromped to their cars. The lack of lights sparked another mental note—floodlights. The meager front porch light was not nearly bright enough.

Tori headed to her office. Not wanting to wait on Cantrell's expense list, she started one of her own. Tori set up a spreadsheet on her computer with headings for the check number, amount, payee, date, and which checkbook. From the stubs in Elly's and Cantrell's checkbooks, she entered the details and added a tick to the check number on the bank statement.

Cross-referencing the checks was a time-consuming task. Tori was far from finished when she decided to quit. But there was no rush. The bank statements, neatly stacked, were left on the desk with the checkbooks on top and her to-do list next to it.

As she shut down the computer, her nails gleamed under the light. What was routine for the four women was a rare occasion for her. She'd had fun, a sensation she didn't expect to experience at the Swanson party. Polished nails and a high-dollar dress wouldn't change that. It wasn't who she was. And, to be honest, it wasn't who she wanted to be.

"Why am I doing it?" Tori muttered. The answer that rose in her mind was one she didn't like. Mia had told her, "take a stand, don't let them run over you." Yet, that's what she was letting someone do by trying to fit in, mold herself into another person. A firm resolve settled over her. Tomorrow, she'd buy what she wanted, not what was expected. And, if they didn't like it, well, she'd take a page out of Elly's book, don't take BS from anyone.

After checking the front door, she headed to her bedroom. As much as she enjoyed a relaxing bath, after crawling out of the tub, Tori made another mental note—install shower.

Startled from a deep sleep, Tori shot out of bed. Her hand tugged the lamp cord as her gaze swept the room. The door was still closed. Tori moved to the side and reached for the knob. With a quick twist, she swung the door open. She peered into the hall. Something woke her, but what? Then she heard that odd scraping noise. Where was it coming from?

Her heart pounding, she waited. Finally, she closed the door. Without a lock, there wasn't any way to secure it other than to stick a chair under the knob. It wasn't much, but at least she'd have some warning if anyone tried to break in.

Chapter 11

After a short meeting with her team the next morning, Mia strolled into the kitchen.

Tori poured a cup of coffee and handed it to her. "Everything okay?"

Mia swallowed a swig. "Oh, yes. A slight adjustment. Tina and Cammie will be gone for a few hours. They have another house to clean today."

"Do you need to stay? It didn't occur to me that I could be screwing up your schedule."

"No. I'm good. Heidi is the assistant manager."

Tori refilled her cup. "I want to talk to you about something before we leave."

Mia dropped onto a chair.

As she leaned against the counter, Tori had to grin at Mia's actions before her tone turned serious. "What you said yesterday, about not letting people run over me, taking a stand, stuck in my mind. It made me stop and think about expensive clothes and all that goes with them. It's not me, never will be. In fact, and I hate to admit it, I panicked. My solution, turn myself into a Myra or Carly. So much of what has happened over the last few weeks has been surreal. It's taking me a while to find my footing." Her face scrunched. "Does any of this make sense to you?"

"Oh, yes. What do you plan to do?"

"I don't know. I don't have many clothes, so I still need to go shopping. And, I like the idea of kicking butt as you so appropriately phrased it. But I want to do it my way. I don't want to buy some expensive outfit, that I might never wear again, for a party I really don't want to go to in the first place."

"I might have a solution. I have a friend, Dina Rizzuto, who started a line of tie-dye garments. A couple of months back, I was in her studio. She has some amazing clothes, including evening apparel. They are unique and, right now, one of a kind. I'm betting they might be what you want."

A buzz of excitement raced through Tori as she listened to Mia's end of the phone call to her friend.

After disconnecting, Mia said, "Grab your stuff and let's go. She has an appointment at eleven. I'll let Heidi know we're leaving."

As Mia backed out, she said, "Dina's shop is in Benbrook, southside of Fort Worth, so it's only a thirty or so minute drive."

Tori snapped her seat belt. "Tell me about her."

"I met Dina in college, and we became good friends. She was working on a degree in Arts. She's truly a talented person. After graduation, Dina decided to try her hand at designing clothing. She started in her garage, recently moved into a small warehouse, and has two employees. Whenever I'm up that way, I stop, and we have lunch or coffee."

Mia turned onto the main highway. "We commiserate over the difficulties of owning a business."

"I can't imagine how difficult it must be."

"Probably no more so than being a nurse. Pros and cons to most everything, no matter what you do."

"Do you have family here, Mia?"

"Yep. Mom is a teacher, and dad works at the city power plant. I have a sister, a pain in the ass, but in spite of it, we love her. She just graduated high school. How about you?"

"Of course, you know my dad was killed in Iraq. Mom died a few months ago. No other family, or at least none I knew about until I got the letter from Jonah."

"It must have been a real shocker to learn about Elly."

"Cripes, it's the understatement of the year."

"So, what are your plans for the B&B?"

"I wish I knew. As you heard yesterday, I've still got estate issues I need to fix. I don't suppose you know a good CPA? I may need one."

Mia laughed as she changed lanes to pass an eighteen-wheeler. "It so happens I do. Jeff Archer. He's the type of person who'll tell you if an account isn't in his wheelhouse. Jeff doesn't pull any punches."

"Sounds like he's what I need. Mia, is there anyone you don't know?"

Mia chuckled. "I'm not sure."

Turning onto a side street, she parked in front of a small warehouse. The name, emblazoned in multiple colors next to the door, read—*In Sync Designs*.

"Catchy name," Tori observed as she slid out of the car.

Inside, the large room was a beehive of activity. Two women sat behind sewing machines, and another stood at a large table cutting a bolt of cloth. Scattered around the room, dummies in various shapes were draped with pieces of fabric.

A tall woman, built on queenly lines, with long dark hair swinging around her shoulders, strode toward them. Her arms outstretched, she grabbed Mia, hugging and exclaiming, "What a wonderful surprise to get your phone call."

"My gosh, you've made a lot of changes since the last time I was here." Mia's gaze swept the room.

"And more to come. I hired another employee today. She'll be here next week."

"Dina, this is Tori Winters. She just moved to Granbury from Missouri. There is a formal event tonight, and she needs an outfit. I suggested we stop here first before heading to the mall."

Dina extended her hand. "Nice to meet you." Her eyes skimmed over Tori with an assessing look.

As they shook hands, Tori said, "This is very impressive. Mia has been singing your praises."

With a tinkle of laughter, Dina said, "She's always been one of my strongest supporters. In fact, she was the one who suggested I should consider designing clothes." Her hands waved toward the room. "Here I am, designing clothes."

A mischievous grin crossed Tori's face. "She didn't mention that tidbit. I'd say she's a dang good idea person. She suggested I turn an old house I inherited into a B&B, and it's what I plan to do."

"What can I say? When I'm good, I'm good." Mia held her fingers to her mouth, puffed, then buffed the nails on her shirt.

"Nothing bashful about our Mia." Another chuckle erupted from Dina. "Okay, let's see what I can do for you. What do you have in mind?"

"I'm open to any suggestion."

"How formal is formal?"

Tori looked to Mia for help.

"I'd bet all the women will be rigged out to the nines, even though it's only a dinner party."

Tori added, "I'm a nurse and have never attended a formal function. This is all new. But I've decided not to start off by simply falling into line with the accepted mode of dress. It's not me. It's why Mia suggested I might be interested in your designs."

"Come with me. We'll see if anything strikes your fancy."

Dina led them into another room where clothes hung from hangers on multiple racks. "Everything is separated by style." She pointed as she talked. "Shirts on those racks, pants there, skirts over there, and here are the dresses."

Tori stepped to a rack, pushing hangers aside. Amazed, her eyes scanned the beautiful, vibrant colors of the tie-dye material. A full-length dress caught her attention. It seemed to change color with the movement of the silky fabric. A sash crisscrossed the bodice, emphasizing the v-neckline. From the sash, the material fell in graceful folds. She pulled it out and held it up against her body.

"Wow!" Mia said. "The colors bring out the red highlights in your hair."

"I agree," Dina said. "It's a bit long for you, but it's easily fixed." She motioned with her hand toward another open door. "I'm not set up with a dressing room, but you can use my office."

Eager to see how it looked, Tori rushed inside. When she slid it over her head, the dress felt like it had been made for her, though Dina was right. It was too long. Holding up the hem so she wouldn't trip, she walked out.

"Oh, my god, it's perfect," Mia exclaimed.

Dina pointed. "There's a mirror against that wall."

Standing in front of it, Tori gazed at her image in awe. The dress was exactly what she wanted. It was different and unique. "I'll take it," Tori said.

"Don't you want to know how much?"

"Nope."

Dina called to one of the women seated at the sewing machine. "Leticia, I need your help."

The two women tucked and pinned for the next few minutes, tailoring the fit to Tori's body. When they finished, Dina went with her into the office to help her change.

After handing the dress to Leticia, Dina said, "This will

take thirty minutes or so, then you can try it on again, to be sure it's right."

"That's good because I want to look at the other clothes."

By the time Tori and Mia were ready to leave, the evening gown and several other dresses hung in garment bags. Tori had also acquired numerous shirts, skirts, and pants.

It took all three women to carry the boxes and garment bags to the car. Once they were stowed, Mia gave Dina another hug.

The woman stepped toward Tori to hug her. "This was an unexpected bonus to meet you."

Tori said, "I'll be back."

As Mia backed out, Tori settled into the seat with a deep sigh. "Dang, that was fun."

"Yes, it was." Mia had also picked out two shirts and a pair of pants. "Now, we need to decide on shoes."

"Rats, I hadn't thought about that. So, where too?"

"Hulen mall is not far from here. Lots of shoe stores."

Mia parked near one of the main entrances. Inside, it took a few stops before they found what Tori needed. Well satisfied with the day's results, they headed back to Granbury.

At the house, their arms overloaded with the clothes and bags of shoes, they headed to Tori's bedroom. After dropping everything on the bed, Mia walked out to check on her team.

Tori started to put the clothes away when footsteps clattered in the hallway. Three women, followed by Mia, burst into the room.

Heidi, in front, exclaimed, "Okay, you've got to show us."

Tori pulled the evening gown from the garment bag on the bed and held it up.

Cammie said, "Oh, my, gosh, it's perfect. I love it. You'll knock them dead in it."

"Show us the rest of the stuff," Tina said.

Enjoying the show and tell, Tori pulled out the clothes she'd just put away.

Tina held up a skirt. "Mia, I've heard you mention Dina several times, but I didn't know she was this talented. The way she designs the clothing around the colors is amazing. I can see why she named her business, In Sync Designs."

Mia grinned. "Here's the really good news. She's giving us a fifty percent discount."

"Really?" the women chimed in chorus.

Tina said, "We need to schedule a day for a road trip. In the meantime, ladies, save up your money."

Mia glanced at her watch. "Hey, it's getting late. While we finish upstairs, you get ready."

After bathing, Tori blow-dried her hair and slipped into underwear. Bundled in a robe, she walked out shouting, "Ready when you are."

In the kitchen, after ordering Tori to sit, Heidi spread a towel over her shoulders. Once she finished curling Tori's hair, Heidi started on the makeup. When everyone chimed in with suggestions, she said, "Tori doesn't need a lot. Her skin texture is perfect. A light touch of makeup will work."

After a brush of rouge across the cheekbones, eye

shadow, a pat of powder, and lipstick, Heidi stepped back to look Tori over. Ringed on each side, Mia, Cammie, and Tina closely scrutinized her face and hair.

Tori had to laugh.

"What's so funny?" Mia asked.

"I feel like a bug under a microscope."

Heidi told Mia, "Get the dress and shoes."

With Heidi on one side and Mia on the other, they gently eased the dress over Tori's head and face. Once it fell into place, Mia snapped the sash.

Cammie said, "Mirror. Where is a mirror?"

Mia piped up. "The etagere. It has the biggest mirror in the house."

Tori slipped into the new sandals and followed them up the stairs. Bunched together, they watched as Tori stepped in front of the mirror, only to stare in stunned surprise. With the hair, makeup, and dress, Tori almost didn't recognize herself. The dress clung, accentuating the curves of her body, capped off by the high-heeled sandals.

Tori looked past her image to the four women behind her, each with an expression of exuberance. They genuinely rejoiced in her good fortune, no envy or jealousy. Suddenly, she was consumed by a rush of emotion. Tears gathered, and she gulped. She couldn't spoil Heidi's work.

The doorbell chimed.

Mia said, "I bet that's Linc. Downstairs everyone. Let's see his reaction when Tori walks down the stairs. Wait until you hear his voice before you come down."

"Yes, ma'am." Her laughter followed them out the door.

Linc's voice could be heard a few minutes later as he greeted everyone. She walked to the stairs. Holding onto the railing with one hand, the other held up the hem of the dress as she started down. Looking down at Linc, she had to admit he looked dang good. His dark hair curled over the collar of a black, form-fitting tuxedo.

Linc looked up. His flirtatious laughter died as a stunned expression crossed his face. He watched her descend before rushing to take her hand at the last two steps. He raised it to his lips and said, "Wow! You look … absolutely amazing."

Behind him, Tori saw the women grinning from ear to ear.

Tori said, "Let me get my bag, and I'll be ready to go."

"I'll get it," Heidi said. "I need to get my bag too."

Tori waited on the front porch. Mia was the last out the door. She hugged Tori and whispered, "You got this. Kick some ass."

The women waved as they got into their vehicles, though they had to wait until Linc backed out. Tori made a mental note—widen the driveway.

On the way, Linc asked, "Where did you find that dress? I can't say I am a fashion expert, but it's extraordinary."

"From a friend of Mia's."

"Mia!"

She smiled. "You'd be surprised at who Mia knows. Tell me what I should expect tonight."

"Myra has invited a few friends to meet you. There will

be a couple of rounds of pre-dinner drinks before we eat. Don't worry. If you run into any snags, I'll bail you out."

Tori wasn't sure she wanted Linc's help, but there wasn't much she could do about it.

"Who are the friends?"

"I'm not sure who Myra has invited. I guess we'll both be surprised."

Linc pulled in front of a large two-story house. The land behind it sloped to the lake. Cars lined both sides of the street.

Her brows twitched upward. "A few. I should have asked for your definition. In my books, it's three or four."

As he slid out, Linc flashed a grin over his shoulder. "Don't worry. It won't be that bad."

A reassurance Tori didn't believe as they walked inside.

The large entryway led to a room where the swell of voices resonated. Myra appeared in the archway. Her attention on Linc, she didn't immediately look at Tori. "Linc, I was wondering when you would get here."

Her gaze shifted to Tori. To say her eyes bulged might be an overstatement. Still, one Tori felt adequately described the woman's reaction.

Myra quickly recovered. "My dear, don't you look nice," giving Tori an air kiss.

Tori's lips twitched in a smile as phony as the one plastered on Myra's face.

"Thank you. It's nice to see you again."

"Linc, introduce Tori to our guests. I need to check on dinner."

As he pulled her forward, the low hum of conversation

momentarily faded as guests caught sight of her.

In a black, off-the-shoulder gown more suited for a fancy ball than a dinner party, Carly turned as they approached. Dumbfounded, her gaze scanned Tori from head to foot before the look turned to one of avid dislike.

Linc said, "Tori, I believe you've met Carly. This is her father, Judd."

Tori nodded.

A heavy-set man, not much taller than his daughter, greeted her. Dark hair was trimmed into a short, military-style cut. In a broad swarthy face, dark eyes had a calculating look, though his voice boomed with joviality.

"Tori, I'm delighted to finally meet you. I've wanted to talk to you." He winked. "I'm certain you'll be interested."

"Later, Judd," Linc said as he steered her to another couple.

Across the room, she noticed Sam watching her. Hostility smoldered in his eyes.

Unnerved, she murmured, "I've already met Sam."

"I heard," Linc said, his tone dry.

She soon gave up trying to remember the names. It was hopeless. Though everyone welcomed her, several eyed her with a supercilious assessment.

It was a welcome relief to see someone she knew. David stood next to Malcolm Reynolds. The metal-grey suit and black shirt with an open collar David wore seemed casual. Yet he wasn't out of place in a room full of men in tuxedos. It suited his brashness.

Greeting her, David's eyebrow cocked up as his gaze

wandered over her. His mouth twisted in a roguish grin. Unnerved by the gleam in his eyes, she pushed aside a tingling awareness that tugged at her. She turned her attention to Linc as he introduced Malcolm's wife.

Once she'd met everyone, Linc left her by the fireplace to get two glasses of wine.

Myra stopped next to her. "I must say your dress is unusual. Not something I would expect to see at a formal dinner party. Where did you buy it? I can't imagine it's an haute-couture design."

"In Sync Designs, and yes, it is." It wasn't a total lie since the dress had to be altered.

Carly stepped up. "I've never heard of the designer."

Tori shrugged as if the statement were unimportant, adding to Carly's ire.

"I'm surprised you're not decked out in Elly's jewelry." Carly sniped.

Tori's gaze locked on the woman. "What jewelry?"

Delighted to air knowledge Tori didn't know, Carly rushed to say, "She had quite a collection. Whenever she went out, she looked like a walking jewelry store."

"This is the first I've heard of any jewelry. Hopefully, Jonah will be able to explain why."

Myra said, "Tori, please make yourself at home. There is a powder room at the end of the hallway." She grabbed Carly's arm, dragging her away while whispering in her daughter's ear. Whatever was said put a mulish look on Carly's face.

David, a glass in his hand, passed the two women. He

slightly angled his body when he stopped to watch them walk away. "From their expressions, I'd say you won that round.

He turned back to her. "No wonder Carly is bent out of shape. You've upstaged every woman here." The warm gleam was back in his eyes.

His compliment set off another tingle, one she decidedly ignored. "I didn't expect to see you since Jonah is here. I thought you didn't like him."

"No. I said Jonah and I don't always agree. I've known the family since dad married Lea. Rumor has it that Jonah's father was in love with Elly. I don't know if there is any truth to it, but it's still talked about."

He took a sip of his drink. "But I'm not the surprise here. It's you." He lifted his glass as if to toast her.

"Me! Why? Didn't they know I would be here?"

"Of course, they knew. Myra proclaimed it from the rooftops. Come meet the poor nurse from Missouri who inherited Elly's money and house. Why do you think more than half of them are here? A mercenary lot. You're not what they expected to see."

"That's rather contemptuous."

"Probably. But it's true. Here comes good ole' Linc. I'll leave you to his meaningless ministrations. If you need help, wiggle your fingers. I'll come running."

What was that all about, she wondered. Why the note of animosity toward Linc? Her curiosity would have to wait as Linc handed her a glass of wine.

Over the next hour, various individuals walked up. It

didn't take Tori long to realize David was right. They weren't interested in her. It was a fishing expedition to find out her plans. Refusing to satisfy their curiosity, she was ambiguous and vague in her answers.

When Carly pulled Linc away, saying she had something important to tell him, Judd cornered her.

"I've heard you plan to sell," Judd said.

"No, it's not true." Tori took a sip of wine.

"You don't need to be coy with me to drive up the price. It really isn't necessary. I'm prepared to make a very generous offer. I'm certain you'll find it's in your best interest."

She was getting tired of hearing what was in her best interest. Irritated, her tone was sharp. "Judd, I'm not selling."

"Now, now," he said as if patting a recalcitrant child on the head. "You say that now, but you haven't heard my offer. What's a good time to come by the house?"

"Judd, it's a waste of time, yours and mine."

"I absolutely insist you hear me out."

"No, there's no point. Please excuse me."

Tori found her way to the powder room. She wondered how long she could hide inside before someone started looking for her. Then decided she wasn't a coward. After freshening up, she slowly strolled along the hallway, looking at the pictures on the walls.

As she neared the living room, she heard Carly's strident voice. Tori stopped, hoping the woman would move away from the doorway.

"Sam, tacky is the only way to describe that dress and

shows how out of place she is. It's utterly appalling Elly left the entire estate to her instead of David."

Sam said, "My dear, let me tell you, the woman doesn't have a clue about what she's doing. She came to my office to discuss the estate's finances, insisting she was taking over. Tori actually had a list of questions she constantly referred to as if she couldn't remember them. I predict it'll only take a few months for her to run the estate into the ground."

Anger built inside Tori as she stepped into the room. Sam and Carly turned toward her. Both looked at her with a cold stare.

With a mocking tone, she said, "I've always been taught organization is the key to any success. A principle a CPA should know. By the way, you are fired. If I find that you hinder or damage my takeover of the administration, I will slap you with a lawsuit. I also believe your continued handling of the tax returns for the probate is a conflict of interest. If Jonah is unwilling to remove you, I will hire another CPA to review your filings."

Myra, having heard the heated exchange, rushed up.

As Tori strolled away, Myra said in a hushed tone, "What the hell is wrong with you two? Carly, your claws are showing. As for you, Sam, have you forgotten what's at stake?"

My, my, Tori thought. The 'butter won't melt in my mouth' woman actually said a swear word. But what did she mean by, "What's at stake?"

The dinner bell chimed. Her thoughts about the

confrontation would have to wait as Linc stepped up to escort Tori into the dining room. Much to her dismay, she was seated next to Judd.

Unaccustomed to alcohol, she asked for water when the waiter tried to fill her wine glass. Judging by the number of bottles sitting on a sideboard, consuming endless refills wasn't a good idea.

With each course, time crawled. Everyone seemed more focused on her than the food. Even Judd continually tried to draw her into a conversation about the sale of the house.

A woman, Tori couldn't remember her name, asked if she had family who would be arriving. Tori, in between bites of braised chicken, told her no.

The woman persisted. "I know your father was killed years ago, but what about your mother? Surely you must have other relatives?"

With difficulty, she controlled her impatience, simply saying, "My mother passed away a few months ago."

"Oh, I'm sorry for your loss. It's hard to lose a family member. Then what *are* you going to do with that huge house and no family?"

Tori said, "I haven't decided."

Another woman joined the conversation. "I heard you planned to sell. That's a wise move. The place is really too much for a woman by herself to handle. I told Miss Elly so on many occasions."

Too much for a woman by herself to handle. Really! The

woman might as well have dashed in front of a bull, waving a red flag, Tori thought.

She laid the fork down and leaned forward to look at the woman. Incensed, she said, "I must disagree."

At her tone, all conversation came to an abrupt halt. Eyes turned toward her. "I believe there's nothing a woman can't accomplish when she sets her mind to it."

Uneasy, looking around, the woman squirmed.

"Everyone has been walking around this issue since I got here, so let me make it abundantly clear. I am not selling the house. In fact, I intend to turn it into a bed and breakfast inn."

Several people gasped. Down the table, David gave her a mocking salute. Voices erupted. Next to her, Judd's was the loudest protest of all. "Why on earth would you even consider such a notion?"

Tori ignored them as she picked up the napkin spread across her lap and folded it. She laid it next to her plate. Looking at Jonah seated across from her, she said, "I'll call you in the morning. I have an issue to discuss with you."

Stunned, he only nodded.

She looked at Linc seated further down the table. "Linc, I hate to pull you away from the party, but I'd like to go home."

When Linc hesitated, looking at Judd, David jumped to his feet. "I'm finished and need to leave early anyway. I'll be glad to oblige."

"Thank you, David. Let me get my purse."

Linc started to protest, but Tori waved him off. "I

appreciate your bringing me, but I don't want to further disrupt the party."

There was nothing he could do except gracefully subside, though he shot an annoyed look at David.

Despite the scowl on Myra's face, she rose and walked with Tori to the door, with David on their heels. After thanking the woman, Tori strode outside.

Inside David's truck, she leaned back and breathed a deep sigh of relief.

Laughing, David pulled away from the curb. "You certainly tossed a fox into the hen house with that declaration. You mentioned it before. Do you really mean it, or was it so much bluff?"

"I meant every word."

"I wish you luck. I think you'll need it."

Her eyes narrowed as she looked at him. Her tone bitter, she asked, "Why? Is it because you believe I can't do it because I'm a woman?"

He gave her a look of sympathy. "Not at all. I expect your turning the house into an inn will be a roaring success, assuming you get the chance. I'm referring to the fact the deck may be stacked against you. You didn't make any friends tonight. You could come up against obstacles you won't expect."

Her chin lifted with grim determination. "Just let someone try and stop me."

Chapter 12

When Mia and the crew arrived, they tromped into the kitchen instead of heading to their assignments.

While everyone grabbed a cup of coffee and donuts, Mia said, "Give it up. We want the gritty details. How was the party?"

Tori groaned. "Not so good. For the most part, the dress went over well. Several women were interested and wanted to know where I got it. I referred them to Dina. I hope it generates some sales."

Mia grinned. "Who didn't like it? Wait a minute, let me guess." She drum rolled her fingers on the table. "Wait for it … Myra and Carly."

"You nailed it. There were a couple of snide remarks."

"To be expected."

"So what happened?" Heidi asked before biting into a donut, setting off a cloud of powder.

"It was a setup. This little party, which wasn't so little, was all about my plans for the house. That's all anyone wanted to talk about. Most of it I handled without any problems until dinner. It went downhill from there."

Wide-eyed, Tina asked, "Why?"

"One of the guests said that selling the house was the smart thing to do. A woman, *by herself*, couldn't handle it."

"And, what did you do?" Mia asked with a wicked grin.

"A rocket. That was me going off."

Cammie chuckled. "I wish I had been a fly on the wall."

"I told them I wasn't going to sell. In fact, I planned to turn the house into a B&B. That stopped the conversations, at least for a few minutes."

Mia said, "Oh, my gosh—"

Heidi interrupted. "You're going to make this place a B&B?" Stunned, she, Tina and Cammie stared at Tori.

"Yep," she said, then took a swig of coffee.

They started to talk. Mia flung her hand in the air. "We can't all talk at once. What did they do?"

"Nothing. I got up and left. David brought me home."

"David? That's interesting," Heidi said. "What happened to Linc?"

"It was toward the end of the dinner, and he wasn't fast enough when I said I wanted to leave. David volunteered. I have a feeling I won't be invited back."

Mia laughed. "I wouldn't bet on it. If nothing else, Myra is tenacious. Wow! The rumor mill must be humming this morning. Everyone will have heard. You know you can still back out?"

"No way, no how. I'm one hundred percent convinced.

As I told David, I'm not letting anyone stop me."

Cammie spoke up. "Did he believe someone would?"

"He said there could be obstacles."

Mia leaned back with a thoughtful air. "He could be right."

"How?" Tori asked.

"Zoning and construction permits, inspectors. Anyone along the line balks, it would stop you dead in the water."

"Maybe so, but that doesn't mean I can't fight back. And I will. Why would Judd Swanson want this property?"

Tina straightened. "I can answer that. My brother works for Holt Construction. He overheard a conversation about plans to use this property for a high-rise condominium. He knew I was working here and thought I might be interested."

"Dang," Mia exclaimed. "I bet Judd is behind this."

"The man was quite persistent about wanting to make an offer for the property. He wasn't taking no for an answer."

"This could be what David meant," Mia said. "Judd has a lot of pull in this town. If anyone could block you from renovating this place, he could."

Tori's phone chimed. She pulled it from her pocket. "I'd better answer this." She waved her hand at the table. "I'll take care of cleaning up."

Mia rose, saying, "Time for us to get to work."

Tori hit the button. "Good morning, Jonah."

"Is it possible for you to stop by the office today? Or I can come to the house. Just let me know when."

Tori didn't want to meet with him until after she met with the Fort Worth attorney. "No. I'm sorry I can't. But we are still on for tomorrow, right?"

He sighed. "Yes, we are. I am quite concerned by the events that transpired last night."

"I'm certain you are. I had planned to tell you about my plans tomorrow. I still have several questions for you. In the meantime, there was an incident with Sam Cantrell at the party. I fired him. It's why I wanted to speak with you this morning. I would prefer he doesn't have any further dealings with the estate, including the probate."

"Before he left last night, Sam told me he quit, not that you fired him."

"I'm sure he was trying to save face. Please let me know who you plan to hire."

"We'll discuss it tomorrow."

"Also, Carly mentioned Elly's jewelry last night. What happened to it?"

There was a short silence before Jonah said, "I don't know. After Elly's death, we couldn't find it."

"Do you have a record of what she had?"

"An old list from several years ago. If you haven't opened the safe, they could be there."

"I haven't found the combination, but why are you just now telling me?"

"It didn't occur to me until you asked. We can talk about it tomorrow."

As she disconnected, finding a locksmith went from low priority to high. Tori poured the last of the coffee, leaning against the counter. At every turn, there was another disturbing issue about the estate. How could you forget missing jewelry? Unless it wasn't that valuable, though she didn't believe it. Then there was the pressure to sell. Could she be stopped from renovating? The sense of disquiet only deepened as she wondered what she could do.

The chime of the doorbell broke into her musings. Setting the cup on the counter, she headed to the front door. When she opened it, a man faced her holding a large box. "Ms. Winters?"

"Yes."

"I work for Sam Cantrell. This is the information you requested." She stepped back to let him set the box down. Then he turned and trotted back to his van.

Tori closed the door and reached down to pick up the box. It saved her a trip since she really didn't want another encounter with the man. Heavier than she expected, she staggered to the office and dropped it. It hit the floor with a thud. She pushed it against the wall. She'd look through it when she had more time, which wasn't today.

When she walked behind the desk, the box of bank statements on the floor caught her eye. Puzzled, Tori stared at it for a few moments. It was sitting further away from the chair, and the statement on top wasn't where she left off. She reached down, grabbed several and quickly thumbed through them. The top four pages were out of order.

Disturbed, she tossed them back down. Is this what woke her the other night? Did someone trip over the box? No, it wasn't possible. She'd checked the windows and doors before going to bed. With everything going on, she probably forgot to put them in the correct order.

Seated, she pulled her to-do list toward her, adding the new items. The list was growing faster than she was crossing them off. With a sigh, she booted up the computer. A search pulled up two locksmiths. She wrote the names and telephone numbers on her pad. When she got back, she'd call.

She pulled the folder from the desk drawer containing a copy of Elly's will. Had she told Mia she'd be gone? It was a good example about forgetting.

Feeling reassured about the box of statements, she strode toward the music room to find Mia. For a moment, she stopped, taking in the gleaming furniture. It even smelled clean. Mia was wiping down the woodwork.

"Hey, need something?" she asked.

"Did I tell you I had to go to Fort Worth?"

"No."

"Hmm ... thought so. I'm getting ready to leave. I should be back before you're done for the day."

"If not, I'll make sure the place is locked up before we leave. I had everyone park on the street."

"Thanks."

Tori gathered her files, tote bag and left. Following the GPS directions, she soon pulled into the parking lot. She stared up at the metal and glass, multi-storied building as she exited the car. It certainly was a contrast to the unpretentious building for the Greer law firm.

From what little Tori knew about Elly, she didn't seem

to be the type of person to act without a reason. What drove her grandmother to come here? As the elevator shot upward to the fifth floor, she couldn't quell her uneasiness.

The glass-fronted door opened into a luxurious waiting room. An older woman seated behind a desk asked, "May I help you?"

Her look of approval was a decided boost to settle Tori's nerves. She was glad she'd worn one of her new outfits.

"I'm Tori Winters. I have an appointment with Mr. Foote."

"I thought you might be. There is an amazing resemblance."

"You knew Elly Leichter, my grandmother?"

"Yes, she was here on several occasions. A delightful lady in every sense of the word."

This was certainly different from the descriptions she had thus far of Elly.

"Mr. Foote is waiting for you. I'll let him know you are here. Would you like coffee or a soda?"

"Coffee, please."

"Cream or sugar?"

"Just black."

The woman left. A few minutes later, a man in his middle forties walked toward her, his hand extended.

"Daniel Foote. So nice to meet you."

Tall, slim, and conservatively dressed, his thin face had a calming look.

"We'll be in the conference room."

On the way, they passed several large offices. "This is a big firm," Tori observed.

"We have eight attorneys plus the staff." He motioned to a doorway. He followed, saying, "Please have a seat wherever you like."

Tori sat on one side of the large oval table as the attorney settled in a chair across from her. A large envelope and a file folder were already on the table.

The woman who greeted her walked in with two cups.

She placed one in front of Tori and handed the other to the attorney.

"Thank you, Emma."

On her way out, she closed the door.

For a moment, he looked at her. "The resemblance is uncanny." He briefly shook his head as if to clear his thoughts. "Let's make it Dan and Tori."

She nodded and took a sip of the rich, dark brew.

He got down to business after a brief conversation about the trip from Missouri to Texas.

"I'm sure you must have questions. Why don't we start with those?"

"I assume your will replaced one prepared by Jonah Greer."

"Yes, it did."

"Did David Tucker inherit in the original will?"

"Yes."

"Why did Elly hire you?"

He took a sip of coffee. "She found out about you and wanted to set up a new will."

"That still doesn't explain why she hired a new attorney."

"No, it doesn't. Elly was afraid."

Her nerves twitched. Whatever Tori expected, it wasn't this.

"Your grandmother was sharp as a tack. Mentally, there was nothing wrong with her. She had difficulty walking but didn't want anyone fussing over her. Your grandmother was a proud and independent woman."

He took another sip. "Jonah Greer and Sam Cantrell, her CPA, had been pressuring her to sell the house. David Tucker and some others joined in. She began to hear strange noises in the house."

The twitch deepened. The same thing was happening to her. A chilling thought arose. "Dan, is it possible someone shoved her down those stairs?"

"The thought did cross my mind. But it was ruled an accidental death."

"Did she contact the police?"

"No. Elly said she was on to something but wasn't ready to talk to the police. She'd already heard rumors that she was senile. Elly didn't want to add to them with vague claims about noises. She needed an independent person who could testify that she was in full possession of her mental faculties. If anyone tried to have her declared incompetent, she wanted someone on her side. It's why she came here."

He paused and took another sip as he considered whether to tell her the rest. Watching her sit, stiff-backed, her chin pushed up in determination, just as Elly had done, made his decision.

"Greer knew nothing about the new will until after Elly died. He was the executor. I forwarded him a copy when I learned of her death. He called. During the conversation, he mentioned Elly's mental abilities, that she had become unstable. Greer expressed a concern that the will might not hold up in court. I informed him that Elly was fully competent in not-so-polite terms. Not only would I swear to it in court, but so would several of my staff. It was the last conversation I had with him. He didn't know it, but I kept tabs on him. I knew he was looking for you but didn't know you'd been located until I got your call. It was quite a relief."

Distressed by the revelation, she said, "Did he really believe Elly was senile?"

"I don't know. We never got that far in the conversation. As far as I was concerned, it wasn't a topic open for debate."

"Dan, if Elly had been declared incompetent, what happened to the will?" She was certain she knew but wanted to hear his answer.

"The will would have been invalidated. Everything would revert to the previous will."

"David would have inherited?"

"Yes."

Her level of disquiet grew, but she'd have to wait until later to sort out why this fact was so disturbing.

"When did you find out you had inherited?"

"Jonah sent me a letter, asking me to call. When I did,

he wanted to fly to Springfield, Missouri, to meet me. He said it involved an inheritance and couldn't discuss it over the phone. I had some rather bad problems at the time and put him off. Due to my circumstances, I decided to move to Texas. I called the day before I hit town."

He threw back his head and laughed. "I bet that took him by surprise. In my opinion, Greer probably hoped that by flying to Missouri, he could hand over the money and get you to sign a deal to sell the house."

She frowned. "That didn't occur to me, though you could be right. Several people, including Jonah, his son, Linc, and David, have pressured me to sell. I found out this morning that a developer wants to buy my land for a high-rise condominium."

"Are you going to?"

"No. But no one wants to believe me. Dan, from the moment I laid eyes on the house, I fell in love with it. I want to turn it into a B&B inn."

"Ambitious project, but you've got the money to underwrite it."

"Yes, I do. But I've also been warned I may hit some roadblocks I can't get around."

With a serious look, he leaned forward. "What do you mean?"

"I don't know a lot about construction, but there are ways someone could stop me if I can't get a permit or whatever."

He tapped a finger on the table as he thought. "Here's what we can do. Let people know you have hired another law firm to help you with the contracts and such for the renovation. Greer won't like it, but you have a very logical reason. His ties to the business community could be a conflict of interest. As the long-time attorney for the family, you don't want to create any problems for him."

Tori liked the way this man thought. "Consider yourself hired."

"Do you have any other questions about the will?"

"Not about the will per se, but I think I'll follow up on Elly's accident and get copies of the reports."

At his surprised look, she said, "I'm a nurse. For the last several months, I worked for hospice." With Horace in mind, she said, "I've had some experience with murder."

"Another fact I didn't know. Let me know what you find out."

"Here's something else. I've been hearing strange noises at night. Elly wasn't making it up. So far, I haven't found out why."

Alarmed, he said, "Then it's not safe to stay there."

A hard look flashed in her eyes. "There's a big difference. I'm not defenseless like Elly. No one is going to drive me out of that house."

How sad Elly had never known this remarkable young woman, he thought.

"For your information, I fired the CPA, Sam Cantrell." She went on to explain why.

"Under the circumstances, it's probably a wise move. I have a couple of firms I could recommend."

"I'll keep that in mind. Thank you."

"I do have one other item of business." He motioned toward the envelope. "Elly gave me this with instructions to give it to you in person."

Tori stared at the envelope with her name written across the front, *Tori Elly Winters*. She looked up at Dan with a questioning look.

He smiled. "I don't know what is inside. But Elly was most insistent it was to be given to you."

Tori reached for it and carefully placed it in her tote bag.

Dan escorted her to the front door. "If you need any help, call. I don't want to tell you not to worry about issues with the renovation. Problems are going to pop up, but they can be fixed. Concentrate on getting it done the way you want."

She shook his hand. "Thank you."

Reassured, she couldn't help comparing her reaction to her grandmother's. Like Elly, Tori now had someone in her corner. All the way home, though, the envelope weighed on her mind. What was inside? Why did Elly leave it with Dan?

When she pulled up to the drive, the crew hadn't left yet. A strange vehicle was in the driveway. She parked on the street. As she walked inside, her gut twisted at the sound of Myra Swanson's shrill voice.

"We really don't mind waiting until Tori gets home. It's vitally important we speak with her."

If last night wasn't bad enough, now she had the woman in her house. Irritated by the intrusion, she stepped into the room. Not only was Myra on the couch, but so was

Carly. Judd sat in one of the chairs. With a look of consternation on her face, Mia stood at the end of the sofa.

"Hello."

Everyone looked toward her.

Mia rushed toward the door. "I need to check on my crew." They ignored her.

"There you are," Myra said. "Good gracious. It seems we've been waiting forever. What on earth could you have been doing?"

Her tone cold, Tori said, "I wasn't expecting company."

"Well, why should you? After all, you know so few people."

Tori settled in a chair, dropping the tote bag to the floor. Her gaze scanned Carly, then Judd's face. She had to give them credit for determination. They weren't giving up.

When she didn't respond, Myra said, her voice bright and chipper. "We truly are concerned about you. After your statement last night and the way you rushed out of the room … well, we had to come by and try to get all this straightened out."

"Get what straightened out?"

"All that business with Thea."

"Thea?"

"Why, yes. The lady, quite frankly, you verbally attacked. Poor woman, she was beside herself with embarrassment. Then you went off on a ridiculous tangent to prove a point."

A slow burn built. It certainly didn't take Myra long to push her buttons. "What point is that?"

"Well, all this silly business about you renovating this rickety old house. It's nothing but a liability. It should be torn down instead of letting people stay here."

So this was going to be their new tactic, attack the house. David had nailed it.

Judd spoke up. "Myra's right, Tori. This house is a liability. We tried to get Elly to sell, but she was just as adamant. If she had, she'd still be alive."

Her voice harsh, Tori said, "What do you mean by that?"

With a look of astonishment, Myra's hands waved in the air. "What are you trying to imply? Everyone knows Elly wouldn't have had that horrible accident if she had been living somewhere else."

Judd said, "It would be dangerous to rent it out. If someone were hurt or injured, you'd be facing huge lawsuits. There are two well-qualified contractors in town. You should have the house examined before you decide to sink any money in it. You'll find out I'm right. I can have them out here tomorrow."

"It's not necessary. I already have a contractor in mind, one recommended by my attorney. I will pass on your concerns." While she didn't have one, it was a minor detail she planned to correct.

Judd's eyes narrowed. "What are you talking about? I spoke with Jonah this morning. He never mentioned a contractor. He's just as concerned about the liability as I am."

"Judd, I'm not referring to Jonah. I hired a law firm in

Fort Worth to handle the contractual issues involved with the renovation."

Grim-faced, he said, "Firing Jonah isn't going to gain you any friends in this town, Tori. He's very well-respected and liked."

Of course, Myra had to add her two cents while Carly sat there with a smug look.

"Judd's right. First, you fire Sam, and now Jonah. He has handled your grandmother's affairs for years. It's shameful, a slap in the face."

"I have not fired Jonah. He is still my attorney, not that it is any of your business. But I don't want any wild or false rumors going around. I took this step because of Jonah's reputation in this community. I don't want to create a conflict of interest that would create a problem for him."

Judd asked, "Who is the attorney?"

"Daniel Foote, with Atkins, Foote, and Smart in Fort Worth."

He stood and took a step forward, looming over her. His eyes glinted with a menacing look. "I've heard of them. A high-priced attorney isn't going to change anything. You'd better heed my warning about the house. It's not safe. There could be another accident … like the one that killed Elly."

A chill raced over her. She slowly stood, forcing Judd to step back. Her tone unyielding, she looked him in the eye. "Let *me* add a warning of my own. I'm not an elderly, frail woman. I plan to live here. If not in this house, then I'll build a new one. It's as simple as that. The property is not for sale. Have I made it clear?"

His jaw rigid with anger, he looked at his wife, jerking his head toward the door. Turning, he marched out of the room.

Not bothering to say goodbye, both women shot her an ugly look as they followed.

Still seething, Tori locked the door behind them. Had they finally gotten the message? Hearing a sound, she looked up. Four women hung over the railing with a look of admiration.

Chapter 13

Mia led the way as they clamored down the stairs. "We were getting ready to leave and didn't want to interrupt. My god, woman, you came out with all guns blazing. Whew!" She fanned herself with her hand.

Heidi proclaimed, "That was a total rout. I never thought I'd see the day the Swanson's were so effectively discombobulated."

Their reaction helped ease the anger rolling inside her. "Mia, you were right when you said Myra was tenacious."

"She is. I opened the door, and they rolled right past me. Short of physical force, nothing was stopping them."

Cammie asked, "Did you really mean all that stuff you told them about the house?"

"I most certainly did."

Mia chortled. "So, when did you hire a contractor?"

Tori laughed. "I sort of fudged there. It's on my list, though I can't trust a local one now."

Mia said, "You could be right. Okay, I've had my fun

for the day. I'm out of here. See you in the morning." The team followed her out the door.

Anxious to open Elly's envelope, Tori hastened to move her car. After racing back inside, she grabbed her tote bag from the living room. Settled in her office chair, she removed the envelope from her bag and slit it open. Tipping it, four envelopes slid onto the desk. One with her name on the outside. A second from her mother, post-marked about eight months before she died. The third had *safe combination* written across the front, and something rattled in the fourth.

Tori opened the one with her name and removed a letter. Unfolding it, she began to read.

My dearest Tori,

I am your grandmother, Elly Leichter. The reason you don't know me is my stiff-necked pride has been my downfall on more than one occasion. No more so than the estrangement from your father.

I was opposed to Michael joining the Army. I tried to force the issue, even with a few threats of which I am not proud. But I was desperate, fearful I would lose him just as I lost your grandfather. In the end, my machinations only brought about what I tried to prevent. Michael left, proclaiming he'd live his own life, and I wasn't part of it.

I let him go. I never knew he married, let alone had a child. By the time I learned Michael had been killed, he'd already been buried in the Arlington National Cemetery in Washington D.C. In my grief, I didn't want to know more.

I received a letter from your mother. In it, she said she was dying of cancer and that I had a granddaughter. She also said that you had never been told about Michael's side of the family.

Though I long to meet you, I must wait a while longer. Until I know it's safe, I don't dare contact you. It could be dangerous. I can't say more as I am uncertain as to the reason for my fear. I don't know who to trust anymore. In the event I can't contact you, this letter will be left with my attorney.

In the meantime, I am taking steps to change my will. Everything I have will be yours. It is the only legacy I can give you. The house has been my life. I hope it will become yours. Built by my father, it has secrets, ones I've kept all these years. They will be yours as well.

All my love,

Elly

Tears streamed down her cheeks as Tori read it a second time before folding it and replacing it in the envelope. Her grandmother hadn't known about her. She hadn't cut Tori out of her life. Oh, if only. But then life was full of—if only. Yet, in the end, what a precious gift Elly had left her. Not the house or the fortune, but her love.

Her grandmother's letter gave her a new sense of determination, a resolve that the house would stand, even if it took every dime Elly had left her. Yet, it also raised new and troubling questions.

This wasn't the ramblings of a senile old woman. The attorney had said Elly was afraid, and Elly didn't want to contact Tori until she knew it was safe. How could a house have secrets, and why did Elly protect them?

Next, she pulled out her mother's letter. A picture

dropped out. It was taken the day Tori graduated from college. The writing was uneven, the letters twisted. In the final months, it became increasingly difficult for her mother to hold a pen.

Dear Ms. Leichter

This letter will no doubt come as a shock. I'm still not sure what I am doing is right. Your son, Michael Winters, was my husband. We met when he was stationed in Fort Leonard Wood, Missouri. During the few years we had before he was killed, I learned a lot about his background and family. Michael, however, was adamant he didn't want to contact you. I disagreed, but it was his decision.

I know he was deeply hurt by what happened between the two of you, just as I am certain you were also hurt. Michael was a proud, stubborn man, and once he set a course, it was difficult to change his direction. I suspect he got that from you.

We have a daughter, Tori Elly Winters. She was born two years before Michael was killed. Michael insisted on naming her Elly. She's a beautiful young woman, kind and warm, but at times, just as proud and stubborn as her father. Tori is a nurse assigned to the emergency room at the Joplin hospital. She graduated at the top of her class from the University of Missouri. I believe you would be proud of her. I certainly am. The picture is when she graduated.

I am dying. I only have months, if even that. I've never told Tori about you. But now, even though I've honored Michael's decision all these years, I question whether it is in Tori's best interest. When I am gone, she will be alone. I have included a copy of her birth certificate.

I will leave it in your hands to decide.

Karen Winters

Tori laid her head on the table as she cried. She wasn't sure if she wept for herself, her grandmother, or her parents. So much pain, so much waste of precious time.

Hiccupping, she opened the bottom drawer and grabbed a wad of tissues from a box. Wiping her eyes, the grief slowly receded. Tomorrow, she'd take the letters to the bank. They were too precious to leave in the house.

Tori picked up the third envelope and opened it. The letter detailed the location of the safe. A small slip of paper dropped on the desk. On it was a series of numbers. She stuffed the letter back inside the envelope and headed to the library with the slip of paper in hand. Somehow, she knew she'd find the missing jewelry. Once the wood panel door swung open, Tori mumbled the numbers, slowly turning the lock. At the last one, she pushed down on the lever and pulled. The door opened. Inside was a metal box.

Before shutting the door, Tori double-checked the inside to make sure it was empty. Locking it, she spun the dial and closed the wood panel.

After setting the box on the desk, she flipped up the lid. Inside were boxes of various sizes. She picked up one and opened it. Under the lights, a diamond bracelet sparkled. Another contained a necklace, one a ring.

When Tori finished opening the boxes, mesmerized, she stared at necklaces, bracelets, watches, brooches, and rings nestled in cotton. One by one, she picked them up. On a few, the clasps were worn and needed to be replaced. She slid an opal ring on her finger. Surprisingly, it fit. Another connection to Elly.

Tomorrow, she'd get a copy of Jonah's list and compare it to what she had. For now, it might be a good idea to make her own list. Tori started a new spreadsheet on her computer, adding a number and a short description for each piece. Then she took a picture with the phone. Once she finished, she transferred the images to the computer.

Satisfied she had done all she could, her next concern was what to do with them. The best place was the safety deposit box. But what about tonight? The strange sounds resonated in her mind, and paranoia again raised its ugly head. Did she want to take a chance on putting them back into the safe?

With a rueful laugh, Tori headed to the perfect place to hide something—the dryer. After setting the box inside, she tossed a couple of towels on top of it. Earl and Farley had torn her house apart, ripped up every piece of clothing she had, but missed what was in the dryer.

She still had one envelope to open. When she did, three red and white objects fell out. Baffled, Tori fingered them. RD was printed on one side. On the back, one had several handwritten numbers, but on the other two, only a single digit, 1 and 3. How odd.

RD sounded familiar. Then an idea hit. Was she right? She typed her great-grandfather's name into the computer. When the short bio appeared, she eagerly read it. Red Door was the name of Frankie's gambling casino. Astounded, she stared at what had to be poker chips. The fact they even existed was astonishing. Why did someone save them all these years? And why did Elly entrust three poker chips to an attorney? And what was the significance of the written numbers? None of it made sense, yet there had to be a reason, a pattern. She just couldn't see it yet.

Then she remembered a comment David made. He told her Elly was a secretive person. Tori groaned. If her grandmother expected her to keep the secrets, it might be good to know what they were. How was she supposed to find out? She was the new kid on the block. She didn't even know most of the players. Now, she could add a mysterious set of poker chips to the puzzle.

After putting the chips in the envelope, she laid it on top of the other three. She'd keep them with her tonight.

Caught up in her discoveries, the rumble of her stomach was a reminder that she hadn't eaten. Tori made a sandwich, grabbed a bottle of water, and took them to the office. Her to-do list waited, and she wanted to continue itemizing the bills. And she still needed to look at the contents of Cantrell's box.

While she ate her sandwich, she started two new lists, one for daily activities and one for ideas for the renovation. Remembering Cantrell's snide remark about her lists, Tori sniffed in disdain. Once she finished, she opened the spreadsheet with the check numbers and picked up where she left off.

It took over two hours, but when she was done, at least she had an idea of the monthly expenses. What was confusing were checks on the bank statements that didn't have a matching stub in Cantrell's or Elly's checkbook. It was too late tonight to figure out why. Tomorrow, she'd look at the documents in Cantrell's box.

Besides, Tori had one more task, her list of questions for the meeting with Jonah. After jotting down several, she laid it aside. She neatly stacked her piles of paper and lists, then shut down the computer.

Tori picked up the envelopes. Before making her nightly trek through the lower-floor rooms, she checked the front door.

She paused for a moment at the piano, only to turn away with a sigh of regret. It was late, and she was emotionally drained. Tonight, she didn't think even her music would help.

She shut the bedroom door and picked up the chair, propping it under the doorknob. Better safe than sorry.

Chapter 14

Seated at the kitchen table the next morning, Tori had a notepad in front of her and the phone to her ear. "Yes, ma'am. That's the correct address. I appreciate your help." She hit the disconnect button and sighed.

Mia walked in. "You're at it early."

"Since I fired Cantrell, I've got to get the utilities switched over, so I get the bills. There's coffee, but I'm out of donuts and cookies."

"You should have mentioned it. I could have picked some up."

"Thanks, but I have several errands to run. I'll stop by the store. How is the cleaning going?"

"Slow but steady," Mia answered, filling a cup. "Later today, I'm headed to the dry cleaners. The first batch of drapes is ready." Mia motioned with her cup toward Tori's list. "I'll leave you to your calls. I have a new polish I want to try on the paneling in the library."

Tori nodded and looked at the next number on her list, the gas company. She tapped the number.

A few minutes later, Mia rushed in. Impatiently, she waited for Tori to finish the call. "Did you open the panel to the safe?"

"Yes. I found the combination. Why?"

"It's open."

"I'm certain I shut it." Alarmed, she followed Mia into the library. She stared at the wood panel door slightly ajar. "Did you touch it?"

"No, that's the way I found it."

Tori walked to the wall. Thinking back, she was positive that she had closed the panel. She even remembered spinning the dial before shutting it. Tori reached for the handle. The safe was unlocked. A chill trickled over her.

Concerned by the expression on Tori's face, Mia asked, "What is it, Tori?"

"I'm not sure. I want to check my office."

She rushed into the room, and her gaze swept the top of her desk. The computer was closed. But the neat stacks of papers, the bank statements and her lists were slightly skewed, not how she left them. Then she spotted the slip of paper with the combination sticking out from under a list. Like an idiot, she'd forgotten and left it on the desk.

Alarmed, Mia cried out. "Something's wrong. I can see it on your face. What is it?"

"Was the front door locked when you came in this morning?" Tori had given Mia a spare key.

"Yes, it was."

"You check the windows. I'll check the back door."

"Okay, but then you need to tell me why."

Finding the back door locked, Tori slowly walked to the kitchen. The certainty someone had broken into the house set off a rush of fear. But how? She eased onto a chair.

Since the directions to the location of the safe were in the nightstand, to open it meant the person had to already know where it was. Only two people, outside of Mia and her crew, knew. She certainly didn't believe it was one of the women. It had to be David or Linc. Maybe even Jonah, since Linc probably told his dad. Tori felt physically ill at the possibility.

Mia walked in. "They are all locked." With an uneasy look at Tori's pasty face, she sat down.

"So was the back door. I've been hearing strange noises during the night. At first, I thought it was the wind rattling something on the outside of the house. Now, I don't think so. A couple of nights ago, I wandered around the house with a glass of wine. I went into the attic and left the glass at the bottom of the stairs near the wall. I forgot about it, but the next morning it was broken."

Her eyes held a touch of fear as she looked at Mia. "I know I locked that safe. But the combination was on the desk. My papers aren't the way I left them. Someone is getting into the house! But how? Before I go to bed, I check the windows and doors to make sure they are locked."

"Should you call the police?"

"I've thought about it, but what can I tell them? I hear noises, a glass was broken. Not what could be called solid evidence. Even the safe isn't proof."

"What about an alarm system?"

"Thought about that too. But all the doors and windows are always locked, so what good would it do?"

"Hmm ... I see your point. How could someone get in?"

"I don't know." A look of dismay crossed her face, and she smacked her forehead with the palm of her hand. "Keys." She groaned. "What an idiot I am. How many people have a key to this place? David did, which I got back. My, god, I need to change all the locks."

She looked at her watch. "Dang it. I've got an appointment with Jonah and need to make a stop at the bank first. I'll call and get a locksmith out here when I get back."

Mia said, "I can do it for you."

A weak laugh broke through Tori's apprehension. "I know ... you know someone. You are a lifesaver. Thank you. Please have a lock put on my bedroom door and ask if the combination to the safe can be changed."

"What about the master bedroom?"

"Let's wait. I don't plan on moving up there anytime soon."

Tori headed to the bedroom to get ready. Whatever her fears, she had to push them aside. After changing into one of her new outfits, the wide-legged pants and tank top with a long-sleeved light shirt, she began to feel better. She picked up the three envelopes, then hesitated. Maybe she should keep the poker chips. She stuck the envelope back into the drawer.

Mia stopped in the doorway. "Okay, you want to explain why there is a metal box in the dryer?"

"Good lord. I forgot about it."

Mia followed her to the kitchen. "I put it on the table."

"It's Elly's jewelry. The box was in the safe."

"Really! It still doesn't explain why it was in the dryer."

"Last night, I was paranoid. A good thing since someone opened the safe. I stuck the box in the dryer until I could take it to the bank today."

Mia laughed. "Good thinking. It's the last place someone might look. You have to let me see the jewelry before you leave. Do you mind if the others look?"

"Of course not."

Mia rushed out. She shouted, "Get your butts down here. Tori has something to show you."

Footsteps clattered. Tori flipped open the lid and began to take out the boxes. The women gathered around the table.

Mia said, "It's Elly's jewelry."

One by one, Tori removed the lids. A chorus of exclamations filled the room.

Cammie asked, "Can we pick them up?"

"Oh, my gosh, yes."

The pieces were passed around before being carefully tucked back into the boxes.

"What are you going to do with it?" Heidi asked.

"For the time being, stash them in my safety deposit box. I think someone is getting into the house at night. Mia's going to get a locksmith to change all the locks."

Stupefied, the three women looked at Mia, then Tori.

"Why would someone break-in?" Heidi asked.

"I don't know, maybe the jewelry. I'm going to make it known it's at the bank."

Tina spoke up. "That's a good idea. We can help spread the word. It won't take long for it to hit the grapevine."

Still talking about the jewelry, they headed upstairs.

Tori picked up the metal box and slung the tote bag over her shoulder. "Dang, the cars."

"Not a problem. We parked on the street."

"A large parking lot is another item on my list. See you later," Tori said and walked out.

The traffic was light, and it didn't take long before she pulled into the bank's parking lot.

Malcolm stood near one of the tellers when she strode into the bank with the metal box in her arms. Seeing her, he immediately approached. He eyed the box with interest.

After exchanging greetings, Malcolm asked, "How may I help you?"

She was beginning to realize the difference money made. Not once had a bank president talked to her until Tori came to Granbury. Though, she didn't miss that he didn't mention Myra's dinner party.

Suppressing a grin at the thought, she said, "I need to get into my safety deposit box. This is Elly's jewelry, and I want to keep it here." The visit was another way to spread the word that the jewelry wasn't in the house.

An eyebrow slightly rose. "You won't be wearing it?" A look of embarrassment crossed his face. "I'm sorry. I didn't mean to be presumptuous."

"No, it's okay. Maybe down the line, but I'm not a jewelry type person."

It only took a few minutes to stow the box and envelopes.

Despite the delay at the house over the jewelry, Tori still had enough time to stop at the office supply store. The shopping cart was loaded when she reached the checkout line. Elly's office had been woefully short on what Tori considered essential supplies.

Not finding a place to park near Jonah's office, she pulled around the corner into a vacant lot where several cars were parked. She gathered up her tote bag and file folder. The warm sun and light breeze felt good on her face as she strolled along the sidewalk.

Inside, Linda greeted her with a cheerful smile. "Go on back. Jonah's expecting you. Would you like a cup of coffee?"

"Please. I don't feel I had my adequate caffeine fix this morning."

Hearing her voice, Jonah stepped into the hallway to greet her.

"Tori, you certainly are a ray of sunshine this morning."

He motioned toward a chair as they entered his office.

She sat and laid the file folder on the corner of the desk.

Linda walked in with two cups of coffee. When she walked out, she closed the door.

Jonah cleared his throat. "Before we get started, I want

to apologize about the dinner party. When Myra broached the idea, I thought it was a good way to introduce you. I certainly didn't want to put you in an embarrassing position."

She suppressed a sardonic remark. There wasn't any reason to point out that Myra claimed it was Jonah who suggested the dinner party.

Instead, she smiled. "You didn't. I'm the one who should apologize for my disruption. I tend to be outspoken, especially when my buttons get pushed."

"You are more like Elly than just in looks."

"Thank you. That may be one of the nicest compliments you could pay me." She took a sip of the hot brew, savoring the rich taste. "I found Elly's jewelry."

"Where?"

"In the safe. I came across the combination in some of Elly's papers." No point in telling him she got it from Dan. It would only raise questions she didn't want to answer.

"That's a relief. Linc and I, even Sam, searched the house. Many of the pieces are valuable."

Her spine prickled at the mention of Cantrell. She took a sip, then casually asked, "How was Sam able to help?"

"He'd been to the house often to consult with Elly on business. I thought he might have an idea. Did you bring the jewelry with you?"

"No, I stopped at the bank on my way and put it in my safety deposit box. I made a list describing each piece and took a picture. It's on my computer if you need it. I would like a copy of your list, so I can compare."

"I'll have Linda email you a copy. I'm surprised you

didn't keep the collection at the house. They are yours to wear. Seldom was Elly seen without some of the jewelry."

Remembering Carly's snide comment, she said, "So I heard. I'm not accustomed to wearing jewelry. As a nurse, it wasn't practical. If I need a piece for a special occasion, I can easily retrieve it from the bank."

"I see," is all he said.

Though from his expression, Tori was sure he thought it was odd.

"Why didn't you tell me about the jewelry or that it was missing? I'm surprised you didn't report it to the police."

He hesitated, pursing his lips as he thought. "I had planned to tell you, but it's a difficult subject to discuss. I've known Elly all my life. She was a very dear friend. She changed the last few months before she died. She had always been tight-lipped. But Elly became very guarded, almost distrustful. I must admit I was concerned about her mental stability, and so were others."

He paused, waiting to see if she'd respond. When she didn't, he added, "I did discuss the issue with Dan Foote, but he was emphatic Elly was mentally competent when she signed the will. Still, when the jewelry turned up missing, my only thought was she had disposed of it, maybe given it away. Especially when I didn't see her wearing any. But I didn't know about the safe. I hope you understand."

Though she wasn't satisfied, what could she say? Instead, she asked, "Do you know why Elly had another attorney draw up a new will?"

"No. I don't. It was a complete surprise when Dan

called and said he was sending over a copy of Elly's will. It seemed odd and out-of-character for her, adding to my anxieties about her competency."

He took a sip of coffee as a worrisome look crossed his face. "Tori, I'm still concerned about the situation with Sam and the estate's tax returns. He has been a close friend for a long time. Sam has successfully managed Elly's business affairs for many years. I believe you should rethink his termination."

"Jonah, I don't feel comfortable with him. Quite frankly, I don't like his overbearing attitude. I need an individual with whom I can build a good working relationship. It isn't Sam Cantrell."

"While I dislike the disruption, I'll abide by your decision. Even though you said you plan to turn the house into an inn, I wish you would reconsider. The house is a liability, but the land is valuable. You could be looking at several million dollars. You could build a lot of houses elsewhere."

"Jonah, I'm not selling. My decision is final."

She hesitated, taking a sip of coffee. "I'm sure Myra or Judd must have mentioned I hired Dan to handle any contractual issues during the renovation."

His face grave, he nodded. "He did. I planned to ask if you were going to discontinue my services."

"No, I'm not. I believe it's important that I have an independent attorney. With your connection in the business community, I don't want to create a conflict of interest that could boomerang on you."

He leaned back, a hard look in his eyes as he studied her.

"Judd's also concerned you thought he threatened you."

Tori wasn't about to tell him that is precisely what Judd Swanson did. "I simply attempted to make my position clear regarding the sale of the property. If I can't use the house for some reason, I'll tear it down and build a new one. Either way, the property is still not for sale." She didn't tell him it would be a cold day in hell before she tore it down.

Evidently, seeing the resolve on her face, he said, "If that's your decision, if I can be of service in any way, please let Dan know."

"Thank you. I will."

He picked up a file and passed it to her.

"These are copies of Elly's financial records for her stock investments. There are several companies. I'm sure you will get a copy from Sam as well. The quarterly reports are currently being sent to Sam. Would you like me to send a change of address notice to the companies? It will cut through the red tape to prove you are the new owner."

Grateful there was one task she didn't have to add to her growing list, Tori said, "Yes, please. I'm still working on getting the utilities switched over to me. Did Elly have any bank accounts other than the one at Liberty Bank?"

"Not that I know about. As a routine procedure in the probate, Linc and I queried several financial companies. We didn't find another account."

"What about her credit cards?"

"She had three. Those have been canceled."

That confirmed what Cantrell told her. "Do you have a copy of the autopsy report?"

Tori was met with a blank stare when she looked up from her list.

"Autopsy report? There wasn't one."

"Then who certified the death?"

"Judge Hartfield, a Justice of the Peace." Seeing her confused look, he said, "Texas has a dual system, coroners and medical examiners. If a county isn't large enough to support a medical examiner, the Justice of the Peace serves as the coroner. If there is no suspicion of foul play in an unattended death, there is no autopsy, only a brief inquest. Elly died from a fall down the stairs. Judge Hartfield ruled it an accidental death. Why are you asking?"

Not wanting to explain the real reason, Tori said, "Because I'm a nurse, and Elly was my grandmother, one I never knew."

Unfamiliar with the procedures Jonah described, she asked, "Is it possible to obtain a copy of any reports? I'd also like a copy of Elly's medical records."

Jonah cast another wary look toward her. "I'll get a copy of the findings from Judge Hartfield and Elly's doctor."

"Where is she buried?"

Jonah pulled a pad toward him and wrote on it. Tearing off the sheet, he handed it to her. "The address of the cemetery."

After glancing at her list, she said, "That should do it for today."

Jonah escorted her to the front door. "Let me know if there is anything else you need."

The small note fell out when Tori dropped the folders

on the front seat. She picked it up and stared at it for a few seconds. Since she wasn't in a hurry to get home, Tori tapped the address into the GPS system. Following the voice commands, she drove out of town.

It wasn't until she turned onto a winding county road that she felt a problem with the steering. The car kept pulling to the left. As she eased off the accelerator, there was a loud explosion. The car swerved, heading into the oncoming lane. Panicking, she slammed on the brakes. The car fishtailed, spinning out of control. Tori clung to the wheel and pumped the brakes. The car tilted, then dropped back onto all four wheels as it slid off the road. Each beat of her heart felt like a hammer strike in her chest. The car was headed straight toward large trees, and she couldn't stop it. She jerked the wheel. The car slid sideways and started to roll.

Chapter 15

As the car slammed sideways against a thick tree trunk, it buckled. All motion screeched to an abrupt stop. Dirt and dust rained down in the silence.

Dazed and disoriented from the impact of the airbag, she swam on the edge before she could pull herself back from the dark abyss. How bad was she hurt? Before moving, Tori took stock of her body. Her face felt wet, and pain shot down her leg.

She lightly probed her head with her fingers. A nose bleed, probably from the airbag. Then her hand slid to her knee, jammed against the door. Tori gently felt the knee cap. No blood and she didn't think it was broken.

Tori slowly turned her head. The car was crushed against the tree. A limb had crashed through the back passenger window. She shifted to look at the road, not a car in sight. Her phone. Where was it? She'd set it in the cup holder on the console. Frantic, her gaze swept the passenger side and papers strewn across the front floorboard. Her hands shoved the remains of the airbag aside to look under her feet. The phone was up against the brake pedal. She unbuckled the seat belt and reached down to pick it up.

Relieved it wasn't broken, Tori shoved the door open, crawled out and landed on her belly. For several moments, everything spun. She wanted to lie there and not move. But it was up to her to get help. Once the lightheadedness eased, she pushed herself up. Limping, she made it across the ditch before collapsing on the side of the road. Tori tapped the emergency speed dial.

"911. What is your emergency?" a woman's voice said.

She croaked, "I've had an accident."

"What is your location?"

Her mind went blank. Tori couldn't remember.

Persistent, the dispatcher said, "Ma'am! Where are you?'

"Uh … I can't remember the road number. I was headed to Watkins Cemetery."

"What direction were you going?"

The question set off another spark of panic. What if there was more than one road? "I don't know. I was coming from town."

"Are you in the car?"

"No."

"An ambulance is on the way. Don't hang up. Are you hurt?"

"My knee. I can't feel any blood other than a nose bleed. I'm a nurse."

"Good to know. Can you describe what happened?"

The dispatcher's questions helped focus her thoughts and ease the panic, though her nerves still thrummed.

In the distance, the sound of sirens wailed. "I can hear the sirens."

"Stay on the line with me until I know they are there."

A few minutes later, a highway patrol car screeched to a stop, followed by an ambulance. Two medics rushed toward her. The cop headed to the car. Tori thanked the dispatcher and disconnected.

"Where are you hurt?" an EMT asked.

"My knee seems to be the only injury."

"Dispatch told us you were a nurse. That helps."

The medic's hands quickly moved over her body, assessing her condition. He pulled up the leg of her pants to examine her knee. It was already swelling.

The other medic said, "I'll get the stretcher."

Tori shook her head. "I can walk."

The paramedic kneeling beside her shot her a grim look. "No. You get to ride. I'm not taking a chance on that leg."

Once the stretcher was next to her, the two men eased her onto it. Inside the ambulance, one medic hopped out while the other strapped a blood pressure cuff around her arm.

The highway patrol officer appeared at the back of the ambulance. His gaze raked her. "I'm Trooper Bert Moore. What is your name?"

"Tori Winters. My driver's license is in my tote bag. The insurance card is in the glove box."

He nodded, writing on a form attached to a clipboard. "How do you feel?"

"Other than my knee, I think I'm okay."

"I was told you are a nurse."

"Yes. For several years I worked in the ER."

"You have Missouri license plates. Are you visiting?"

"No. I've moved here."

"What is your address?"

When she answered, the paramedic said in a surprised tone, "That's the Leichter house."

"I'm Elly Leichter's granddaughter."

"I'll be damned," the medic exclaimed. "We heard a woman appeared out of the blue and inherited the whole shebang."

Trooper Moore said, "Tell me what happened."

"I'm not sure. I had a problem with the steering, then there was a loud popping noise. I lost control."

"Your front tire blew."

Tori's voice rose in protest. "That's a new car! I bought it before I left Missouri. Why would a brand new tire have blown?"

The trooper shrugged his shoulders. "The tire could have been defective. Once the wrecker hooks up, I'll be able to take a closer look."

Moore left. When he returned, he had the tote bag and insurance card. Propped on one elbow, Tori rummaged inside the bag until she found her driver's license. Once Moore recorded the information, he handed them back to her. She dropped them in the bag.

"Where are you taking the car?"

"A wrecking yard. I'll write down the address for you."

"Could you do me a favor?"

"If I can."

"Would you gather up all the papers on the floorboard and give them to me?"

"Okay. There are several bags and boxes in the back. What are they?" At her questioning look, he added, "I have to inventory the vehicle's contents."

As she itemized her purchases, he wrote them down.

"You'll be able to pick them up once the car is at the wrecking yard."

He walked away. The next time he returned, he had the file folders filled with papers and her keys.

When he handed them to her, he also gave her a card. "This is your report number and where you can obtain a copy of the crash report. It'll take a day or two before you can download a copy. On the back is the address of the wrecking yard. Do you have any questions?"

"Not yet."

"You were fortunate. If the car had hit the tree head-on, we might not be having this conversation."

On the way to the hospital, she called Mia.

When Mia answered, she asked, "Hey, what are those sirens?"

"I had an accident and am on the way to the hospital."

Mia gasped, "How bad?"

"Just my knee, but the EMTs insist I get it checked."

"On my way." Mia disconnected before Tori could say

anything else. *Dang,* she thought, hating to make a fuss over a bruised knee, even if she felt like needles were jabbing her leg.

Once she had been wheeled into the emergency room, she was shifted to a bed. The paramedic who had driven the ambulance said, "I'm sorry for your loss. Miss Elly was a good friend. Every Christmas, the fire department received a huge box of toys for our children's Christmas drive and a meal for each shift from KB's Barbeque. She did the same for the police department. She will be missed."

A sheen of tears appeared in Tori's eyes. Another side to Elly. "Thank you for sharing that with me." It would be another item to add to her to-do list.

After the doctor finished his examination, he said, "Nothing seems to be broken, though I want an x-ray to be certain. I'll give you something for the pain. You've got a visitor anxiously pacing in the waiting room."

As he walked out, Mia hurried in. "Oh, my god, are you sure you're okay? The nurse wouldn't tell me anything."

Though she was hurting, Tori didn't want Mia to know. "Yes, I am. I didn't mean for you to rush over here. I wanted to tell you I'd be late."

Mia shot her a scorching look. "Good lord. You've got a lot to learn about small towns. Of course, I'd be here. Even if I didn't already consider you a friend, I'll be danged if I let someone languish in a hospital if I could do something about it. So what does the doctor say?"

"A bruised knee, but I have to get it x-rayed."

The nurse walked in, giving Mia a strong look of

disapproval. "Mia, time for *you* to leave." She handed Tori a small cup with a pill. In her other hand, she held a bottle of water.

"Don't get in a tizzy, Charlotte." Mia looked at Tori, winked, and whispered in sotto, "Don't let her bully you. She's been good at it since we were in grade school."

At a snort from Charlotte, Mia threw her hands in the air. "I'm going. Tori, I'll be in the waiting room when you're ready to leave."

Certain the pill was a powerful pain killer, Tori didn't want the side effects and handed back the cup. "I'll wait until I get home to take something."

As she suspected, the x-ray proved negative, nothing was broken. Before she was allowed to leave, Charlotte wrapped her knee with an elastic bandage for support. "You'll need to wear this for a couple of days, but I'm sure you know that." The news had spread that Tori was a nurse.

Settled in a wheelchair, her file folders and tote bag on her lap, Charlotte wheeled her out the front door where Mia waited. After thanking the woman, Tori hobbled into the car. Mia handed her the tote bag and folders she had grabbed.

"How's your knee doing?" Mia asked as she pulled out of the parking lot.

"It'll be sore for a few days, but it could have been much worse. According to the highway patrol officer, I was lucky the car ended up sideways against the tree and not head-on."

"Why did you lose control?"

"The officer said a tire blew."

"Highway patrol. That means it happened in the county. Where were you going?"

"The cemetery where Elly is buried. Could we make a detour before we go home? I stopped at the office supply place. The stuff I bought is in the car."

"Sure. Where is it?"

Tori reached inside the bag, digging to find the card the trooper gave her. Flipping it over, she said, "Baybrook's wrecking yard."

"It's not that far out of the way."

Surrounded by a high, solid wood fence, the wrecking yard was located on the outskirts of Granbury. Tori limped inside the small office with Mia hovering next to her.

Tori grinned. "Don't worry. I'm not about to keel over."

A man in a stained t-shirt and bib overalls stood behind a counter. "Can I help you?"

"I'm Tori Winters. My car was towed here earlier. I'd like to get my possessions out of it."

He eyed her with a jaundiced look. A splat of tobacco juice landed in a paper coffee cup. "It's here. It's pretty rough in the lot. You sure you can walk out there?"

"I'll be fine."

"I need your driver's license. Gotta make sure you're legit."

"It's in my bag in the car. I'll be right back."

Mia chided her. "No. You stay here. I'll get it."

A few minutes later, Mia returned and handed it to him.

After a brief look, he picked up a clipboard. He stuck a

blank form under the clip and noted the number before handing the license back.

Tori stuck it in her pocket.

"I got to list everything you remove." He eyed their empty hands. "You might need a sack or two. I've got some in the back. I'll meet you at the gate."

The man led the way to where Tori's car had been dropped.

Seeing it, Mia gasped, "Good lord. It's a miracle you weren't hurt worse than you are or killed."

For the first time, Tori saw the extent of the damage, the side crushed in, the u-shape from wrapping around the tree. Fear squeezed her insides as she relived those moments when the car raced toward the trees.

"Yeah, a tire blowing can be deadly," the man said.

Shaking off the nightmarish images, she turned her attention to getting her possessions out of the car.

When Tori tried to reach inside, Mia stopped her. In her firm but no-nonsense voice, she said, "You stay put. Tell me what you want."

Tori said, "What's in the glove box and console," not bothering to waste energy arguing. The man handed a sack to Mia. She filled it, then a second one, setting them on the ground. The boxes and bags stashed in the back of the SUV were placed alongside the sacks.

"Did you buy out the entire store?" Mia grumbled.

Tori, watching from a few feet away, weakly chuckled. "A few items for my office."

"A few! You could start your own business."

Mia and the man carried the boxes and sacks to the car. Tori snapped pictures with her phone as she eased her way around the vehicle. She'd never had an accident, but maybe the insurance company needed them. She took several close-up shots of the culprit, the tire. Satisfied, she slowly stepped over the ruts and around the debris that littered the lot as she limped back to the car. With a sigh of relief to get her weight off the leg, she leaned back in the seat.

Mia shot her a look of concern as she backed out. "You need to stay off your feet for a couple of days."

"I have plenty to do at home. I'll take it easy."

With another quick look at Tori's pale, drawn face, Mia muttered, "I intend to see that you do."

The front door opened as Mia pulled to a stop in the driveway. Heidi, Cammie, and Tina rushed out. Heidi was faster, darting to the passenger side to open the door. Her eyes filled with concern as she eyed Tori's blood-stained clothes.

Mia said, "Careful. Her knee is banged up."

"Here, hang on to my arm," Heidi told her as Tori slid out of the car. A groan of pain erupted when her foot hit the ground.

"Let's get you inside." Heidi's arm slid around Tori's waist.

Cammie rushed up to help.

"Okay, everyone. I'm not crippled. I can get inside under my own steam."

"Don't be stubborn. We'll help," Heidi informed her in the same stern tone Mia had used.

With Cammie on one side and Heidi on the other, they practically picked her up and carried her inside. Tina and Mia followed, carrying the boxes and sacks.

A rush of emotion coursed through her. Tori had never had many friends. During the years before her mother died, what with graduating, starting a new job and caring for her mother, there wasn't much time left for anyone else. The friendship she felt for the four women overwhelmed her. Not wanting them to see, she choked back the tears.

Heidi asked, "Where to?"

She looked down at her clothes, wondering whether she'd ever get the bloodstains out of the tie-dye material. "The bedroom."

After changing into sweats and a t-shirt, Tori swallowed two Tylenol from the bottle in her bag. She grabbed her phone and hobbled into the hallway, heading to her office. Mia waited by the door to help her. Once Tori was ensconced in her chair, Mia pulled the small couch around to face the desk, then pushed the easy chairs to form a semicircle.

Heidi walked in with a large pitcher of iced tea and several glasses. Behind her, Tina carried a tray of sandwiches, plates, and napkins.

"Why didn't you tell me. We could have stayed in the kitchen."

Cammie said, "Not a big deal. As a matter of fact, we thought we'd be doing this in your bedroom." She glared at her friend. "Mia wasn't exactly forthcoming when she called to let us know you were on the way, so we weren't certain how bad you were hurt."

When everyone had a drink and sandwich, Heidi said, "Tell us what happened."

In between bites, Tori filled them in on the accident.

Cammie asked, "What about the car?"

Tori picked up her phone and brought up the pictures. The phone, passed from person to person, prompted exclamations of concern.

Heidi said, "It's a total loss." A wicked smile crossed her face. "You've still got Miss Elly's car. It's always made me think of the movie *Driving Miss Daisy*."

Tori groaned.

Swallowing a bite of sandwich, Mia choked, coughing as she giggled. "Tori will be going about town in grand style in the Tank."

Cammie, seated next to Mia on the couch, thumped her back. "Hey guys, it's not *that* bad."

Tina chimed in. "You should get a truck."

Tori shot her a skeptical look.

"Think about it. A pickup would be mighty handy since you plan to turn this place into a B&B."

Maybe it was a good idea. Tori reached for her pad and wrote—pickup.

Once they finished eating, the four women refused to let Tori help straighten the room and quickly cleaned up the impromptu meal. Before they left, they trooped into the office, standing in a line in front of the desk.

Suspicious, Tori eyed their somber faces.

Mia said, "Okay, here's the deal. Unless you promise to

stay off your feet, except for what is absolutely necessary, one of us is staying the night. We flipped." She grinned. "I won."

Tori groaned. "There is no need. I'm—"

Mia's hands flashed in the air as she interrupted, "Tori, this isn't open for debate. We've decided. You've only got two choices here."

Knowing it was a lost cause, she grumbled, "I promise."

Mia studied her and finally said, "Okay. We're holding you to it."

From her pocket, Mia pulled out several keys. "The locks have all been changed. Your bedroom has a deadbolt. All are keyed the same. I wasn't sure how many copies you might want, so I got four." She laid them on the desk.

"I forgot all about it."

With a wry smile, Mia said, "I can't imagine why."

Tori pushed one toward her. "You need one."

"Are you sure?"

With a smile, Tori said, "Absolutely. What about the safe?"

"New combination. I dropped the card with the numbers in your center drawer along with Eddie's bill."

"Someone you know, right?"

Mia grinned. "We'll see you in the morning."

Tori started to rise.

Mia's hand flashed upward. "Don't get up. I'll lock the door when we leave."

As they trooped out, Tori called out. "Thank you."

In response, they waggled their fingers in the air. Once they left, the house suddenly seemed empty. Too restless to sit, Tori slowly made her way to the music room. Her hands caressed the piano before sliding onto the bench seat. Her fingers trickled over the keys as memories resurfaced.

Most of her mother's furniture had to be sold when Tori moved, including the old upright piano. Purchased for her when she was in the fifth grade, Tori had taken to learning with a passion. She'd practice for hours. As her expertise grew, she soon played for local weddings and church functions.

The day her piano was hauled out of her home, Tori felt she'd lost another connection with her mother. Now, as she played, she felt a sense of peace and renewal, almost as if her mother was listening.

Tired, her muscles aching, she rose. Turning off the lights as she went, she headed to the bedroom. With an air of relief, she flipped the new deadbolt lock. Whatever was going on in the house, she felt safe.

Since she couldn't navigate the tub, she took a sponge bath. It wasn't until she was in bed that her thoughts reverted to the horrific crash. Despite the trooper's claim that new tires could be defective, it seemed a remote possibility. But how else could it have happened? The question kept swirling in her mind, even as sleep overtook her.

Chapter 16

A clatter in the kitchen brought her out of a sound sleep. Despite the closed drapes, the room was awash with bright sunlight streaming around the edges.

"Dang, what time is it?" she muttered. Rolling onto her side, the clock came into view. It was mid-morning. Tori didn't remember the last time she'd slept this late. But then, her body had never been subjected to the trauma of a car crash.

Sharp jabs of pain and sore muscles were an awakening reminder as she swung her legs over the side. Gently, Tori pressed the knee cap and the muscles around it. Swollen and bruised, it would take several days before she'd be back to normal. Tori rewrapped it with the elastic bandage she'd removed the night before.

Mia was pouring a cup of coffee when Tori ambled into the kitchen.

A broad smile lit up her face as her eyes assessed Tori. "I heard you stumbling around in there." She handed the cup to Tori. "I made it extra strong. Figured you might need it. You look a lot better than yesterday. How are you feeling?"

"Like a truck ran over me."

"I've never had an accident, but I've heard other people claim it's what they felt like the next day."

Tori settled in a chair, took a sip, and moaned with pleasure. "Oh, so good. Woman, you are a lifesaver. Sorry to be late getting started."

"When we got here and found you were still in bed, we decided to let you sleep. You've already had one visitor. Jonah stopped by on the way to his office. I reassured him that you were doing fine. He wants you to call when you feel up to it."

"I will. Where is everyone?"

"Heidi is upstairs in the master bedroom. Tina and Cammie left. We have two other houses to clean today," she said as she wiped the counter. "I'm going to be gone for a couple of hours." She glanced at her watch. "I'd better get a move on, or I'll be late. I have a meeting with a prospective client." She cast an uncertain look at Tori.

"Hey, I'm good. You can stop worrying about me."

"Okay. Be back later. Oh, there's an omelet warming in the oven." She grabbed her purse from the counter and rushed out the door.

Tori hollered, "Good luck."

For a few minutes, her elbows propped on the table, Tori cradled the cup in her hands, enjoying the coffee's strong, almost bitter taste. Her gaze swept the weeds and tall grass through the large double windows overlooking the backyard. She needed to call the fireman.

First was breakfast, though she didn't have much of an appetite until she opened the oven. The sight of the golden omelet with bits of ham and green peppers set her taste buds to watering.

Eating, she tried to focus on her ideas for the house to keep her thoughts of the crash at bay. It didn't work. Images rolled in her head. With a groan of frustration, she swallowed the last bite and cleaned up her mess. The doorbell chimed. Overhead, the sound of running footsteps had her calling out. "Heidi, I got it."

Heidi leaned over the railing and smiled down at her. "I didn't know you were up. How are you doing?"

"Two cups of Mia's coffee, and I'm good to go."

Heidi laughed. "She likes it strong."

The doorbell rang, again. Someone was getting impatient. When she opened the door, David grinned at her over the top of a large vase of flowers. He strolled inside.

Still hanging over the rail, Heidi called out, "Hey, David. Nice flowers." He looked up and grinned before she turned away.

Dumbfounded, she stared. Flowers? No one had ever given her flowers.

David looked at her. "I didn't mean to send you into shock. You might want to close the door."

A flush of embarrassment warmed her cheeks as she quickly shut it.

"Where do you want me to put them?"

"Uh … oh, I guess in the living room. No, the office. Maybe the music room."

"Make up your mind, woman."

"Oh, the living room, then."

He walked in and set them on a table at the end of the sofa.

"David, they are beautiful." She limped over to smell the delicate blooms. The only ones she recognized were the yellow rosebuds.

Pleasure lit up her face as she turned toward him. "Thank you. But I'm not really hurt, you know. Just banged up my knee."

"All the same, flowers brighten the day. Elly loved them. When I was growing up, she had a standing order with a florist. Every Friday, vases of flowers would arrive." Seeing she was balancing herself on one leg, he said, "You'd better sit down."

As she collapsed on the couch, he settled into a chair.

"I'm supposed to stay off my feet as much as possible for a few days. There's coffee in the kitchen if you'd like a cup."

"No. I can't stay. I have a couple of appointments. What happened? All I've heard is you had an accident."

As she told him, a frown crossed his face.

When she finished, he said, "I had no idea it was so serious or that you wrapped the car around a tree. It's a miracle you weren't killed. Did the trooper give you any explanation for the blowout?"

"Since the car is new, he said it could be a

manufacturing defect. I bought it before I left Springfield. If the tire was bad, why didn't I have a problem with it on the drive from Missouri? It doesn't make sense."

"I wouldn't worry about it. Sometimes accidents happen, and you never know the reason why."

Still bothered, she said, "I suppose so."

"What are you going to do about getting a car?"

"Elly's, if it still runs."

He threw back his head and laughed. "The Tank. Be prepared for the looks when you start driving it around town."

"I've heard." She hesitated, wondering whether to broach the subject, before saying, "David, did Elly ever say anything about being afraid?"

His eyebrows shot upward. "A strange question. Why would you think she was afraid?"

"Dan Foote mentioned it. I've wondered if she ever said anything to you." She didn't want to tell him about Elly's letter.

"No, she didn't. Did the attorney tell you?"

"He wasn't sure. I wanted a copy of the autopsy report, but there isn't one."

"Why in god's name would you want to see the autopsy report?"

With a wave of her hand, she said, "I'm just curious. Were you here when she died?"

"If you mean in the house, no. But I was in town. Linc called me. What is this all about?"

"Oh, I don't know. Just an odd feeling I have. It's probably nothing. Forget I even mentioned it."

Glancing at the vase of flowers, Tori didn't see the narrowing of David's eyes or the hard look that flashed across his face. When she turned back, he stared at her with concern.

"Like I said, sometimes accidents happen. You were lucky. Elly wasn't." He rose. "I need to get back to my office." At the doorway, he stopped and looked back. "Do you like Chinese food?"

"Yes, I do."

"There's a great place downtown. Since I can't take you there, how about I pick up take out, and bring it back this evening?"

Conflicted by her suspicions and an unwanted awareness of him, she hesitated before saying, "Okay."

"What do you like?"

"Anything hot and spicy."

"I'll see you about seven."

Tori followed him to the front door, closing it after he left. Uneasy and not certain why, she thought back over the conversation. David hadn't said or done anything to trigger the uneasiness, but it persisted. Something felt off, but what? Maybe it was the way he blew off her concerns about the tire. It was time she got some answers. A little judicious investigation tonight might get them.

Tori limped to her bedroom to get her tote bag. In the kitchen, she grabbed a bottle of water. Pain radiated down her leg by the time she got to her office. If she wasn't careful, she could end up on crutches.

Sitting didn't help since it bent the knee. She needed to support the leg. But with what? Tori couldn't remember seeing a stool anywhere in the house.

She eyed the box with the blank paper. It might work. After shoving it under the desk, she hoisted her foot on top of the box. It eased some of the pain in her leg, but the knee still throbbed.

Inside the tote bag, her hand rummaged for the bottle of Tylenol. Buried at the bottom, she found it along with the insurance paper, driver's license, and Trooper Moore's card. It was a reminder she had to call the insurance company. Waiting to be transferred to an adjuster, she shook two pills into her hand, followed by a gulp of water.

It took longer than expected to answer the woman's questions. Relieved to have the claim filed, she turned to Cantrell's box. She pulled out the folders and documents, looking for a record of payments for the unaccounted checks on the bank statements.

Frustrated when she didn't find any documentation, she drummed the table with her fingers. Should she call Cantrell? Ask him if there was another checkbook? *No*, she thought. She really didn't want any further contact with the man. There was another way. Tori called the bank.

When Malcolm came on the line, he said, "How are you doing. I heard about your accident."

"I'm fine. I was lucky, only a banged-up knee."

"That's good to hear. How may I help you?"

"I need a copy of the canceled checks for Elly's account for the last two years. Is that something you can provide?"

"I already have the copies. Miss Elly made the same request."

"When?" Tori asked with a sinking feeling.

"A couple of days before she died. I held on to them in case someone needed them."

"I hate to inconvenience you, but is it possible to have them delivered?"

"I'll have them dropped off this afternoon."

"Thank you."

Her senses hummed. Why did Elly ask for the canceled checks? Until she got them, there was nothing she could do.

Stymied, she turned to her to-do list. She pulled out the business card the fireman gave her and tapped the number.

When he answered, she asked, "Is this Doug?"

"Yes. Who is this?"

"Tori Winters. I'm calling about my yard. Could you stop by the house in a couple of days?" With her knee in mind, roaming around ten acres wasn't the best of ideas.

"Yes. How about the day after tomorrow?"

"That would work. If you could be here early in the afternoon, I would appreciate it."

"How about two o'clock?"

"I'll see you then." She noted it on her calendar.

After crossing off the landscaper from her list, Jeff Archer was next. Booting up her computer, Tori pulled up his firm. The *About* page included a picture of all the employees and a list of an impressive set of credentials. She called. A young woman answered, "Archer Financial Services, how may I direct your call."

"I would like to speak with Mr. Archer."

"He's out of the office. May I take a message?"

"Please have him call Tori Winters." She rattled off her number.

"May I tell him what this is about?"

"I am Elly Leichter's granddaughter. It's in connection to her estate."

With a new note of urgency, the woman said, "I'll make sure he gets the message."

As Tori disconnected, she couldn't help but smile. She was starting to sense the power in Elly's name. Money talked.

A few minutes later, the phone rang. She picked it up. "Tori Winters speaking."

"Ms. Winters, this is Jeff Archer."

"Mr. Archer, I am Elly Leichter's granddaughter. I would like to make an appointment."

"When would be a good time. I can come to your house or meet you here at the office. Whichever is most convenient for you."

"I had a car accident yesterday and won't be able to get out and about for a few days. I certainly would appreciate it if you could come to my home."

"I hadn't heard. I hope it wasn't anything serious."

You may be the only person in town who doesn't know, she thought. "No, it wasn't. When is a good time for you?"

They set a time for later that afternoon. Tori added another appointment to the planner as Heidi walked in.

She plopped into the chair. "I hauled two trash bags outside. Do you know you have quite a stack out back?"

"Mia mentioned it. I keep forgetting to call the trash people. Where are they located?" She pulled her to-do list in front of her.

"Call the city's waste management division. With what's there, it will be a special pickup. I got a call from Mia. She's on her way back. Don't worry if you hear the front door open."

"Good to know. Oh, I have an appointment this afternoon. If you hear the doorbell, don't worry about rushing downstairs. I'll get it."

"I don't mind, and quite frankly, I can get there a whole hell of a lot faster than you can." She shot Tori the stink eye. "Stay off the leg. Do you want something from the kitchen? I'm headed there."

"Another bottle of water."

As Heidi walked out, her phone rang. Seeing the number, she couldn't stop the anxiety that tightened her gut.

"Tori, this is Kermit Layton. I have an update for you. You'll be glad to know Earl and Farley Russell are in jail and will be there for the next five years. The woman who pawned the jewelry is Earl's girlfriend. She rolled on them when she was brought in for questioning. She also had the rest of your jewelry."

As she listened, a sense of relief overwhelmed her. It was finally over. With the Russells in jail, she could put all of this behind her. No more looking over her shoulder.

There was a pause, dead silence, before Layton said, "I've debated whether to let you know about a disturbing twist to your case."

In a flash, the trepidation was back. "What happened?"

"The Russells admitted to slashing your tires, the phone calls, and trashing your house as part of the plea bargain. They are adamant they didn't shoot at you and don't know who did. Even though I told them it won't change their conviction, they still deny it. If they're telling the truth, someone else tried to kill you."

An icy chill clutched at her. Elly was afraid. Elly died. And now she was afraid.

Chapter 17

Her heart lurched. "Why would anyone else want to kill me? It had to be the Russells."

Layton said, "At the time, it struck me as odd. Before the trial, it was scare tactics. But the trial was over, and *now* they decide to kill you? It didn't make sense, but I didn't have any reason to believe it wasn't Earl or Farley. Tori, I can't prove this one way or the other. If it is true, then someone else fired that shot. Your leaving may have been a wise move. I still can't release the jewelry. I will call you when I can. Do you have any questions?"

She didn't, and they disconnected. Dazed, her mind grappled with the terrifying implications. Not the Russells, then who? And why? She didn't like the answers—Elly's estate and David. But what would he have to gain at this point? She was in control of the estate, or at least she believed she was. Surely, he wouldn't have gone so far as to kill her. Or would he? As she learned from Horace's death, greed was a powerful motivator.

Another specter reared its ugly head, the car crash.

Before she could think this one through, the doorbell rang.

Heidi shouted, "I'll get it." The rumble of voices grew louder.

"You've got another visitor." Heidi walked in, followed by Linc, who carried a large vase of flowers.

"Hey, you okay?" Heidi frowned as she set the bottle of water on the desk. "You look a bit peaked all of a sudden."

Unable to explain, Tori fobbed off the question with a glib answer. "Just a twinge." Hoping to divert her attention, Tori gushed over the flowers, which wasn't difficult since there had to be at least two dozen pink and white roses. "Wow, those are gorgeous!"

Heidi's eyes twinkled with humor. "Linc's always had good taste. I'm headed upstairs."

With a hesitant expression, Linc looked around. "Where should I put them?"

"On the table against the wall."

After setting the vase down, he settled into a chair.

"I love them. Thank you." She nodded toward the flowers.

"They're from Dad and me. I was deputized to bring them by, not that I really resisted." He chuckled.

"It was very thoughtful. There may still be some coffee in the kitchen."

Crossing his legs, he said, ""I'll pass. Let's hear the tale. What happened?"

Tori was beginning to feel beleaguered, wondering how often she'd have to repeat it.

When she finished, Linc said, "You were lucky. We've

handled a few lawsuits involving a vehicular collision. Let me know if you need any legal advice. Did you contact the insurance company?"

"Yes. An adjuster will go by and look at the car. I was told it would be several days before they would get back to me."

"In the meantime, what are you doing for a car?"

"If Elly's is in working condition, I guess I'll drive hers. Do you happen to know where the keys are?"

His eyes twinkled in merriment. "That will be something to see. I haven't seen the keys. I'll ask Dad."

"I don't want to rent one unless I have to."

"Why ever not?"

"An unnecessary expense."

Linc let his look of disbelief do his talking.

Her hand fluttered in the air. "I know. I've got the money, but that doesn't mean I will heedlessly toss it away."

"What's this about your questions regarding Miss Elly's death? Dad said you asked about an autopsy report."

More questions. Tori was getting tired of answering them. "Linc, don't forget I am a nurse. I simply wanted to see what the ME said. It's not that important."

He frowned. "I'd say it is if you want the inquest report and medical records."

"I'm trying to get a sense of who Elly was and what happened. Don't forget, I never met her. Which reminds me? Who found her?"

"Dad did. He had an appointment with her that

morning. When she didn't answer the door, he became concerned."

"How did he get in?"

"Miss Elly gave him a key sometime back."

Just how many people had a key, she wondered. At least she had solved that problem.

"Well, I'd better be going. As soon as that knee gets well, I'd like to take you to dinner."

"All right. Thank you again for the flowers."

After he left, her thoughts reverted to Layton's call. Someone tried to kill her in Missouri. And now she has an accident that doesn't make sense. Was it another attempt to kill her? But why?

Whatever was going on, she needed facts. From a desk drawer, she retrieved Trooper Moore's card. She typed the website address into the computer.

A page for the Texas Department of Transportation popped up with the steps to obtain a copy of the crash report. Hoping it was in the system, she entered the required information. When she found it, she paid with her credit card and clicked to download a two-page report and summary explaining the numbering system.

The back of the report contained a narrative and diagram of the collision. Trooper Moore had written that the crash was due to a sidewall blowout of the left front tire, the result of underinflation. He further added that no evidence of punctures or damage to the tire was observed.

A flat tire? This was a brand new car. She knew the tire wasn't flat when she pulled out of the parking lot. The steering didn't get flaky until right before the blowout.

On the front of the card was a phone number for the trooper. She called and left a message.

Startled by the sound of the front door opening, she jumped. A moment later, she heard Mia's voice talking to Heidi. She had to get a hold of herself. At this rate, she'd turn into a babbling bundle of nerves.

Mia breezed in. "I could smell them before I reached the door." She walked to the vase. "Lordy be, these are beautiful. Who brought them?"

"Linc."

"I saw the ones in the living room. David?"

"Yep, how'd you know?"

"I've seen the way those two look at you."

With an expression of disbelief, Tori protested, "It's nothing more than I'm the new kid on the block."

Mia chuckled. "Right. Time will tell."

"Speaking of Linc and David, do you know what's going on with them? At the party, I picked up on some bad vibes."

"There was an incident after the funeral service at the cemetery. Maybe it's why. David got in Linc's face, but I was too far away to hear. For a moment, I thought he would deck Linc, but then he walked off in a huff. I really didn't give it much thought. They grew up together, each trying to outdo the other. Even though they're friends, they've tangled on more than one occasion. It's probably nothing important."

Tori wasn't sure she agreed.

"How are you doing? Heidi said she'd been keeping an eye on you."

"Knee's sore, but it's improving." She wasn't about to mention pill-popping to stop the pain.

Tori pushed her chair back, setting the propped foot on the floor.

"Where are you going?" Mia asked.

"The kitchen. I've got to get out of this chair for a while."

As Tori slowly walked, Mia stayed close to her side.

"Quit fussing over me. It's getting better."

"For someone who is a nurse, you make a lousy patient. So get over it."

"I guess I do." Tori chuckled.

The doorbell rang. Mia rushed to open the door. A man dressed in a suit stood on the porch with a large box. "This is for Tori Winters. It's from the bank."

Mia gripped it with both hands and thanked him. He trotted down the steps. Swinging her hip, she shut the door.

"Do you want me to put this in the office for you?"

"Yes, thank you," Tori said.

Mia snorted. "That's better."

When she returned, Tori stood at the counter with slices of bread, cheese, and turkey in front of her. "Sandwiches and chips okay for lunch?"

Mia looked at her and groaned.

With a wide-eyed look of innocence, Tori said, "What?"

Mia said, "Okay, I give up," throwing her hands in the air. "I'll get the chips."

"Do I need to make one for Tina and Cammie?"

"No, I don't expect them back today. One of the houses took longer than expected. The kids decided to have a water fight with ketchup bottles. And they weren't filled with water." Even Tori had to shudder at the image it invoked.

Once the plates were on the table, Mia stepped out to call Heidi, who soon trotted down the stairs.

When they were seated, Mia asked, "How are you coming on the upstairs?"

"Slowly," Heidi answered. "I hauled more bags of sheets, blankets and other assorted items to the stack by the garage. Tori, I didn't figure you'd want them." She bit into her sandwich.

"Ah, heck," Tori exclaimed. "I forgot, *again,* to call about the trash pickup. I'll do it as soon as we finish. If you think it needs to go, throw it out. I'll be buying new stuff anyway."

Heidi swallowed. "I came across several crocheted doilies and a couple of handmade bedspreads. I've laid them aside. They'd be great to use in the B&B."

"That's a good idea. By tomorrow, I'll be able to climb the stairs and take a look." Tori turned to Mia. "How'd your interview go?"

With a note of pride, Mia said, "We got the job. For once, I beat out Myra's proposal. It felt good since it doesn't happen often. I can't compete with her prices. She can undercut me, and I can't do anything about it."

Tori swallowed. "What made the difference this time?"

"Scheduling. The client liked mine."

The discussion set off an idea in Tori's mind. When the

B&B opened, she would need a full-time cleaning service. This wasn't the time to broach the subject. She had a long way to go before she reached that decision. But it was food for thought.

"What are your plans for the rest of the day?" Mia asked.

"Jeff Archer is coming over this afternoon."

"Oh, you will like him. He's competent and a down-to-earth, no-nonsense type of guy."

Heidi chimed in. "I've never heard a single complaint about him from anyone. And another thing, he's not in Myra's clique."

"Makes for a good recommendation," Tori said.

Mia rose, picking up the plates. "I'll clean this up. Would you like me to get anything out of the pantry for your supper?"

Her thoughts on the meeting with Archer, she absent-mindedly said, "No. David is bringing Chinese food."

Heidi let out a hoot. "David. Now isn't that interesting."

Mia added her two cents' worth. "I told her, but she didn't believe me."

In astonishment, Tori stared at the two women. "Have you two been talking about this?"

Mia and Heidi broke out laughing. "Not just the two of us, all four of us."

"It's nothing but a meal," Tori grumbled, attempting to head off any more speculations. She certainly couldn't tell them David was on her list of suspects.

Mia's eyes twinkled. "We'll see."

The two women headed upstairs, and Tori toddled to her office. Mia had set the box next to her chair. Seated, Tori stripped off the tape. Filled to the brim, sheets of paper were imprinted with rows of checks. She hoped they were in some kind of order.

She booted up her computer and accessed the spreadsheet. One by one, she compared the copy of the canceled check to her list of check numbers. A time-consuming and laborious task. When the doorbell rang, she'd barely made a dent in the box of papers.

Tori glanced at her watch. Dang, she'd let the time get away from her. It was probably Archer. She'd planned to make a new pot of coffee.

Not sure why she didn't want Archer to see the copies of the canceled checks, she hurriedly stacked them, dropping them onto the box beside her. As footsteps approached, she pulled out a fresh notepad and laid it beside her computer. Her hands smoothed her hair. Why was she nervous? Maybe because she knew how far out of her depth she was.

Short and plump, with a receding hairline and slightly rumpled clothing, Jeff Archer's appearance wasn't one to spark confidence until you looked into his eyes. Dark, they gleamed with astuteness and even a hard-core toughness. Kermit Layton, the district attorney, had the same look.

"Ms. Winters, please don't get up." He stopped in front of the desk and extended his hand. "So nice to meet you."

"Nice to meet you too, and it's Tori. Please have a seat."

Standing in the doorway, Mia said, "I made a fresh pot of coffee. Would either of you like a cup?"

Tori shot her a grateful look. "Yes."

Jeff said, "Coffee sounds good. Black, please."

With an air of comfortability, he looked around the room. "I've never had an opportunity to visit here. The house is even more impressive than what I've heard."

Tori said, "I fell in love with it the first moment I saw it."

"I can see why. My condolences on your loss."

"Thank you, Mr. Archer."

"It's Jeff. Are you getting settled in? I heard this is your first trip to Texas."

"It is. A big change from Missouri."

"No doubt. I think you'll find Texas is rather unique, not only for its size but also the variety of the terrain. Everything from pine trees to palm trees to arid desert."

Mia walked in carrying a tray with coffee cups, small plates, cookies, and napkins. She handed a cup to Jeff and set the tray on the corner of the desk.

Astonished, Tori said, "Where did you find the tray?"

"Dining room hutch. Figured this was a good time to make use of it."

"Oh, my gosh, look at the scrollwork. It's beautiful. Tell me it is the real deal, not silver-plated."

Mia nodded. "Yes. It's sterling silver."

"Are there any more pieces?"

"Several."

"Wow, we can make good use of these." Belatedly, in

her enthusiasm, she forgot Jeff, who quietly sipped his coffee while he watched the two women.

"Sorry, I didn't mean to get carried away," Tori said. "Mia and her team have been here almost from the day I arrived. The house has become a journey of discovery for all of us. Quite frankly, the best decision I've made so far was calling her for help."

A look of merriment lit Mia's face. From the pocket of her smock, she pulled out a small silver bell and shook it. It tinkled. "If you need anything, just ring," and set it on the desk.

The gesture was so Myra-like that whoops of laughter rolled from Tori. Mia joined in.

Lordy be, Tori thought as she brought herself under control. *Jeff will think we're nuts.* She glanced his way. He was laughing with them.

With a swipe of her hand, Mia wiped her eyes. "Okay, since I've managed to liven up this little shindig, I'll leave you to your discussion," and strolled out.

Tori took a sip of the coffee to give her time to gather herself.

"For someone new, you've already made a solid friendship. Mia is one of the best. I've known her for many years. Now, what can I help you with?"

She took a deep breath and said, "You might as well know up-front. Sam Cantrell is no longer my CPA."

Surprised, he said, "I hadn't heard. May I ask why?"

Since she had no idea what was floating on the rumor mill or how much Archer might know about Cantrell's activities, she said, "Let's just say we didn't seem to be on the same page. I know I have a lot to learn about managing the estate. But I fully intend to do just that. I don't want to sit back and let someone else do it for me. I will make the final decisions, but I'd be pretty dumb not to know I'll need help with input to those decisions."

Jeff nodded with a shrewd look. He had a pretty good idea that Cantrell probably tried to run roughshod over her. Obviously, it didn't work. Despite her unpretentious appearance, she seemed to have an inner layer of resilience and determination. "A lot of rumors are floating that you plan to sell. It doesn't sound as if it's the case."

"No, Jeff. It's not. The property is not for sale. In fact, I plan to turn this house into a bed and breakfast style inn. I've hired Atkins, Foote, and Smart, a law firm in Fort Worth, to oversee the contractual issues with the renovations. I need financial guidance for the accounting and operational issues."

A look of shock crossed his face. "A huge undertaking. Though I must say, the house is suited to the concept. What about Jonah Greer?"

"He's still my attorney. After considering his ties to the business community, I don't want to create a conflict of interest for him. Which is why I hired Dan Foote."

A look of respect sparked in Jeff's eyes. "In my opinion, a very smart move." He set the cup on the desk, then popped a cookie in his mouth. As he chewed, he opened the briefcase next to his chair and pulled out a notepad. He swallowed. "When do you plan to start?"

She smiled. "As soon as I hire a contractor, I want to have everything in place to start the actual renovations."

"That's the long term. What do you need in the short term?"

"Someone to work with me on the current structure of the estate."

Over the next hour, they discussed Tori's ideas and concerns. Thankful she had set up the printer, she was able to give him a copy of the financial statements and the last tax return.

When they finished, the cookies were gone. Jeff perused the notes he'd made, then looked at her. "I don't see any difficulty in transitioning the financial oversight of Elly's investments to my firm or setting up a business model to manage the renovations. If you want to move forward, I'll work up a proposal. If you're satisfied, we'll get started."

"Next time, I will come to your office. This knee isn't going to keep me down for long."

Jeff grinned. While he hadn't known Tori's grandmother well, he'd always been struck by her determination and strength of character. It seemed her granddaughter was from the same mold. "No, I don't think it will."

Jeff gathered up his notes, putting them in the briefcase. He handed her a business card. "I appreciate the opportunity you are giving me. Personally, I think it's exciting. It's going to be interesting to see what you do with this place. I'm looking forward to helping you make it happen."

"Next time you're here, I'll give you a tour."

Tori walked him to the door, albeit slowly. When it

closed behind him, she fist-pumped the air. "Yes!"

Behind her, Mia laughed. "I take it the meeting went well."

Tori turned, and her eyes sparkled. "Oh, you were right. He's what I needed."

"Good. I thought he would be. Heidi and I are getting ready to leave. Anything you need before we go?"

"No. Thank you for the coffee and the omelet this morning. It's not part of our bargain, but I appreciate it."

"Wasn't that big of a deal. Consider it a favor."

Heidi trotted down the stairs. "How's the knee?"

"Better. In a couple of days, I'll be back to normal."

"Don't push it. But you know that. I'm preaching to the choir," Heidi told her.

Once they left, Tori wandered through the rooms, envisioning the changes she wanted to make. Should she keep the large dining room table that seated twelve or have smaller tables? Maybe both, the smaller tables against the wall. She needed her notepad. As she headed to the office to grab one, the doorbell rang.

Now, who could it be? When she opened the door, David strolled in with a large box. The smells emanating from inside enticed her taste buds.

Lost in thoughts of snowy white tablecloths, gleaming silverware, elegant dinnerware, wine goblets, and candles, she'd forgotten he was coming. No chance to change clothes. Maybe it wasn't so bad she was wearing sweats and a t-shirt. After all, a person didn't dress up to entertain a suspect.

Chapter 18

With an inquiring look, David asked, "Where to, kitchen or dining room?"

"Let's use the kitchen, not as formal," and to her mind, less intimidating.

David dropped the box on the counter and began to pull out sacks. "Since I wasn't sure what you like, I got an assortment of beef and shrimp, wonton and hot and sour soup, egg rolls and steamed rice."

She grabbed plates and silverware, setting them on the table.

His lips twitched. "No forks. I brought chopsticks."

"You can't be serious. I don't know how to eat with chopsticks."

He picked up the forks, dropping them into the drawer. "It's time you learned. Consider this a new adventure."

Grumbling, she said, "These last few months, my whole life has been nothing but an adventure. I don't need an adventure to eat a meal."

"Now, where's the fun in that?"

"How about enjoying the food."

He only laughed as he set food containers on the table.

Still muttering under her breath, she retrieved the bottle of wine from the fridge and two Waterford goblets she stashed in the cupboard.

"Would you like a glass of wine? I also have soda if you'd prefer."

"Wine." He looked up and scowled. "*Where* did you get that bottle?"

Embarrassment struck, sending a rush of heat across her face. It was an eight-dollar bottle of wine. What had she been thinking? That was the problem. She didn't think. Obviously, he expected something more expensive.

"The grocery store," she said.

"Why?" he asked as he finished setting out the food.

Irritated now and with a bit of sharp sarcasm, she said, "Because I wanted a bottle of wine. That's why."

At the tone in her voice, David's head whipped around. The look on her face had him stuttering. "Uh ... sorry. I didn't mean to cast aspersions on the wine. I wondered why you didn't get a bottle from the wine cellar."

"A wine cellar!" Her voice rose just short of a shriek. "I have a wine cellar?"

With a facetious tone in his voice, he said, "Okay. I'm guessing here that you don't know about it."

"Bingo. I don't."

"I thought Linc gave you a tour. I'm surprised he didn't tell you."

"I am too. Where is it?"

"Under the kitchen."

Excited, she said, "Show me."

Dubiously, he looked at her leg. "Can you navigate stairs?"

A gritty determination swelled. "You bet I can."

"If I may suggest, let's eat before the food gets cold. Then, I'll show it to you."

Ignoring her impatience, she poured the grocery store wine before easing onto the chair.

David sat across from her. "Take your pick of soups. I like both."

"I'm taking you up on that." She snagged the cup labeled hot and sour.

He pulled the container of wonton soup toward him. "How is the knee doing?"

"A lot better. I stayed off it most of the day. Even had it propped under my desk. Another couple of days, and I'll be back to normal. Tell me about this wine cellar."

"Have you done any research on your less than illustrious ancestor Frankie Leichter?"

"Some, but don't let it stop you."

In between swallows of soup, he said. "Elly's father controlled the gambling syndicate until he was killed in a shootout. I think she was about fourteen or fifteen when he died. What she didn't know firsthand, she got from her mother, who passed away in the early 1980s."

He scooped rice and kung pao shrimp onto his plate and picked up the chopsticks.

Tori groaned. "You really are going to use those things, aren't you?"

He grinned, picked up a set and handed them to her. Between bites, he explained, "Frankie came out of the prohibition era. Bootlegging was big business. It's how he got the start of his fortune. Even though prohibition was repealed in 1933, many counties in Texas were dry. You couldn't purchase alcohol."

Watching her fumble, the food falling onto the plate, he said, "You're holding them wrong. Do it like this." He demonstrated.

Then he reached across the table to grab her hand and reposition her fingers. Tori felt an unfamiliar rush of warmth. This was crazy. She couldn't let herself be attracted to him. David might be the one trying to kill her, though she couldn't bring herself to really believe it. Still, she had to admit he had an aura that pulled at her. When she finally managed to hang onto a piece of beef, she grinned like a loon before popping it in her mouth.

David picked up where he left off. "Elly told me she could remember cars arriving late at night and men hauling boxes into the cellar. Back then, it wasn't a wine cellar. Even though many local judges, cops, and politicians were getting kickbacks, Frankie was paranoid. According to Elly, he used the cellar to stash his goods to hide them from the Feds. I suspect it was more than liquor, probably guns too, but Elly never admitted it."

After adding a quantity of stir-fried beef and rice to his plate, he continued, "Elly always claimed her father built the house in Granbury because he could buy cheap land after the depression, and if the house was raided, he'd see them coming. Frankie was right. It would have been hard to sneak up on this place back then. Elly renovated the house after her mother passed, fixing up the bathrooms and kitchen. She added paneled walls, a floor, and wine racks in the cellar. Elly was a wine connoisseur, never cared for the hard stuff."

Tori could barely contain her excitement. "It will certainly be a noteworthy addition to the inn."

"Still going ahead with the B&B?"

"Yep, that I am."

"How do you plan to go about it?" he casually asked, refilling their glasses from the bottle on the table.

Focused on her plate, she didn't see the flash of uneasiness in his eyes. "Right now, making lists, getting organized.

"I heard you hired another attorney. Jonah was rather disturbed by the fact."

From his tone, David seemed almost pleased.

"I know. Still, I thought it was the right move. Daniel Foote will oversee any issues with the renovation."

Finished, he laid the chopsticks across his plate. "Interesting. He's the attorney who drew up Elly's new will. Did you find out why?"

For some reason, his probing was disquieting.

"Not really. David, was there some issue with the will?"

"Why do you ask?"

Not wanting to mention what Mia saw at the cemetery, she said, "You've made some comments about Jonah, and there seemed to be an issue with Linc at the party. I just wondered if it was connected to Elly's death."

"At times, Jonah and Linc get a bit officious with their ideas. I don't always agree. That's all. I noticed you have new locks. Was there a reason?"

Tori was beginning to realize that not much escaped his notice. She shrugged and swallowed the last of her wine. "I didn't know who had keys."

She rose to pick up the plates.

David shoved his chair back. "Let me help." When she started to protest, he said, "I'll dump the containers in the trash."

The comment reminded her that she still hadn't called the trash department.

Once the table was cleared and the dishes stowed in the dishwasher, David said, "The door is in the pantry."

"I've never seen a door there."

"Ah, that's because you didn't know where to look."

Inside the room, wooden shelves lined the walls. Most were empty. In the center was a waist-high counter with drawers underneath the marble top.

David walked to one wall and reached behind a shelf. A section of the wall popped open to reveal a staircase. "There's a lever on the backside of this shelf."

"Oh, my gosh," she exclaimed, stepping alongside him to see where he pointed.

"There is another lever in the cellar that opens the door.

Keeps anyone from accidentally getting locked in. You sure you can get up and down the stairs?"

Tori looked down. Though not wide, there was a handrail. "I can manage."

"Let me go first. If you have a problem, I can help."

After flipping a light switch inside the stairwell, he walked down. Tori, her hand on the rail, slowly trailed behind him.

When she stepped off the last step onto a wide, planked floor, she stopped and stared about her in astonishment. Overhead lighting illuminated a wood-paneled room and free-standing shelves filled with dusty wine bottles. "Good lord, how many are there?"

"I don't know. It's a sizeable collection, quite valuable as a matter of fact."

She sauntered along the shelves, occasionally pulling out a bottle to look at the label. Most she'd never heard of. Overwhelmed, she realized how much she had to learn. Her background and education had never prepared her for any of this. Was everyone right? Should she sell? Then her innate logic kicked in. Take it one step at a time. Right now, she didn't need to know anything about wines.

David said, "Check with Jonah. Since he's the executor, he might know more about them. You might also check the inventory for the estate. The collection is probably there."

Inventory? Jonah had never mentioned an inventory. She forced back the irritation, not wanting David to know. First thing in the morning, she'd find out why.

Before they headed upstairs, David grabbed a couple of

bottles and showed her the lever to control the door. Back in the kitchen, he asked, "Would you like me to open one of these?"

"Sure," she said.

David wiped the dust off the bottle. He deftly inserted the corkscrew, pulling out the cork. He filled their glasses, handing one to her.

For a moment, she let the wine settle on her tongue, enjoying the deep rich flavor. "Oh, my, this is good. What does a bottle like this cost?"

"A Rothschild. Probably around a thousand dollars."

Tori choked. Her lungs locked down in shock. For a moment, she couldn't breathe. Wheezing, she said, "Tell me you're joking."

His devilish grin spread. "No, I'm not."

She held up the glass, scrutinizing the deep red liquid. "How much is it per sip? Who pays that much for a bottle of wine?"

"Your grandmother. I'd bet there are even more expensive bottles down there."

A worrisome thought struck. "What about the insurance?"

"Don't worry. Elly had this place insured to the hilt."

Not convinced, Tori made another mental note to find the policy.

"Do you mind if I take a look at the rooms? I'd like to see what Mia has done."

"Not at all."

With glasses in hand, they strolled into the living room.

Tori sat while David wandered. He stopped in front of the fireplace, looking up at the painting. "Elly worshiped her father. Many a time, I'd see her standing here, staring."

"That's odd, considering his background."

"Strangely enough, the old buzzard was very protective of his family. Elly received the finest schooling available at the time." He turned and propped his arm on the mantel. "The room looks good. This is how I remember it."

Tori drank the last sip of wine, ignoring the twinge of guilt about the cost.

"Ready to move on, or do you need to rest the knee?"

"I'm doing fine." She wasn't about to tell him it had begun to ache, likely caused by the jaunt into the cellar.

"What changes are you planning on making?" he asked as they strolled into the music room.

"Hmm … still thinking about it. Earlier I was pondering the dining room. Keep the table, replace it with small ones, or a combination. It's nice the room is so large. Why did Frankie build such a big house?"

"He came from nothing and wanted to be somebody. Frankie had power and made sure everyone knew it. He ran his syndicate with an iron-clad fist. Step out of line, and you'd end up dead in some back alley. This house was the social front. A place where he could entertain in grand style. Elly often recounted the parties. Of course, she was too young to attend, but she'd talk about hanging over the staircase to watch the guests arrive."

They ambled into the music room.

"This was her favorite room," David said as he looked

around, pleased to see the furniture gleam under the chandelier.

"Linc said she enjoyed playing."

"The piano was a birthday gift from her father. I think he had it shipped from New York."

Tori limped over to it. Her hands lovingly stroked the glossy wood. "It is beautiful," she said before sliding onto the bench and positioning her feet on the pedals.

"You play?" David leaned against the side of the piano.

She smiled up at him. "I dabble."

Her fingers picked out the starting notes of one of her favorite pieces, *Clair de Lune.* As the melodic chords filled the air, Tori let herself slide into the music, forgetting the man who watched, feeling only the wistfulness and longing within the sounds.

The notes died away, and for a moment, unconsciously, Tori held her hands in position before removing them from the keyboard. Pulling herself back from the realm of the music, the room was strangely quiet. She looked up. David stared at her with an odd awareness in his eyes.

"I'm sadly out of practice. I haven't spent much time on a keyboard the last couple of years."

"It was amazing. You are quite talented."

Embarrassed by the quiet accolade, she wasn't sure what to say. "Anyone would sound good on this magnificent instrument. I grew up playing on an old upright."

"Some evening, I'd like to hear more. It's getting late. I have an early start in the morning, and I'm sure you do too."

At the door, he stopped. "If you need help or advice, call me."

"Thank you, I will. Thank you for dinner. I enjoyed it."

"So did I." Surprisingly, he meant it.

David sat in his truck, staring at the house. Inside, lights winked out. This was a turn of events he hadn't anticipated.

Her digging into Elly's death was a complication, even a dangerous one. And Tori didn't trust him. Granted, their first meeting wasn't an auspicious start, but he'd done nothing to alert her suspicions.

Tonight, caught by surprise, David had felt a sense of déjà vu, memories of Elly seated at the piano with the same pensive look. Something intense and unwanted had stirred deep inside him.

But the surreal feeling he experienced as he watched her play wasn't the only time. He felt it whenever Tori looked at him with wariness in her eyes.

Elly had looked at him the same way—and Elly had died.

Chapter 19

Refreshed by a solid night's sleep, Tori was up early and at her desk. Not once had she been awakened by odd sounds. It was too early to start making phone calls. So she picked up where she'd left off when Jeff Archer arrived, the stack of canceled checks. As she worked through them, Tori began to find the checks that weren't in Elly's or Cantrell's checkbook. There must be a third one. Why didn't Cantrell give it to her?

Four checks signed by Sam Cantrell were issued to different companies each month in varying amounts. There was no notation on the front of the checks as to the reason. She wrote down the company names, intending to research them.

Alerted by the voices at the front door, she pushed back her chair and walked into the hallway with only a slight limp.

Gathered in the entryway, Mia and the crew greeted her when she approached. Four sets of eyes watched her walk.

"Hey, not bad," Mia said.

"Nope, a lot of the swelling has gone down. It's now turning into an interesting mélange of colors. Coffee's ready."

Tina said, "Good, I need a jolt to jump-start my system. I stayed up late studying for an exam."

Tori had already learned Tina was taking night courses for a degree in computer science.

In the kitchen, she fidgeted, waiting until they had mugs of coffee before making her grand announcement.

Mia, instantly concerned, asked, "Did you still hear noises last night?"

"Nope. Nary a one."

With a look of relief, she nodded.

Heidi eyed her. "I bet the twitchy nerves have something to do with David."

Cammie exclaimed, "Talk. Give it up. What happened?"

With a mischievous grin, Tori said, "Oh, the dinner was nice."

"Nice!" Mia squealed. "Macho man Tucker brings you dinner, and all you can say is it's *nice*?"

"Well, it was. But that's not important."

Heidi threw her hands in the air. "The woman's lost it. Dinner with one of the hottest men in town, and she says it isn't important."

Tori laughed. "I do have something to tell you, though."

All eyes locked on her. Her fingers drum-rolled the counter. "Wait ... wait for it. I have a wine cellar."

Stunned, all four women simply stared at her. Mia was the first to recover. "Where?"

Tori tapped her foot. "Underneath us. Come on. I'll show you."

She opened the door to the pantry.

Behind her, Mia protested, "I've never found a door in here."

Tori reached behind the shelf and tripped the lever. As the section of the wall slowly opened, exclamations resounded.

She flipped on the light. Still mindful of her knee, Tori eased her way down the stairs.

As the wine shelves came into view, behind her, Mia exclaimed, "Oh, my god."

With varying expressions of wonder, the women wandered, fingering the bottles.

Heidi said, "This is amazing. Why have we never heard about a wine cellar?"

Tori said, "From what I have found out, Elly liked to keep secrets. Evidently, this was one of them."

"What little I know about wine is what I've learned working at the grocery store. You've got brands here that I've never even heard of," Mia said. "High-dollar stuff. Any idea what it's worth?"

"Not yet."

From the back of the room, Tina shouted, "You've got champagne back here."

Gazing around her, Mia asked, "What are you going to do with all of it?"

"I've given it a lot of thought and have an idea. Let's go back upstairs."

When they reached the kitchen, the four women settled around the table, watching Tori with an expectant look.

Leaning against the counter, Tori said, "Here's my idea. I think it's a perfect advertising gimmick. It would certainly elevate the inn to something more than the normal B&B."

Excited, Heidi said, "You're right. How many places can claim to have the elegance this place has, including a fabulous, fully stocked, high-dollar wine cellar? Do you think the wine is still good?"

"Hmm … a good question, though I can attest to at least one bottle we opened last night. Nothing wrong with it."

Mia said, "If you plan to promote the wine, I'd suggest getting an expert to take a look. To drink it for personal use is one thing, but for commercial use, you have additional liabilities."

"Good point. The contractor should probably take a look as well. See if there are any changes I need to make to the wine cellar. I'll add it to my list."

"Out of curiosity, how long is your list," Mia asked.

With a chuckle, Tori said, "Long, and getting longer every day."

Mia let out a short laugh before her tone turned serious. "Whenever you feel up to climbing the stairs, we need to decide what you want to do with the boxes."

"I have a few calls to make, then I'll take a look."

Mia and the crew headed upstairs. With another cup of

coffee in her hand, Tori headed to her office. By now, Jonah should be at work. She tapped his number, greeting Linda when she answered.

"Jonah just walked in. Hold on."

A few seconds later, Jonah came on the line. "Good morning. You're getting an early start. How are you feeling?"

"Much better this morning. Another day or so, and I'll be back to normal. Thank you for the flowers. It was very thoughtful. Jonah, something else fell through the cracks. I just found out about the wine cellar."

"I didn't realize you didn't know."

Tori said, "I'm surprised Linc didn't mention it during his tour."

"He probably forgot."

"Do you know anything about the collection? The value?"

"No, I don't. It was included in the inventory, but no value was placed on it."

"That was my next question. I don't have an inventory."

"It's part of the paperwork filed with the courts. I'd planned to give all the documents to you at one time. But I'll make sure you get a copy."

"What about the insurance on the house? I'll need a copy of the policy."

"I'm not sure I have one. I'll check. A copy should be in Elly's files, or Sam might have one."

Oh, great, she thought. "I'll see if I can find it. Do you know if Elly's car is okay to drive? I'd like to use it until I get a new one."

"It should be."

"Do you have the keys?"

"Yes. Linc said you had asked. I'll have him drop off the inventory and the keys. I also have the inquest reports you asked for. Anything else?"

"No, that should do it."

Troubled, Tori laid the phone on the desk. She felt she was flying blind. At every turn, it seemed another document she should have was missing. It wasn't a comfortable feeling.

Since she already knew the policy wasn't in the desk, it had to be in the file cabinets. Finding the folder, she pulled the most recent policy and perused the contents. David was right. She had plenty of insurance. Another item she could cross off her list.

Her phone chimed, a number she didn't recognize.

"Hello, Tori Winters speaking."

"Ms. Winters, this is Trooper Moore returning your phone call. How is your injury doing?"

"Very good, thank you. Since it could have been so much worse, I'm not complaining. I called because of a statement on the crash report regarding underinflation. Would you please explain?"

"The blowout occurred on the sidewall of the tire. It can be caused by age, damage, uneven wear, manufacturing defect or underinflation. If the tire is losing air, heat builds up, causing the tire to explode. It's what I suspected at the time. But it wasn't until I had a chance to examine the tire more closely that I could confirm my suspicion. The tires are new with no wear, so it came down to damage, factory defects or underinflation. I could not find any other damage to the tire, a nail or cut. It also wasn't a factory defect. The lining of the tire was burnt and missing chunks of rubber, which meant the tire was going flat."

"But how could the tire lose air?"

"I can't say with certainty, but it could have been the valve stem. If it was damaged or loose, you'd lose air."

As she listened to the trooper's explanation, she felt a flutter of apprehension. Was it possible?

"Trooper Moore, could someone deliberately tamper with the valve stem, causing it to lose air?"

"Yes. Do you have reason to believe someone did?"

"Proof, no. Suspicion, yes. Is there a way to prove the valve stem was at fault?"

"No. The tire is too badly damaged." For a moment, there was silence before he added, "Without evidence, I'm sorry to say, there is nothing else I can do."

With a bitter note, as memories of what the police could and couldn't do rose in her mind, she said, "I know. I'm very familiar with your limitations."

His tone concerned, he said, "If you have any further questions, please let me know."

"I will. Thank you for your time."

A hysterical thought flicked in her mind. If Layton was right, and one of the Russells didn't fire the shot, then a killer had tried twice. Would the third time be the charm?

Without proof, the cops couldn't help her. Well, she'd get the proof. She didn't know how, but she would. The big question was the reason. Why did someone want her dead?

Who gained by her death?

She picked up the phone and hit the speed dial for Dan.

"Atkins, Foote, and Smart Law Firm. How may I direct your call?"

"I'd like to speak to Daniel Foote. This is Tori Winters."

"Please hold."

A woman's voice came on the line. "Ms. Winters, Dan is in court. May I take a message?"

"Please have him call at his earliest convenience."

"Yes, I will. It will be later this afternoon."

Deeply troubled, Tori laid the phone on the desk. She picked up her cup and wandered to the kitchen. She stared at the pot for a moment, then set the cup aside. Coffee didn't even sound good. She dropped into a chair and blankly stared out the window.

Mia walked in. At the sight of Tori's somber expression, a worried look crossed her face. "What's wrong?" she quietly asked.

Startled, Tori jerked. "I didn't hear you."

"Wherever you were, it wasn't here." Mia sat across from her. Her concern bit deep at the lost look in Tori's eyes. "I've got a good shoulder; if something needs to stay between us, it does."

Tori hesitated. She wasn't used to sharing. But she badly needed a friend. "I think someone is trying to kill me."

Mia gasped. "Oh, my god. How do you know? Wait a minute, the car crash." One thing she was good at was connecting seemingly irrelevant details.

Tori nodded and began to explain.

"So someone might have tampered with the valve stem," Mia said.

"I think so."

"But what makes you suspect the crash?"

"There's more." The next set of explanations took even longer. She ended with the call from the district attorney. "If Layton is right and the Russells didn't try to kill me, it means the person is here, in Granbury. And to think, I rushed, no, ran from Missouri to escape being killed, only to put myself squarely in his sights here. How ironic." She burst into tears.

Mia rose, rushing into the utility room. When she returned, she dropped a handful of tissues in front of Tori. "Let it out. Let it all out." She sat, reaching across the table to grab Tori's hands.

Tori couldn't stop the tears, but slowly she began to gather herself together. After wiping her face with the tissues, she said, "Sorry. I'm really not the type of person who cries at the drop of a hat."

"If there's one thing I've learned in the short time we've known each other, it's that you are one of the strongest persons I've ever met. Look at what you've already accomplished since you've been here."

A weak smile crossed Tori's face. "Thanks, Mia. I think the crying jag is over."

Mia settled back. "So, what's your game plan?"

"Since the cops can't help, I'm going to find out who wants me dead."

"Oh, that's a good one. Just how do you propose to go about it?"

"Find out why. There must be a reason. I'm waiting for a callback from my new attorney. He might be able to shed some light on what happens if I die."

"How would he know?"

Tori suddenly realized Mia didn't know about the will. "He's the one who drew up Elly's will."

With a thoughtful air, Mia stood to get a cup of coffee. "Now that raises all sorts of interesting questions. Do you mind me asking why since Jonah was her attorney?"

"No, it's a logical question. Dan, he's the lawyer, said Elly was afraid and didn't know who she could trust. Evidently, there were rumors about her being senile."

"She was right. I heard them but didn't believe it. Not Miss Elly. I'd see her at the store and around town. Sure she had a problem walking, but senility, no. Never saw it. At the time, I wondered who started the notion and why? But here's something that occurs to me. In Missouri, the person used a gun, but now it looks like an accident. I find that very strange. Why the change?"

"I've thought about it too. What I think is that if I had been killed in Missouri, the cops would have believed it was the Russells. Here it's different. A murder would bring all kinds of scrutiny. But an accident, no."

A look of horror crossed Mia's face. "Miss Elly."

"Yeah. I'm waiting for Jonah to give me copies of the inquest reports, not that I'm sure it will prove anything."

"You already suspected then? Why?"

"First, from what Dan told me. He also gave me a letter, one Elly had written to me. In it, she said it wasn't safe to contact me." As a thought struck her, she abruptly straightened. "You know who I need to talk to?"

Mia said, "Ethel Morris." At Tori's astonished look, Mia shrugged. "Great minds and all that stuff."

"You know her, right?"

"Oh, yes. Ethel and I have been friends since I was a kid. We go to the same church. She was always handing out candy and cookies to the kids. When do you want to go? It's only about fifteen minutes from here."

Tori glanced at her watch. "How about now?"

"Give me a few minutes."

"We'll have to use your car. I still don't have the keys to Elly's."

During the drive, Mia filled Tori in on Ethel's background. "Her father died when Ethel was a child. When Frankie and Irene moved into the house, they hired Ethel's mother as the housekeeper. Ethel was allowed to visit, but she couldn't live there. Instead, her grandmother raised her. When her mother passed away, Ethel took over. She's still pretty mobile, and occasionally I see her at church. I should warn you, though, Ethel has good days and bad days. Her mind wanders. She was devastated by Miss Elly's death."

Ahead, a number of multi-story units came into view. In front was a large auditorium-style building. Mia parked in front.

"The center has all types of activities, bingo, book clubs,

cards, and there's a cafeteria. We'll need to stop at the front desk. I don't know Ethel's apartment number."

As they opened the double glass doors, an elderly woman behind a desk called out, "Mia, girl, get over here and give me a hug. I haven't seen you in a month of Sundays. Where have you been?" She came around from behind the desk.

Mia rushed over and gently wrapped her arms around the frail shoulders. When she pulled back, she smiled down into the weathered face of the small woman. "Francis, you know me. Always busy at something. How's the arthritis doing?"

The woman shrugged as she shuffled to the chair. "Some days good, some not so good. Nothing fun about getting old." Francis wagged her finger at Mia. "You wait. Your time is coming."

Mia grinned. "I hope I hold up as well as you are doing. Francis Kleiber, this is Tori Winters. She's Miss Elly's granddaughter."

Tori, who had purposely lagged behind, stepped alongside Mia.

"Well, kiss my grits if you aren't the spitting image of your grandma. I'd heard you'd come to town." Her brow furrowed in disapproval. "Going to sell the place, are you? I have to say your grandma must be rolling in her grave."

Tori laughed. How long would it take for the rumors to stop? "No, I'm not selling. In fact, I'm going to turn the house into the finest bed and breakfast inn you'd ever want to see."

"Well, now," her face all smiles, "that's good news. I bet you're here to see Ethel."

"Yes, ma'am, we are. I'd like to meet her."

"You just hold on, let me get her on the phone." She winked at the two women. "Need to make sure she's decent to have company. She's going to be tickled pink when she finds out who is here."

From the center drawer, she pulled out a stapled set of papers. "This is all the phone numbers." She flipped pages, running her nail down the columns. Peering over her glasses at the phone lying in front of her, she tapped the number before holding it to her ear. "Ethel, you got company. It's Miss Elly's granddaughter. No, I'm not kidding." She listened, then disconnected.

"She said for you to come on over." She pushed a map of the apartments toward them, tapping on one. "This is her apartment, 108. You can follow the sidewalk or pull around to the back."

The warm sun enticed them to walk, though Mia expressed concern about Tori's knee. After being assured it wasn't a problem, they slowly worked their way toward the apartment.

"How old is she?" Tori asked.

"Hmm … ninety or so. You ask her, and she'll tell you old enough to know better."

As they approached, the door opened. A small, frail woman stood in the doorway. Her gaze scanned Mia's face before she looked at Tori. Her eyes grew wide with shock as she gripped the door. Her voice quaked, "Miss Elly."

Mia quickly stepped forward, guided her into the room, and eased her onto a chair.

The woman's eyes never left Tori's face as she gripped Mia's arm.

In a firm voice, Mia said, "Ethel, this is Tori Winters. She's Miss Elly's granddaughter."

The woman straightened, her voice stronger. "Yes, of course. It's only that ... oh, my dear, you do so look like her, it took me aback for a moment. Where are my manners? Please have a seat." She waved her hand toward the couch.

Once they were seated, she asked, "Would you like some tea? It won't take long to fix."

"I'd love a cup, Ms. Morris," Tori said.

"It's always been Ethel."

Mia jumped up. "Why don't I fix it so you can visit with Tori?"

Ethel said, a look of uncertainty on her face, "Well, if you don't mind."

"I don't," Mia assured her. At which point, Ethel gave her detailed and explicit instructions on the preparation and where to find cups, plates, and a package of cookies. Mia grinned as she listened with an occasional, "Yes, ma'am."

Once Ethel was satisfied that Mia fully understood, she turned her attention to Tori. "Now, my dear, tell me all about yourself. You're Michael's daughter. I can see him in your face."

After Tori gave her an edited version of her

background, Ethel said, "A nurse. How remarkable. I wonder when Miss Elly found out about you?" A sad look settled on her face. "I remember the day Michael left. I didn't believe he'd never come back, but he didn't. For months, Miss Elly watched for the mailman, certain there would be a letter. But there never was one. She lost so much. Her husband killed in that horrible hunting accident. Lea and her husband in a plane crash. And Michael." Her mind seemed to regress into memories. Her eyes had a distant look.

The rattle of cups brought her back. Mia set a tray with a teapot and dishes on the small coffee table. "Would you like me to pour?"

With a regal nod of her head, Ethel said, "Please. My hands these days are a bit shaky."

Ethel watched with an eagle eye as Mia filled the delicate tea cup, setting it on the saucer before handing one to Tori, then Ethel. On a plate, Mia had arranged cookies on the paper doily Ethel insisted she use.

As she sipped, Ethel mused, "Miss Elly loved her afternoon tea. I'd serve it to her in the living room. That's where the picture is of her parents. But of course, you know that. She liked to drink her tea while she looked at the picture."

"I don't know much about her. As a matter of fact, I didn't even know I had a grandmother until a few weeks ago. Shortly before my mother passed away, she sent a letter to Elly, telling her that she had a granddaughter." She picked up a cookie and daintily bit it, carefully keeping the crumbs on her plate.

"It's so tragic you didn't have a chance to meet her. I wonder if it would have changed anything?" Ethel took a sip of tea.

"Changed what?" Tori asked.

"She might still be alive. She was so afraid, you see."

Tori's heart thumped. "Afraid of what?"

"The house and its secrets. It killed her."

Chapter 20

Caught by surprise, Tori threw a look at Mia before she carefully set the plate and cup on the table. Up to now, Ethel had been perfectly lucid. "What do you mean?"

"Why, don't you know? My dear, Miss Elly was murdered."

Not sure how to respond, Tori hesitated.

Mia said, "Ethel, it was an accident. Miss Elly fell down the stairs."

With a look of exasperation, the elderly woman shook her head. "No one wants to listen."

"I'm listening," Tori told her.

"The reason I left was because Miss Elly was afraid. She said she didn't want me in the house, in danger. Of course, I didn't want to leave, but she insisted."

"Why was she afraid, and what did the house have to do with it?" Tori asked.

"The house has secrets. Miss Elly told me so. She didn't fall down those stairs." An unladylike sniff erupted. "Miss

Elly could have walked that house blindfolded and never once stumbled. She was killed, and it was the secrets that killed her."

Next to her, she felt Mia's body tense, though she didn't say anything. "I still don't understand?" Tori said. "What secrets?"

Ethel looked down, shrugging her shoulders. "I don't know."

"Do you remember her father?"

"Well, of course, I do, even though I was a child. Not long after the house was finished, Mother became his housekeeper. A hard, cruel man, though he thought the sun rose and set on Miss Elly. She could do no wrong."

"What about Elly's mother?"

"If ever there was a woman to be pitied, it was his wife. Mr. Leichter abused and continually berated her. I often thought he was the reason the poor woman miscarried twice after Elly was born. Back in those days, women didn't have any rights." She sniffed again.

Even though Tori asked again about the secrets in the house, Ethel only repeated she didn't know. Seeing that she was beginning to tire, Tori knew it was time to leave.

Mia and Tori carried the dishes into the kitchen. They washed and put them in the cupboard. At the door, Ethel's eyes filled with tears. Her hand reached to stroke Tori's face. After kissing the woman's cheek, Tori promised she'd come back and visit again.

As they strolled toward the car, Tori said, "She really believes Elly was murdered."

"Yes, and I'm beginning to agree," Mia said. "What the devil are the secrets she kept referring to? I've never heard about any mystery connected with the house." She stopped, glancing over her shoulder at the apartment. "She knows."

"What!" Tori exclaimed.

Mia nodded, her steps picking up again. "People who work in homes know what's going on. You wouldn't believe some of the stories I could tell you. Ethel lived in the house for many years. There isn't any way she wouldn't have known about the secrets."

"Why wouldn't she tell us?"

"I'm not sure. Maybe a sense of loyalty to Miss Elly. Ethel never married. Her world was Miss Elly and that house. When, for whatever reason, Miss Elly thought it wasn't safe, she sent Ethel away. Any secrets Miss Elly had would have been Ethel's as well."

As they got into the car, Tori said, "I wonder."

"Wonder what?"

"I'll tell you when we get back to the house."

A car in the driveway forced Mia to park on the street. "Linc's here," she said, stopping near the curb.

"I expect he's dropping off papers and Elly's car keys."

Footsteps pounded on the stairs as they walked inside. Linc grinned down at them. "Your knee must be doing better. You're not even limping. Mia, the upstairs is really looking better. How's Ethel doing?" he asked as he jumped the last couple of steps.

Tori wasn't surprised he knew where they had gone.

Mia said, "Good, though she was stunned by how

much Tori looked like her grandmother. For a moment, I think she believed she was seeing a ghost."

Linc's eyes studied Tori. "It is uncanny, but Elly was a stunning woman despite her age."

Uncomfortable with the warm look in his eyes, she quickly changed the subject. "It was a nice visit, and I plan to go back. Did you bring the keys?"

"Yes. On your desk, along with the documents Dad said he was sending you. Do you want to look at them now?"

"No. I'll do it this evening. Would you like something to drink before you leave?"

"I seldom turn down an offer of coffee."

"I could use a cup too. Mia, are you interested?"

"Maybe later. I want to check on the upstairs."

In the kitchen, Tori punched the button to start the coffee machine while Linc settled into a chair.

"I hear I'm on your hit list."

Unnerved, Tori turned. "What!"

"I forgot to tell you about the wine cellar."

"Oh, that."

"What did you think I meant?"

She shrugged. Tori couldn't tell him what flashed in her mind was her suspect list. "Well, I did wonder why, considering what's there."

"With everything else that day, I forgot. How did you find out about it?"

"David."

A note of irritation crept into his voice. "How'd he

manage it? I thought he was tied up on some engineering project."

Tori handed him the cup. "He stopped by last night. What is it with you two?"

Still not bothering to hide his irritation, he said, "David gets high-handed at times. An annoying trait. He's usually off on some trip somewhere. I'm surprised he's sticking around this long."

"He's never said much about his job. Exactly what does he do?"

"He owns Tucker Engineering. Designs new systems for utility companies."

A thought occurred to her. Where was David when someone took a shot at her? Would Linc know? "Where does he go?" she casually asked and took a sip of coffee.

"He was in New Mexico for a while, but this last trip was up north somewhere, Kansas, I think."

Springfield was only eighty or so miles from the Kansas border. With a disquieting feeling, she asked, "Where in Kansas?"

"I'm not sure. I don't keep up with him."

She persisted. "Do you travel much?"

He swallowed a swig. "On occasion."

"Any trips lately?"

"No." He eyed her with suspicion. "Why the questions?"

"Oh, I don't know. Just idle curiosity, I guess. Until I got Jonah's letter, I'd never been outside Missouri. When you mentioned David being out of town, I thought about traveling." Good lord, could she make this explanation sound any more idiotic? Obviously, interrogation wasn't her forte.

"Another reason to sell this place."

At the look of exasperation on her face, he said, "Okay, okay, won't mention it again. By the way, how are the plans for the renovation going?"

She laughed. "Slowly. I'm taking it one step at a time. I'm still getting a feel for the house; what I want to offer in the way of amenities, that kind of stuff."

"Learn anything new from Ethel? She would be a font of information about the house."

"Yes, I think she will. Today, I could see she was tired, and I didn't want to push."

"That's right. I keep forgetting you are a nurse. I would imagine you're more attuned to health issues than most people. I haven't seen her for some time, though I'd heard her mental condition is slipping, forgetful, even irrational."

"If so, I didn't see any evidence of it today. She seemed very lucid."

He rose, stepping to the pot to refill his cup. "No wild accusations?"

A niggling suspicion set her on edge. Was *he* pumping her for information? Ethel had said no one would listen. But had Linc heard her accusations?

"Only that she didn't understand how Elly could have fallen down the stairs." Uncertain why, Tori didn't want him to know Ethel claimed Elly had been murdered. "I'd like to show you something I found. I'll be right back."

Curious to see his reaction, she went to her bedroom and removed the tokens from the nightstand. She hesitated, then dropped the one with the series of numbers back into the drawer before returning to the kitchen. Tori laid the two chips on the table with RD face up.

"Son-of-a gun, poker chips. These must be from Frankie's casino. It was named Red Door. Where did you find them?"

"Oh, I came across them in Elly's things." It would raise undue interest if she said Elly gave them to the attorney.

"It doesn't surprise me that Elly saved them."

She flipped them over. "Any idea what these numbers might mean?"

Puzzled, he studied them. "Odd. Do you have any more?"

"Yes, with more numbers on the back."

"Maybe somebody's lucky number. I'd hang onto them. They could be valuable."

She picked them up, dropping them in her pocket.

He took the last swallow of coffee. "How about dinner one night this week?"

"Let me take a rain check. My paperwork is starting to pile up."

"I could tell by the list of items you've written down. If you need help with any of it, let me know."

As he backed out of the driveway, she stood on the porch. Uneasiness stirred her gut. Was it his questions about Ethel? Could they have been innocent inquiries? Her paranoia was in high gear because of everything that had happened. So, what had set off her apprehension?

Her mind in a muddle, she walked back to the kitchen and sat at the table. Tori laid the tokens in front of her, pushing them around with her finger. What was the meaning behind the numbers? Could it be as simple as Linc said, someone's lucky number? Yet, her instincts told her no. They were important, a key to something. But what?

Mia, Heidi, and Cammie trooped in.

With a smile, she looked up. "Finished for the day?"

"Yep. We're at a good place to stop. Tina has already left. Tomorrow you need to decide on the boxes," Mia said.

Tori held up her hand. "I promise."

Cammie flopped in the chair. "Where did you get these?"

"I found them in an envelope. They are tokens from my great-grandfather's gambling casino, the Red Door."

"Cool," she said as she picked up one.

"Anyone else want a cup of coffee?" Mia asked, pouring herself a cup.

Busy studying the chips, both women shook their heads no.

"Any idea what these numbers are on the back?" Heidi asked.

"No. I don't. Linc thinks they might be someone's lucky number."

Mia picked up one, turning it over in her hand. "Could be. Seems odd Elly would have saved them."

"There is one more, but it has a series of numbers on the back."

"Just got even weirder," Cammie said.

"Okay, guys. I'm out of here." Heidi stood. "See you in the morning."

Mia said, "Cammie, don't forget you and Tina have the Morton house tomorrow."

Cammie tossed her a grin and wagged her fingers on the way out the door.

After washing her cup and setting it aside, Mia said, "I'm going too. I've got to work on my accounts tonight. I can't put it off any longer." She started for the door, then stopped. "You said you had something to tell me when we returned to the house."

Tori pointed to the chips lying on the table. "I wanted to show you these. Could they be connected to the secrets Ethel mentioned? I thought you might make sense of them."

"It's odd, but how could they be important?"

Unsettled, Tori picked them up, slipping them back into her pocket. "I don't know. But it's a mystery why Elly saved them."

When the front door closed, the house seemed to settle into a strange stillness, as if it waited. But for what? With a toss of her head, she shook off the fanciful thoughts. Tori refused to be scared. She needed to keep busy and give her mind something else to dwell on.

After fixing a peanut butter and mayo sandwich, she carried it and a bottle of water into her office. Might as well eat while she worked. The keys and three large envelopes lay on top of the paperwork strewn across the desk.

She stared at the bank statements, checkbooks, and copies of canceled checks for a moment before setting down the plate and bottle. Like before, they'd been moved. The stack of bank statements was slightly askew. Even the ones flipped over, with ticks against the check numbers, were out of line. A checkbook partially covered the note with the company names. It had been left on top.

Though the computer screen was black, a tap on the keyboard brought it to life. There was the spreadsheet listing the check numbers, payment amounts, and who was paid.

Apprehension built as she collapsed into the chair. Someone had searched through the documents. It had to be Linc. He'd commented about her list, and it was under the checkbook.

Like Jonah, he was also her attorney. Linc would have immediately realized that she was crosschecking Elly's account. Even the box sitting next to her chair, full of copies of canceled checks, should have raised all kinds of questions. Yet, he'd made no comment, not asked a single question.

Tori bit into the sandwich and slowly chewed. Could Linc actually believe she wouldn't realize he had looked through the documents? Maybe so. The small changes wouldn't be readily apparent. But then, he didn't know her meticulous, almost obsessive penchant for organization. A natural inclination honed by her training as a nurse.

It's not that she intended to keep all of this a secret. Or did she? My god, she was following in Elly's footsteps.

Secrets. Everyone said Elly had secrets. And now she was the one with them.

Her phone chimed. *Dang,* she thought, her tongue scraping the peanut butter glued to the roof of her mouth. It was Dan. She answered, saying, "Hold on."

She gulped down water and punched the speaker-phone. "Sorry about that. I'm sitting at my desk eating a sandwich."

"I know it's late, but I just got back to my office and expect to be in court all day tomorrow," Dan said.

"I appreciate your calling. I had an accident with my car." At his exclamation, she hurriedly explained she was okay, then added a brief description of what happened before asking, "If something happens to me, what happens to the estate?"

"Good question. Elly included a ninety-day survivorship clause. If anything happens to you, the estate reverts to David. After that, it depends on whether you have a will."

She remembered the section but had glossed over it, thinking it was so much legal mumbo jumbo. Now, it loomed, leaving a nasty taste in her mouth. There was even more reason to suspect David. But he wasn't the only one, as another appalling motivation occurred to her. David would sell and, in fact, had been quite vocal about it. Was someone willing to kill to make it happen, make sure David inherited? It left the door open to others. She could add Judd, Jonah, and Linc to the list. And god knows who else that could be involved in the land development project.

"Tori, are you still there?"

"Yes." Not ready to share her thoughts, she asked, "When does it expire?"

"Hold on, let me check the dates."

She wondered how long she would have to dodge bullets, metaphorically speaking, to stay alive.

"Another six weeks. I suggest we go ahead and get a will in place. Will you call Emma tomorrow and set up an appointment?"

"All right. Dan, in the envelope you gave me were two letters, one from Elly and one my mother wrote to Elly. It's how Elly found out about me. It's Elly's letter that has me concerned. In it, she alluded to her fears. It wasn't safe for her to contact me. And, someone has already tried to kill me, not once but possibly twice."

There was a brief silence before Dan said, "Tell me the details."

It took several minutes to explain about Missouri and the subsequent call from the district attorney before she added, "I think someone tampered with my tire, which caused the blowout. Even the officer who investigated said I could have easily been killed."

"You need to hire a bodyguard."

"No, I don't think it's the solution. The only way I can stop this is to find out why."

Unwilling to abandon his position, Dan said, "Tori, I'm very disturbed about what is happening. I'm going to contact a private investigator I've worked with before. He's good. Expect a call from Parker Hayes. Listen to his advice.

You can trust him."

Though she wasn't thrilled at the idea, she agreed. Then she asked, "Dan, are you aware of Elly's family history, her father?"

"No, I'm not."

"Frankie Leichter was a gangster in the 1930s and 40s. He ran the gambling syndicate in Dallas. In Elly's envelope were three poker chips from his gambling casino. On the back are handwritten numbers. Dan, did Elly mention the poker chips? There must be a reason why she entrusted them to you."

"How odd. Elly didn't tell me what was in the envelope."

"There was also the combination to a hidden safe in the library. I found her jewelry inside, which had been missing."

"What did you do with it?"

"Put all of it in a safety deposit box at the bank."

"Good. Expect a call from Parker."

After disconnecting, the half-eaten sandwich didn't appeal. Pushing the plate aside, she picked up the list of companies Cantrell had paid. One by one, she researched the company name. Each set off red flags, no websites, identification on ownership, or what the company did.

How could she find out? Could Jeff Archer help? Or should she even bring him into this? Cripes, another secret.

Her phone chimed. Engrossed in her dilemma, she considered ignoring the call since she didn't recognize the number. Then remembered Dan said the P.I. would call.

"Tori Winters speaking."

"Ms. Winters, this is Parker Hayes. Dan Foote called me. He's quite concerned about your situation, so I didn't want to wait until tomorrow to contact you."

Maybe Dan had been right. Hayes might be the answer, but not for a bodyguard.

"Yes, Dan told me he planned to contact you. How much did he tell you?"

"Enough that I'm concerned as well. While we can discuss this over the phone, I'd like to meet you. I am about thirty or so minutes away if it's convenient."

"Yes. Please come on over." Despite Dan's recommendation, Tori felt it was imperative to form her own opinion of the man.

"I'm on my way. In the meantime, I do have a website, Hayes Investigations. It will help to introduce me."

"Thank you. I will take a look at it."

"See you shortly."

Tori carried the plate to the kitchen. She made a fresh pot of coffee and went into her bedroom to freshen up. By the time she was back in her office, she only had a few minutes to check out Hayes. What she found was impressive.

Parker Hayes was a thirty-year veteran of the Fort Worth Police Department, most as a homicide detective. He'd received multiple commendations, including two life-saving awards for pulling people out of burning buildings.

The doorbell rang, cutting into her musings. When she opened the door, a nondescript, slightly overweight man with a small bag slung over his shoulder stood on the porch, the type of person she wouldn't give a second glance.

"Ms. Winters, I'm Parker Hayes." His eyes sparkled with humor as if aware of her assessment.

Tori stepped back. "Please come in."

As she closed the door, he gazed around in wonder. "I've heard of this place, but the description certainly doesn't stand up to the reality." He turned to her, extending his hand. "I'm sorry. I didn't mean to get carried away."

As they shook hands, she said, "I felt the same way the first time I walked into the house. I have fresh coffee in the kitchen and would be happy to give you a tour, at least of the downstairs. The upstairs is still in disarray."

"I could use a cup. It's been a long day."

While Tori poured the coffee, his quick gaze took in the windows and short hallway leading to the back of the house.

"Where are the back doors?" After she showed him, he noted, "New locks. That's good. I noticed the front door also has a new lock."

Evidently, not much missed his sharp-eyed gaze. While he seemed to enjoy seeing the rooms, the windows had his attention.

In her office, he eased the bag off his shoulder and settled into a chair. "Come to any conclusions?" he asked and finished the coffee.

"Yes. I would like to hire you."

Chapter 21

He motioned with the cup. "In that case, do you mind if I have a refill? I suspect I'll be here for a while. May I set my computer on your desk?"

"Sure."

When she returned, a small laptop sat open in front of him. Accepting the cup, he took a swig before setting it down. "What I got from Dan was barebones. Please fill in the gaps if you don't mind, starting with what happened in Missouri."

As she talked, he typed, occasionally interjecting a question. Upon hearing about the call from Layton, he asked, "Did he give a reason for believing the two men weren't involved in the shooting?"

"He mentioned the plea bargain, something to the effect that admitting to the shooting wouldn't have changed it."

Parker nodded. "Good point. Okay, tell me about your accident. I don't suppose you have a copy of the report?"

"Yes, I do." She removed the report from the folder on her desk and handed it to him.

He quickly scanned the front, then flipped it over to read the narrative. "Hmm … sidewall."

"I spoke to Trooper Moore about the underinflation comment. Quite frankly, I find it hard to believe a brand new tire just went flat. He was quite emphatic the air pressure was low and mentioned the condition of the liner."

"Yes, it's usually the indicator." His face serious, he looked at her with a penetrating gaze. "What do you believe?"

"I think someone tampered with it."

He nodded, looking once again at the back of the report.

A bit peeved at his lack of a reaction, she said, "You don't believe it."

"No, quite the contrary. I think you're right. It's too coincidental, and I'm not big on coincidences. Plus, it's the left front tire."

"Uh, okay," she said.

He looked up. "The left front tire would pull you into the oncoming traffic lane, more dangerous than the right tire that would pull to the side of the road. I'd go for the left tire if I planned to kill someone."

Unnerved by his opinion, she said, "I felt the car pull to the left. I was luckier than I realized. There wasn't any other traffic."

"I bet you stomped the brakes when the tire blew."

A bit defensive, she said, "Yes, I did."

"A common reaction. It's what caused the car to spin. I get the feeling this isn't everything."

She sucked in a deep breath and took the plunge. "It's possible my grandmother was murdered."

This did rock him back in the seat. "How did she die?'

"Supposedly fell down the stairs."

"Why don't you believe it?"

"Three people told me Elly was afraid, Dan Foote, her housekeeper, and Elly herself in a letter she wrote to me. I've been told she had trouble getting up and down the stairs. Several months ago, she moved into the downstairs bedroom. Her housekeeper, Ethel Morris, is adamant Elly wouldn't have taken a tumble."

"Any idea what she was doing up there?"

"No, I don't. But Elly told Dan she heard strange sounds in the house. I've heard noises, found things moved, even a safe left open. The combination was on my desk. I believe someone is searching the house."

"Ah, the new locks. Anything missing?"

"Not that I can tell, but this is a big house, and I'm not all that familiar with it yet."

"Since you put on the new locks, have you seen any evidence someone got in."

"No."

"Might be a good idea to get a copy of the police report for your grandmother's death."

"I have it and the inquest report. They arrived this afternoon. I haven't had a chance to look at them yet." She picked up the envelope labeled Inquest and Police, slitting it open. She pulled out the documents, handing them to him.

Approval sparked in his eyes. "You don't miss much."

"As a nurse, I can't take anything for granted. It's too easy for someone to push an elderly relative into the grave."

"I get your point."

Tori watched Parker's face for any indication of his thoughts.

He looked up. "Straightforward, nothing here to indicate foul play. She was found lying at the base of the stairs by Jonah Greer. The doctor estimated the time of death between midnight and four o'clock. The inquest report stated death was consistent with a fall down the stairs and ruled an accidental death. If you are right, the sounds could be why she was upstairs in the middle of the night. And now it looks like you're a target. Any idea why?" He handed the reports to her.

"Well, that's the problem. It's all conjecture. I have no proof." She explained David's relationship to Elly and added, "In the original will, he was the heir. Several months ago, Elly found out about me and changed the will. When I talked to Dan earlier, he told me about a ninety-day survivor clause. Anything happens to me, David inherits."

"Do you think he is behind the attempts on your life?"

Confused, she said, "I don't know. But he's not the only one with a motive. Elly was being pressured to sell the property, and so am I. If David had inherited, he made it clear he would sell this place. I won't." A frightening thought arose. Did Elly sign her death warrant when she refused to sell? Had she done the same?

"So someone could want David to inherit. What's so important?"

"Ten acres for a condominium project."

His face thoughtful, he finally said, "Dan wants you to have a bodyguard, though he said you weren't receptive to the idea."

"I don't believe a bodyguard is what I need. Right now, my main focus is this house. I plan to turn it into a bed and breakfast-style inn. Several women are here every day, all working to clean the house. The only time I'll need to be cautious is when I leave, and that's not often. My main problem is that I don't know who I can trust, which is exactly what happened to my grandmother. If the need arises, I want someone I can contact."

"All right." He didn't plan on telling her that Dan had already hired him. By morning, he'd have a team in place to keep an eye on her and the property. "I expect such an occasion has already come up."

"Yes, you're right. Sam Cantrell. He was Elly's CPA and financial advisor. Cantrell was responsible for the payment of the day-to-day expenses for Elly. She had a checkbook, and so did Cantrell. In reconciling Elly's bank account, I've come across a few anomalies, check numbers out of sequence with no matching stub in either checkbook."

She picked up the paper with the names of the four companies and handed it to Parker. "I obtained a copy of the canceled checks from the bank. Every month, Cantrell wrote a check to these companies in varying amounts. I can't find any record of the companies. Can you find out? I want to know what services the company provides and who owns them."

As he listened, he felt an unexpected sense of respect for this unusual woman. Tori Winters was no fool, or a pushover, which in his books added to her credibility.

He typed the names into his computer before handing the paper back. "I'll have something for you tomorrow. Anything else?"

"We haven't discussed your fees?"

"I charge by the hour or a monthly retainer." With Dan Foote's involvement in mind, he said, "I would recommend the per hour fee for now," and quoted the rate. This way, he'd only charge for what time he expended on her requests.

She smiled. "I like that."

From his pocket, he pulled out a business card. On the back, he wrote his cellphone number. "This will reach me any time of day or night. If anything seems off, call."

After closing his computer, he stashed it in his bag. Together they walked to the front door.

"Once you finish renovating, I'd like to see the final results. I have a feeling you're going to set Granbury back on its heels."

"Why, thank you. What a nice compliment."

As he walked out, he said, "I'd make your outside lighting one of your first priorities."

With a laugh, Tori said, "Believe it or not, it's near the top of my list."

"I'd believe it. Have a good evening, and we'll be talking again soon."

Oddly reassured, she watched as he pulled out. Inside, Tori started to switch off the porch light, then decided to leave it on. It wasn't much protection, but better than nothing.

Before calling it a night, she finished totaling the payments to the four companies, which amounted to over three hundred thousand dollars. How long had this been going on? She'd only looked at about eighteen months. The sinking feeling roiling inside her said Cantrell had been robbing Elly blind.

If David had inherited, he'd probably have left everything in place, including Cantrell, until after the probate was complete. As the CPA, Cantrell controlled the estate's financial affairs. Once the probate was finished, and the books closed, who would know about the fraudulent payments? People had been killed for far less.

There was only one problem casting Cantrell in the role of the killer. It didn't add up. One minor detail, a teensy discrepancy she couldn't get around. Her accident didn't happen until after she started digging into the financial records and fired Cantrell. So, why the attempt in Missouri? Back then, how could she have been a threat to Cantrell? And it still didn't answer the question of why someone had searched the house.

Her thoughts reeling, she stacked the copies of the canceled checks back into the box. Though it was a tight fit, she shoved the statements and checkbooks in the bottom drawer. Tori added another entry to the list—buy file cabinet.

On the way to the bedroom, she stopped in the library.

If she was going to get any sleep, she had to divert her thoughts and get her mind off her fears. As she perused the shelves, she discovered several books about her great-grandfather.

As Tori undressed, she felt the chips in her pocket. She dropped them in the nightstand drawer, on top of the one still there.

She stacked the pillows behind her and picked up one of the books she'd laid on the nightstand. Written in 1956, the book detailed Frankie Leichter's criminal career. The author outlined how Frankie, a bootlegger during the latter years of prohibition, slowly took control of the distribution and sale of illegal liquor in the Dallas and Fort Worth area, mainly by killing off his competitors. By the time prohibition ended, he was second-in-command to the kingpin, Luigi Costa. Rumor had it that Costa was linked to the Chicago Mafia. Not long after prohibition ended, Costa was gunned down on a south Dallas street. Frankie took control of Costa's syndicate. While suspected of ordering the hit, nothing was ever proved.

Though he had allegedly amassed a fortune from the illegal sale of liquor, Frankie turned his attention to gambling. As a boy, he'd been introduced to the pastime by horse traders at county fairs. One by one, he took over the smaller casinos. The infamous Red Door Casino was located in an upscale Dallas restaurant Frankie purchased when the owner was killed. This time, an eyewitness claimed Frankie was responsible. While he'd been arrested for the murder, the charges were dropped when the witness disappeared.

Not only did he control the gambling syndicate, but local judges, politicians and even cops were on his payroll.

When Tori glanced at the clock, she groaned. Caught up in the book, it was late. Tomorrow was another early start. Reluctantly, she laid the book aside. Snuggled under the covers, she soon fell asleep.

Her eyes blinked open. What woke her? Then Tori heard it, the creak of wood. Her head shifted toward the sound. A large, dark shape stood in front of the dresser. Fear rippled through her. Could she get to the door? It was her only chance, even though the dresser was closer to the door than the bed. She had to try.

Throwing aside the covers, she swung her legs over the side of the bed. It squeaked. The intruder spun.

Galvanized by a surge of adrenaline and fear, she reached for the only weapon she had, the large brass table lamp. Tori jumped to the floor, ripping the cord from the socket.

As the intruder rushed toward her, she swung the heavy lamp. A very satisfying thud sounded when it struck his head. The man's hands flailed wildly, trying to grab it. When Tori struck another blow, he grunted, turned and ran out the door.

Still hanging onto the lamp, the cord dragging behind her, she ran after him. The front door stood open. She stopped on the porch.

A voice shouted, "Tori! Are you all right?"

"David?"

He ran up the steps. "What happened?"

"A man was in my room. I fought with him, but he got away." The shock and fear began to subside as she pulled herself together. "What are you doing here?"

"I was on my way home and saw someone run out of the house." David's gaze slid over her. His lips twitched.

Mortified, she realized she was standing under the porch light wearing nothing but her ratty oversized t-shirt. It had been washed so many times, David could probably see right through it. If that wasn't bad enough, she still held the broken lamp with the shade hanging by a wire.

She rushed inside. The cord flopped around her feet as she hollered, "Come on in. I'm going to call the police." She dropped the lamp on the floor.

Cursing herself for not locking her door and leaving the phone in the office, she rushed to get it. After calling 911, she headed to her bedroom. As she passed the kitchen, she stopped to let David know the cops were on the way. Busy filling the coffee machine with water, he nodded.

"I'll be in my bedroom."

"Be careful not to destroy any evidence."

Irritated by the patronizing tone in his voice, she snapped back. "I know. Been there, done that."

"Hey," he said, with his hand palm up, "just trying to be helpful."

"Sorry, this isn't your fault."

Tori flipped on the overhead light and stared at the mess. Pieces of the lamp and light bulb were strewn across the floor. Clothing hung over the side of an open dresser drawer.

With careful steps to avoid the glass, she wondered how she managed to keep from getting cut when she ran out of the room.

Still irate over her stupid mistakes, Tori walked into the bathroom. All the dashing about hadn't helped her knee. She swallowed two pain pills before changing into sweatpants and a sweatshirt.

When she heard the sound of cars, she headed to the front door with David close on her heels. Three cops exited from the two vehicles.

The lead officer asked, "Are you Tori Winters?"

"Yes, please come in." They stood in the entryway while she explained, pointing to the lamp on the floor. While the three men didn't comment, Tori didn't miss their amused exchange of looks. Two left to check the inside of the house, and the other followed her to the bedroom. He asked David to wait in the kitchen.

In the bedroom, the officer gazed around, making notes on a small notepad he pulled from his front pocket. Tori stood in the doorway.

He turned toward her. "Can you describe him?"

"Not really. The room was dark, and something covered his face."

"How about height or weight?"

She thought back. She had to raise her arms to hit his head. Still, it wasn't enough. "I'm not sure."

"Any idea how he got in?"

"I had the locks changed a couple of days ago. Maybe a window."

"Do you know if anything is missing?"

"I haven't had a chance to look."

He pocketed the notepad. "If you do, I'll give you a number to call." He turned and walked out.

David was seated at the table, drinking coffee. The officer stopped, asking a few questions before strolling toward the front of the house.

Tori filled a mug and dropped into a chair across from David.

"Did you get a good look at him?" As he spoke, he turned his head, and the light hit the side of his face. Across the temple was a red mark.

She tensed, the hackles rising. Tori never said where she hit the man. Was David the intruder? He had time to ditch the disguise. But not enough time to get away in his truck. What better way to avoid suspicion than to return to the crime scene.

"What happened to your face?"

He shot her a sheepish look. "I chased him and tripped. I hit the ground pretty hard."

It sounded reasonable, but was it true?

"You never said why you were driving by so late."

He grinned. "Poker night."

"Huh."

"A bunch of us get together for poker night. I was on my way home."

Something about his explanation didn't quite ring true. David just happened to be driving by at the precise moment an intruder ran out of the house. It was a bit of a stretch.

The officer who took the report walked in. "Ms. Winters, we checked all the windows and doors. They are locked, and there is no sign of a forced entry."

He handed her a business card. On it was the case number and a telephone number. "If you find something missing, call this number and ask for the detective assigned to your case. He'll add it to the report."

"You can't get fingerprints?"

"No. Your friend said the man was wearing gloves."

David rose. "I'd better leave also. I'll check on you later today."

Once she cleaned up the mess, it was too late to go back to bed. While she waited for a fresh pot to brew, she sat at the table, watching the sunrise over the trees. Rays sparkled on the dew, albeit it was on weeds, not grass. A brief reminder of her appointment today with the fireman, though it was the intruder who dominated her thoughts.

He could have killed her while she slept, but he didn't. Though she hated to admit it, he could have easily overpowered her. The lamp wasn't much of a weapon. Instead, he turned tail and ran. It seemed to reinforce her notion her death had to look like an accident. Unlike Elly's death, murder would have set off a hue and cry. Tori also had another grim reminder, Horace's death. Russell would have gotten away with killing Horace if her suspicions hadn't triggered a closer look.

The machine beeped. Tori rose, filled a cup and leaned against the counter.

Since murder wasn't his purpose, what was he looking for in her bedroom? She'd searched the drawers, and nothing was missing. The troubling fact was the room was pitch-black. He couldn't see anything. She mulled the thought as she sipped the coffee.

"What if he didn't need to see, only feel," she muttered. It meant he was searching for a specific object. But what? All that was in the bedroom was her clothing. There wasn't even any jewelry since the Russells had stolen hers, and Elly's was in the bank. What was left?

Tori stiffened as an idea took on legs. The only unusual objects were the poker chips, immediately recognizable by touch. She talked about the chips but only showed two of them. Then someone searched her bedroom. Another coincidence she didn't like.

David didn't know about the chips, a fact in his favor, though she was still suspicious about his just driving by explanation. Linc knew about them and that they were in her bedroom. She even mentioned there were more chips. Linc probably told his dad.

If Jonah told Judd, she could add him to the mix. Mia said Jonah and Judd were tight, and she was right. Judd was in the middle of this. She could still feel the icy chill when Judd threatened her, saying there could be another accident like the one that killed Elly. Was he the intruder?

Consumed by the terrifying moment when the man rushed toward her, she idly topped off her cup. She sighed. It happened so fast, she didn't know. It could just as easily have been Linc or Jonah.

But what did the chips have to do with the sale of the house, the attempts to kill her, or even Elly's murder? Like Ethel, deep down, she believed someone had killed her grandmother.

Coming into her bedroom was risky, or it seemed so to her. So, why were the chips so important?

And how did he get into the house? She'd allowed herself to be lulled into thinking re-keying the locks was the answer.

All she had were questions and no answers. But the more she thought about it, everything seemed to point to three men, Jonah, Linc, or Judd. The only problem, it was all conjecture. She didn't have one iota of proof.

She wasn't kidding when she told Parker Hayes she needed someone she could trust.

Chapter 22

Since she had a new combination to the safe, Tori decided it was the best place for the chips. With them safely stowed, she slowly strolled back to the kitchen, mindful of her knee. It still ached from her late-night scamper. While she waited for Mia and the crew to arrive, she wandered out the back door.

Her gaze swept the guesthouse and garage as she breathed deep, enjoying the light breeze. In her mind, Tori envisioned smooth green grass, flower beds, maybe a gazebo, and footpaths. She had enough space to build walkways for visitors.

A lot of work, but it would be worth it in the end. For now, it was overgrown grass and weeds. And she definitely had to get rid of the well house near the back of the property.

Voices from the front of the house broke into her musings. She chuckled as she wondered how many times she'd have to recount the details of the break-in. Inside, she greeted Mia and Heidi when they entered the kitchen.

"What's the vacuum doing in the hallway?"

Trust Mia to go to the heart of the matter.

"I had a little excitement last night."

Heidi stashed her purse in the cupboard. "Do tell."

"Someone broke into the house."

Startled, hot coffee from the pot splashed on Mia's hand. Muttering a few unsavory words, she stuck her hand under the faucet, letting cold water flow over it. "What happened?"

"I woke up and saw a black shape in front of the dresser. I clobbered him with that old brass lamp."

Agog, they stared. When Tori paused to swallow a swig of coffee, Mia whirled her wet hand in the air. Water droplets flew. "Come on. What else?"

"That's all. He ran out, headed to the front door."

"You weren't hurt?"

"No."

Heidi observed, "Nothing more intrepid than our Tori. Beats the bad guy with a dang lamp."

The women burst into laughter, though Mia's eyes were still shadowed with concern.

It dawned on Tori just how ridiculous it did sound. Laughter bubbled as she joined in.

She held up a hand. "But that's not all. I chased after him, and guess who was outside? David! All I had on was my ratty old nightshirt."

Heidi's lips curved upward in a wicked grin. "I bet you put on quite a show."

"Let's just say, I don't consider it one of my finer moments. Though I don't think he even noticed. I suspect he was too busy laughing about the lamp I still had in my hand. At least I was able to change before the cops arrived."

With a troubled look, Mia asked, "Was anything stolen?"

"No."

"How did he get in? You changed the locks."

"I don't know. The officers checked the windows and doors. All were locked."

"What was David doing here?" Heidi asked.

"Something about being on the way home from a poker game and saw the man running out the front door."

Mia nodded. "Whenever David is in town, he plays poker with a group of friends. They rotate the game from house to house. I'm surprised they had a game last night."

Instantly suspicious, Tori asked, "Why?"

"Wrong day of the week."

About that time, the front doorbell rang, and Tori couldn't pursue the conversation. Still, she filed it away to ask about later. Maybe Mia could find out if there was a game.

Tina and Cammie had arrived. Before Mia went upstairs, she reminded Tori about the boxes.

In her office, Tori followed up on her call with Dan and made an appointment. While she had the secretary on the line, she said, "When you talk to Dan, let him know someone broke into the house last night." After reassuring the woman that she hadn't been harmed and nothing was stolen, she disconnected.

From the center drawer, she retrieved Parker Hayes' business card. He answered on the first ring.

She filled him in on the details about the break-in. After asking a couple of questions about David's presence, he hung up. Odd, she thought. Prepared to get hit with another round of arguments about a bodyguard, Parker didn't mention it.

Next up was the call on the trash. Another entry Tori could cross off the list. It was the next one she dreaded, having gone through the same process with her mother's possessions. Now, she had to do the same for Elly.

She headed up the stairs. In the far back room, Tori heard their voices. When she walked in, several boxes had been opened.

Mia said, "From the looks of it, there is no rhyme nor reason. Clothes are jammed inside. I suggest we pull everything out, give it a quick glance and go from there."

While much of the clothing was useable, Tori decided to throw it all away. Somehow, the idea of Elly's clothes in a thrift shop wasn't a pleasant thought. Mia had brought up a box of trash bags, and as each box was emptied, the clothes went into a bag.

Heidi and Cammie hauled them outside. After one of the trips, Heidi said, "Please tell me you made arrangements to have all those bags picked up."

With a grin, Tori assured her it was scheduled for later in the week. It wasn't until they neared the end and found the evening gowns that Tori changed her mind.

Mia said, "Oh, these are gorgeous. I think you should keep them. Stand up."

She held a black silk gown, trimmed with seeded pearls across the bodice, in front of Tori. "I bet you could wear all of these."

Tori nodded. "I hope they haven't been damaged with the rough treatment."

"They need to go to the cleaners," Heidi said.

Each one was carefully folded and carried downstairs. Since the dining room table was the largest one in the house, they were laid on top.

Tina opened the last two boxes. "Purses."

"Wow," Mia said as she began to remove them. "Some match the gowns."

"Let's keep those." The ones to be thrown away were opened. Most were empty, but one had a few items.

"This may be the one Elly was using," Mia said, pulling out tissues, a pen, coin purse, and lipstick. In a zippered pocket, she found a small notebook.

Mia handed it to Tori, who quickly flipped through it. "I'll keep this. Anything else?"

"No, that's all."

Grateful they were finished, Tori headed downstairs. As she started toward the office, the doorbell rang. She shouted, "I've got it."

Parker stood on the front porch. "I hope this is okay. I tried calling, but you didn't answer."

"I've been upstairs. The phone is in the office. Coffee?"

"I'm a typical cop. Never turn down a cup."

He followed her to the kitchen. Surprised to see a fresh pot, evidently, someone on their trek downstairs had stopped to make it, she poured two mugs.

Hearing the sounds overhead, he said, "Let's go to your office."

A quiver of concern raced through her at his serious tone. When he closed the double doors, she knew bad news was coming. Still carrying Elly's notebook, she dropped it in a desk drawer.

Parker settled into the chair, setting the cup on the corner of the desk. From the bag slung over his shoulder, he pulled out a file folder. "The reason you couldn't find anything on the four companies is because they're shell companies. A shell company has no offices or employees. It's usually formed for financial transactions and is owned by a parent company."

He slid a piece of paper across the desk. "This is the parent company, and it's owned by Sam Cantrell."

A cold feeling settled over her. "He was stealing from Elly."

"That's my conclusion. I'd like to see those canceled checks."

From the box, she picked up the ones she'd left on top.

He slowly looked through them. "Did you get a copy of the backside of the checks?"

"The front is all I got. When I called the bank president, he already had the copies. Said Elly had asked for them."

Parker leaned forward. An intense look crossed his face. "Did he say when she asked for them?"

"A couple of days before she died. It never occurred to me to ask if they were front and back."

"We need to find out who endorsed the checks."

"I'll get them."

"Anything else?"

Tori hesitated and finally asked, "Can you find out if someone made a trip to Springfield?"

His eyebrows twitched upward. "Probably. Who?"

"Jonah Greer, his son, Lincoln, and Judd Swanson." She hesitated, then added, "David Tucker."

"Care to explain why?"

"No, not yet. Let's see what you find out."

Parker didn't push it, knowing he'd run a check on all four. He closed his computer, shoving it into the bag. When he stood, he looked at her with a grim expression. "You've got good instincts. Listen to them. If something seems off, it's probably because there's a reason. I'll be in touch."

He opened the doors and strode out. Tori slowly followed. His comments had stirred up the fear that clung like a bad dream she couldn't shake.

At the sound of the front door closing, Mia tripped down the stairs. She took one look at Tori and said, "Everything all right?"

"I'm not sure," she said in a vague tone, walking back into the office.

Mia followed. "Okay, you've got me scared. What's going on?" She plopped in the chair. "That guy looked familiar, but I can't place him."

"He's a private investigator my attorney hired, some

minor estate issues." Right now, it might be better if no one knew the real reason. It could be unsafe. The thought triggered a blinding reminder. In her letter, Elly said the same thing.

Seeing Mia's suspicious gaze, Tori said, "It really is okay. Just something I can't talk about."

Mia nodded with an understanding expression. "On my way home, I go by the cleaners. Would you like me to drop off the gowns?"

"Yes, thank you. Mia, you are a blessing. I have an errand to run. So, lock up if I'm not back before you leave."

Mia stood. "We have to move cars if you plan to get Elly's car out of the garage."

Once Mia was out of earshot, she tapped the number for the bank. When Malcolm answered, she asked, "How long would it take to get a copy of the backside of the canceled checks. I don't need all of them, only certain check numbers."

"It would only take a few minutes."

"I'm on my way." She downloaded the list of numbers to a thumb drive.

Her phone chimed. "Tori Winters."

"This is Doug Coleman. Are we still on for this afternoon?"

Oh, great. Tori had forgotten the appointment. "I'm sorry. I can't. Can we shift our appointment to tomorrow?"

"Not a problem. Same time?"

"Yes, thank you."

When she was ready to leave, Mia and her gang had

moved their cars. Tori opened the garage door.

Mia laughed as she walked up the drive. "If the Tank doesn't start, I'll play chauffeur."

"Here's hoping," Tori said as she tossed her bag on the front seat and slid behind the wheel.

Surprisingly, the engine turned over on the first try. As Tori backed out, she waved to the four women lined up alongside the driveway, cheering her on.

As soon as Tori backed out, she knew why David dubbed it 'the Tank.' The car was bigger and more powerful than what she was accustomed to. Tori turned onto the main road. As she neared an intersection with lights, she tapped the brake. The car didn't slow down. She pushed harder. The pedal went to the floor. A bolt of panic ripped through her. The busy intersection loomed closer. The light had turned red. She couldn't stop the car. How many people would she kill?

Frantic, Tori spun the wheel toward the curb and spotted a large brick mailbox. She aimed for it. The airbag blew. As she lost consciousness, her only thought was, *not again*.

When she came too, she was lying inside an ambulance. A medic leaned over her. "Glad to see you're back with us."

"I know you," she murmured. He was the medic from the first crash.

"Yes, we have to stop meeting like this. People will talk."

Pain stabbed her head. "How bad am I hurt?"

"Actually, you're in better condition this time than last.

The airbag knocked you out. You're headed to the hospital to check for a concussion."

"The car?"

"Sitting in the middle of the yard of a very irate elderly gentleman. You destroyed his mailbox."

"Had to. The brakes didn't work. Can you get my bag from the car? It has my phone."

"I already did. It's on the floor next to you. You'll have to wait on making a call." He tapped the window. A siren blared as the ambulance pulled out.

My god, she wondered. What were the odds of two accidents? What happened to the brakes? They were working when she left the house.

The medics wheeled her into the emergency room, where she was moved to a bed. Close on their heels were the doctor and a nurse.

When the doctor finished his examination, he stripped off his gloves. "You don't have a concussion, so I'm going to release you. But this is the second time you've been here for a blow to the head, which is cause for concern. You're a nurse and know what to look for. Any symptoms of a head injury, and I want you back here. Take it easy for the next couple of days. Nothing strenuous." A mischievous grin crossed his face as he followed the nurse out the door. "You might consider not driving for a while."

Tori swung her legs over the side and eased off the bed. Her head spun. Afraid she'd land facedown if she took a step, she leaned against the side of the bed until it passed. *Okay,* she thought, *I can walk out and not collapse.* She straightened, reaching for the tote bag on the counter. A groan erupted. How was she going to get home? Cripes, she'd have to call Mia, again.

A police officer approached as she walked out. Behind him was Parker Hayes.

Surprised, she stammered, "Parker, uh … what are you doing here?"

"I'm your ride."

The officer said, "Please have a seat. I have a few questions."

Parker stood back, letting the officer talk.

"How do you feel?"

"Other than the mother of all headaches, I'm okay."

"You were lucky. If you'd been in a smaller car, the engine might have ended up in your lap. That was a good-sized brick mailbox you hit. What happened?"

"The brakes didn't work."

"What do you mean they didn't work?"

"Just that. I pushed on the brake pedal, and it went to the floor. The intersection was ahead. So I steered toward the mailbox, hoping it would stop the car."

Parker turned and walked out of the room with the phone held to his ear.

The officer's voice brought her attention back to him. He asked for her driver's license and the insurance card.

She searched for the documents in the bag. "I inherited the car. I guess my insurance will cover it." Tori handed them to him. While he wrote down the information, she wondered how long it would take before the insurance company canceled the policy.

Parker passed the officer as he made his way back inside. He stepped beside her. "Ready to go home?"

"Yes."

He waited until they were on the road to say, "I'm having the car inspected to find out what happened to the brakes."

"I don't understand. They worked when I left."

"Let's wait until I get the report."

"How'd you know I had an accident?"

Parker pointed to a radio mounted under the dashboard. "Police radio." It wasn't a lie, just not the whole truth. A call had come over the radio about the crash. But he already knew. The man following her had called. "Where were you headed?"

"The bank. I was going to get copies of the back of the canceled checks."

"Do you want to stop there? I don't mind."

After glancing at the bloodstains on her shirt from the nose bleed, she said, "No. I'll call Malcolm when I get home. I can email the numbers to him."

"If he can have them ready today, tell him I will pick them up for you. If Cantrell is behind this, I want to know."

"All right. Thanks for coming to the hospital."

He shot her a quick smile. She was one gutsy woman. He'd stopped at the crash site before going to the hospital. If she had plowed through that intersection, she could have been killed as well as whoever she hit.

As he pulled into the driveway, Mia was walking toward her car. Seeing Tori inside Parker's truck, she rushed up the drive.

When Tori stepped out, she cried, "My God, what happened?" as she stared at the dried blood on Tori's shirt.

"Would you believe another accident?"

"You wrecked Miss Elly's car? How?"

Parker walked around the front of the truck. "There was something wrong with the brakes. Tori hit a mailbox."

"You're the private investigator."

"Mia, meet Parker Hayes." Tori reached inside and grabbed her tote bag.

"I knew I should have driven you. You look exhausted. Let's get you inside."

Unlocking the front door, Mia tried to steer Tori to her bedroom. "You need a hot bath, and that big claw tub is just the ticket."

"I can't, not yet. I have to take care of something." Tori headed for her office, followed by Mia and Parker.

She collapsed in the chair, slipping the tote bag off her shoulder. She pulled out her phone and called Malcolm. When he answered, she said, "Malcolm, I can't get to the bank. If you'll give me your email address, I'll send you those numbers."

As she spoke, she turned on the computer. Tori set up an email and attached the list. "Can I still get the copies today?"

There was a pause while Malcolm waited for the email to arrive. "It shouldn't be a problem."

"A friend of mine, Parker Hayes, will pick them up. How soon will they be ready?"

When she disconnected, she said, "About thirty minutes."

"I'll be back." Parker turned and walked out.

A worrisome look settled over Mia's face. "You look like you are about to pass out. I'm going to run that tub of water and no protests. Let's go."

Mia started the water in the tub, then got a clean towel from the cupboard. "Did you go to the hospital?"

"Yes, another trip." She told her about the comment from the EMT, which prompted a laugh.

"What did the doc say?"

"No concussion." She wasn't about to tell her what else the doctor had said.

"Can you get in the tub by yourself?"

"Yes, I can."

"I'll be in the kitchen. Holler if you need anything."

"You don't need to stay. I'll be fine."

Mia gave her the stink eye and walked out.

Tori undressed, tossed her clothes in the hamper and eased into the tub. As the hot water flowed around her, she sighed with relief. Tomorrow, she would feel like a truck ran over her—again. She was getting damn tired of it.

Chapter 23

Sinking under the water, she leaned her head back and tried to relax, not let herself think about what happened. An impossibility, as the images replayed in her head. Did someone tamper with the brakes? If so, it must have occurred while the car was parked in the garage. Belatedly, she realized that while she had changed the locks on the house, she didn't think about the garage. Anyone with an old set of keys could get inside.

Once the water cooled down, Tori crawled out and dried off. Dressed in sweatpants and a sweatshirt, she wandered into the kitchen.

Her feet propped on a chair, Mia was engrossed in a book.

"When I didn't hear any sounds, I thought you had left."

Mia looked up. "Nope. Been sitting here enjoying a few quiet moments, drinking your wine, and getting a chance to do a little reading." She laid the book aside, her gaze scrutinizing Tori. "You look a heck of a lot better than when you got out of the truck."

"I am. Thanks for the tub idea. It worked."

She said smugly, "I knew it would, though I wasn't sure I could convince you. Has anyone ever told you that you are a wee bit hard-headed?"

"Many times. Did Parker get back?"

"Not yet." Her feet dropped to the floor. A worrisome look settled on her face. "Tori, was this an accident?"

"I don't know. Parker is checking the car to find out why the brakes didn't work. It might be because the car was old and not in good condition."

"I'm worried about you being alone in this house. And tomorrow, we won't be here."

"Don't be. Tonight, I'll lock myself in my bedroom. Tomorrow, I have an appointment with Doug Coleman about the yard. I will keep my phone with me."

Mia stood. "I still don't like it. I'm going to call and check on you. So you had damn well better answer, or I'll be calling out the troops."

While she washed the wineglass, Mia added, "Time for me to head home. There's a turkey sandwich in the fridge. I didn't think you'd feel like fixing anything."

Tears clogged her throat. Tori quickly turned away, not wanting Mia to see. "Thank you. You know you didn't have to do all of this."

An arm came around her shoulder, and Mia gave her a quick hug.

"If there's one thing you can take to the bank, it is that

I don't do anything I don't want to. If you need anything, call."

As Mia walked out the door, Parker drove up. With a wave, she trotted down the driveway.

Parker stepped onto the porch, glancing over his shoulder. "You've got a good friend there."

"Yes. Yes, I do."

"If you're up to it, let's look at these checks. I don't suppose you have any coffee?"

Tori laughed, and it felt good. "No, but it will only take a few minutes."

Seated at the desk, she opened the large envelope and pulled out the papers. Malcolm had made a copy of the front and back of each of the checks. She looked at one and handed the rest to Parker, who set his cup aside to flip through them.

"Cantrell has endorsed every one of them."

"Okay, where do we go from here?"

"Dig some more. He could say he had Elly's permission, and we don't have a way to disprove his statement. I suggest you go through Elly's records and correspondence. See if you can find anything about these payments. I'm going to talk to a friend of mine in the FBI. It might be interesting to see if Cantrell has claimed the money on his tax return. I wonder if you hadn't investigated, would the embezzlement have been discovered. Who is doing the tax returns for the estate?"

"Until I fired him, it was Cantrell. I don't know if Jonah Greer has hired a new firm. Jonah is the executor and was

Elly's attorney for many years."

"How did Dan enter the picture?"

"A few months ago, my grandmother went to Dan for a new will. That's when everything was left to me."

He whistled. "Odd that she would bypass Greer."

Tori went on to explain the rumors Elly was senile.

"Sounds like she didn't trust anyone close to her, and with good reason. You did mention your grandmother told Dan she was afraid. Now you're in the same boat. Make sure your bedroom door is locked and keep your cellphone with you."

The doorbell rang as they approached the door. When Tori opened it, David charged inside. His gaze swept over her. "I heard about the accident. Are you all right?"

"Yes, I am. Though I can't say the same for Elly's car."

"Who cares about the car. All that matters is that you weren't hurt." Suddenly, his head turned, spotting Parker for the first time. His eyes narrowed.

Tori introduced the two men, adding that Parker was an associate of the Fort Worth attorney. She hoped to head off any uncomfortable questions.

Parker, playing along, said, "I was dropping off some papers." With a nod to David, he walked out.

Still holding the door open, Tori said, "David, I'm not up to having company. It's been a rough few days." She was tired and didn't want to answer any more questions. Besides, she couldn't rid herself of the niggling suspicions he was involved.

His face furrowed with concern. "I understand. But if

you need anything, you call me."

"I will."

He turned and trotted down the steps.

After cleaning the coffee pot, even though she had no appetite, she ate the sandwich Mia had made. Tired of the endless thoughts that went nowhere, she grabbed a notepad from her office. Tori prowled through the rooms, writing down ideas for changes to each of them.

Upstairs, she stepped into the master bedroom. Did she really want to move? With a few changes, this room would make a great suite for the inn.

In the other bedrooms, she pondered the size, envisioning how she could turn each one into a more attractive room. Two of the bedrooms were certainly a lot smaller than the others. Maybe she should knock out the wall and make it one room.

It wasn't until Tori headed to the staircase that an odd sense of awareness tickled her spine, as if someone watched. She turned, looking at the long dark hallway. Even the dim glow of the wall sconces was ineffective against the dark shadows. Who did they hide?

For cripes sake, she thought. She was letting herself get spooked over nothing.

Still, as her hand reached to turn off the lights, she hesitated. *It wouldn't hurt to leave them on,* she thought. She raced down the stairs, heading to the bedroom.

It wasn't until she turned the lock on her door that she felt safe. Undressing, she slid into her nightshirt and crawled into bed. Propped against the pillows, she flipped pages to where she had left off in the book about Frankie.

Names like Machine Gun Kelly and Bonnie and Clyde were part of her great-grandfather's world. As Frankie's casinos grew, so did his ruthless reputation. It was, play by my rules, or you don't play at all. Infamous for the bright red door, his casino became the go-to social club for movie stars and the wealthy echelon. Though gambling was illegal in Texas, no one, including the cops, messed with Frankie.

The Red Door Casino was located in the basement of the restaurant. In case of a raid, he had secret passageways and rooms. Gambling tables, roulette wheels and other paraphernalia could quickly be moved into the hidden rooms through doors concealed in the wood-paneled walls. Guests could escape through a tunnel into the dance hall connected to the restaurant.

By the early forties, attempting to avoid crackdowns by the FBI, Frankie began to legitimize his operation. He bought large parcels of land in the Dallas area, which in later years accounted for a major portion of the Leichter fortune, ultimately inherited by his daughter, Elly.

The Granbury house was the start of the real estate business. After the depression, land was cheap, and he bought ten acres on what was then the outskirts of town. The house became a testament to his money and power.

One chapter dealt with the legends of the Leichter era. Riveted, Tori read the account of a shootout, old west style, on a Dallas street. Frankie and one of his enforcers faced off with a local competitor trying to muscle his way into the syndicate. When the smoke cleared, three men lay dead in the street. Frankie and his enforcer walked away. It was reported that Frankie left word with the cops to pick up the bodies.

Other stories dealt with the gambling casinos. Legend had it that gambling losses were often paid with valuable paintings and jewelry. The author recounted one story of a wealthy, well-known New York socialite. The woman supposedly pulled a tiara from her hair and tossed it on the table to cover her bets. The Ludivich tiara that dated back to the Napoleonic era was never seen again. While the author recounted similar stories, since none of the jewelry or artifacts had ever been found, he discredited them as nothing more than legends.

Slowly, Tori put down the book. Her mind linked up tidbits of information, secret passages, hidden rooms, missing jewelry and artwork worth millions in today's market.

A house with secrets, Elly had written. Ethel said the house had secrets. Was it possible this was the answer? Secret rooms and hidden passages? But how did the chips fit in? There had to be a reason why Elly gave them to Dan. She didn't give him her jewelry, left all of it in the safe, then gave him the combination. Why didn't she leave the chips in the safe?

She grabbed the notepad from the nightstand and wrote the numbers. As she stared at them, an idea occurred to her. What if the chip with multiple numbers was the middle one? Whatever it referred to was between 1 and 3. It felt like something was just out of her grasp that she was missing. "Wait a minute. Could that be it?" she muttered. A combination? Another hidden safe? But where and what did the 1 and 3 tell her?

A muffled sound, that odd scraping noise, echoed. Chills raced down her back as she thought of that odd moment of awareness on the staircase. Had someone watched? Her gaze locked on the knob of the door. She reached for the phone, ready to hit the emergency call button. With bated breath, she waited. After several minutes and nothing happened, she let out a sigh of relief. No longer willing to believe the odd noises were the wind or the house creaking, she planned to search it from top to bottom tomorrow. There had to be a secret way to get into the house, and she was going to find it.

She laid the phone down and reached to turn off a lamp she had removed from an upstairs bedroom. Then she pulled her hand back. Despite the locked door, she felt safer with the light on. This time, if whoever was out there tried to get to her, she'd see him coming.

Chapter 24

By the time Tori started the day, the morning was half gone. Reluctant but determined, she pulled her aching body out of bed. After a quick glance at the phone and the missed calls, it occurred to her that she shouldn't have put the phone on mute. The last two were from Mia. Perched on the edge of the bed, she quickly called.

"I was just about to call the cops," Mia said.

"Sorry. I put my phone on mute and just got up." After reassuring Mia she was okay, she called Parker.

"Tori, I was starting to get worried about you."

"I slept in and just saw your call." Between Mia and Parker, it was a wonder the cops weren't already pounding on her door.

"I have bad news. The report came in from the mechanic. Someone did muck with your brakes."

Unnerved, the phone trembled in her hand. "How?"

"I'll explain when I see you. I want to take a look at the garage. When can I come by?"

They set up a time later that afternoon, and he disconnected.

She sat, staring at nothing. Someone had tried to kill her a third time. Tori laughed almost hysterically. *Guess the third time wasn't the charm, after all,* she thought.

As logic slowly pushed back the fear, Tori realized she wasn't solving anything by freaking out on the edge of the bed. She wasn't going to let fear rule her life.

Tori glanced at the rest of the missed calls. They could wait. Since she'd be tramping around the property, she dressed in jeans, a sweatshirt, and the new boots she bought during the trip to the mall.

With a sense of purpose, she sat at the kitchen table and returned Dan's call.

"Parker called me about the accident. Anything I can do?"

"No, though I appreciate the call. Did he tell you someone tampered with the brakes?"

"Yes, he did. Tori, you need a bodyguard."

"No. As long as I'm home, I'm safe." Then she quipped, with a quick laugh, "I might consider a chauffeur." Tori decided not to mention her suspicions about the house until she found proof. He'd insist on having a bodyguard inside the house.

Next up, Jonah. Tori reassured him she was all right but didn't tell him what Parker had discovered. He'd find out soon enough.

While she wasn't hungry, she fixed toast and scrambled eggs. The food and a couple of cups of coffee gave her a much-needed boost of energy. With plenty of time before the fireman arrived, Tori shoved her phone in her back pocket and headed into the wine cellar. She tapped walls, crawled along the floor, and ran her hands under every shelf. If there was a hidden door, it wasn't in the cellar. Next was the library. Tori tugged and twisted pieces of wood and inspected the floor for a trapdoor, all to no avail. She did the same to the other rooms. Even her office got a cursory search.

When Tori reached the kitchen, her energy flagging, she stopped to rest. The bending and stretching didn't help her sore muscles. She'd just settled into a chair when the doorbell rang.

With a groan, Tori made her way to the door. When she opened it, Doug Coleman stood on the front porch.

"I'm early, but I hope it's okay."

She said, "Certainly. I'll meet you out back."

Grabbing a pad and pen, she walked out the back door. Doug stood near the guesthouse, looking toward the rear of the property.

"You've got a lot of land here. What did you have in mind?"

"For right now, the lawn in the front and back."

He walked to the back edge of the lawn and then looked toward the house. "Is this as far as you want me to go?"

"Yes."

His gaze swept the area. "It will take several applications of weed killer, fertilizer and reseeding. I may even have to bring in sod."

They started back and slowly worked their way around the house. When they finished, she had a list of changes. Doug said he'd work up a proposal and bring it by the next time he was off duty. As he strode to his truck, the sight of the garage was a reminder that Parker was on his way to look at it. She went back inside, dropped the pad on the table and grabbed the keys hanging on a hook by the back door.

Inside, Tori stared where Elly's car had been parked. On the floor was a stain that appeared to be fresh. Was it connected to the problem with the brakes? Parker would know. She left the overhead door open and walked out.

Her gaze swept the side of the house. It needed a new coat of paint. As she looked at the second floor, she spotted something peculiar. The windows for the master bedroom and the bedroom next to it seemed misaligned, not centered. Odd, she'd never noticed it from inside.

Intrigued, Tori headed into the house. She laid the keys to the garage on the table in the entryway before trotting up the stairs. She walked into the master bedroom. The windows were centered. Then she looked in the second bedroom, one of the smaller rooms. The window was perfectly centered. It didn't make sense. Maybe the closet in the master bedroom made the difference.

She hurried down the stairs and outside to look again at the windows. Even accounting for the closet, it still didn't look right. In fact, the closet seemed larger.

An epiphany struck—the chips. Did the single

numbers, one and three, refer to the two bedrooms? If so, was something in between? A safe?

Oblivious to her sore muscles, Tori raced back inside. This time she stopped in the hallway to study the distance between the doors to the two bedrooms.

"Oh, my gosh!" she muttered.

The walls didn't line up. Something was between them, a space wide enough for a small room. So where was the door?

Bubbling with excitement, she rushed into the second room. The wall common to the master bedroom was wood-paneled. Mindful of the safe in the library, she slowly scanned it, tapping the wood. Her fingers felt the carved edges, twisting and pushing. On her knees, she crept along the baseboard, looking for cracks.

Stymied, she dashed to the master bedroom and into the empty closet. It wasn't large, with shelves on each end and a narrow row on the back wall. She ran her hands along each shelf, looking for a locking mechanism similar to the one in the pantry. Nothing. On her knees, she studied the baseboard and almost immediately spotted faint hairline cracks. She followed them up the wall. Hidden along the edges of the short section of shelves, the width of a door, they were near invisible.

Jacked beyond excited, she spun, trying to figure out how to open it. Somewhere in this closet had to be a trigger. She started over, examining the walls. Nothing. She dropped to her knees. Tori's hands stroked the baseboard. She had stopped when she found the cracks. This time, she examined the rest of the woodwork. It wasn't until she reached the opposite corner that her fingertips felt a slight depression.

It appeared to be about the size of one of the chips. Tori pushed. Astonished, she watched the narrow section of shelves swing inward. Slowly, she stood and stepped toward the opening. The faint light from the closet barely extended into the darkened room. Thrilled by what she might find, Tori pushed the shelves back and stepped inside.

Her hands fumbled for a light switch, finding it next to the doorway. Dangling from the ceiling, a light dimly lit up the small room, slightly larger than the closet.

Two oil paintings hung on a wall. Stacks of boxes sat on the floor, and in one corner was a safe. She didn't have to go downstairs to retrieve the combination from the chip. It was imprinted in her brain. Tori twirled the dial, sucked in a deep breath of anticipation, and twisted the handle. The heavy door swung open.

Boxes filled the shelves. Tori opened the largest one. Even in the dim light, jewels in a tiara sparkled. Was it the Ludivich tiara? She picked it up. If it was, she held an irreplaceable piece of history. Carefully, she returned it to the box. The other boxes contained rings, bracelets, necklaces, and a few loose jewels.

Her thoughts whirled at the incredible find. Who could she tell? It had to be Parker since he was the only one she trusted. He'd know what to do. She started to close the safe door. A footstep sounded behind her. Before Tori could turn, something struck her head.

A sharp pain twisted viciously at the back of her head. Lying crumpled and bent, Tori wanted to touch her head but couldn't. Why? Then a horrifying awareness struck. Her hands and feet were bound. Opening her eyes, she stared into pitch-black darkness.

A mindless, intense wave of fear engulfed her. It clawed through her insides, choking the breath from her lungs. Her senses swimming, a black mist swirled at the edges of her mind. Self-preservation clung to one thought, stop the panic attack, or she would die.

Fighting through the pain and horror, Tori forced herself to take slow, deep breaths. As the debilitating fear slowly eased, her mind began to work. Curled on her side, her hands were jammed against a wall. The side of her face was wet. A familiar metallic odor filled her nose. Blood! It had to be from the blow to her head, though it didn't feel like the wound was still bleeding.

Tori slowly scooted, using her legs to thrust her body into a sitting position. Dizzy, her strength sapped by the painful blow to the head and yesterday's accident, Tori leaned back, her legs stretched out in front of her. She could rid herself of one horrifying thought. She hadn't been buried alive, which meant she had a chance to escape.

A door opened, and a light beam struck her eyes, setting off another round of sharp stabs of pain. Tori moaned.

A voice, distorted and ghostly, said, "You're awake."

Tori croaked, "Where am I?"

The light wavered as he came closer. "A place where no one will ever find you."

All she could see were shoes, but she recognized the voice—Sam Cantrell.

He stopped. "Ever since I first heard your name, you've been a thorn in my side. Now, I'm finally going to be rid of you. Though I'm grateful to you for finding the treasure."

The calm conviction in his voice sent another wave of fear crashing over her.

"How did you find it? I've searched for months," Sam asked.

Her voice stronger, she countered, "How did you know about it?"

"From an old diary, I found in Elly's office. It belonged to her mother. I stuck it in my briefcase when I realized what was in it. The woman wrote about the treasure, even described it, the paintings and jewelry, but not where it was located."

"Then it was you in my bedroom. Why?"

"The poker chips from Leichter's casino. Jonah told me about them. He was curious about the numbers and even said you had more. I knew they had to be a clue to the treasure's location.

"Why didn't you kill me and just take them?"

"Hmm ... it won't hurt to tell you." A laugh erupted. "You won't be doing any talking. It had to look like an accident. I didn't want to risk a murder investigation. It's why I damaged the valve stem on your tire and cut the brake lines on Elly's car. Either of those accidents should have killed you. But now, I don't have any choice."

"Did you try to kill me in Missouri?" Tori twisted as if to ease her position. Despite the bright light, she tried to look past the edge of the beam into the room. What little she saw was nothing but a bare floor.

Sam mused, "It was a brilliant plan, if I may say so. I found out about the trial. I could kill you and get away with it. The cops would think it was tied to the murder case. A pity I missed. Everything would have been so much simpler."

"But why?"

Impatient, his feet shifted, causing the light to flicker. Tori could see more of the room. Not that it did any good.

"Simple. If you died, the estate reverted to David. Everyone knew he'd sell. One way or the other, you were going to die before the survivor clause expired."

Tori shivered from a bone-deep chill at the unemotional tone in his voice. "Who else was involved in your scheme to kill me? Jonah? Judd?"

Sam snorted in disgust. "Those two. It would never have entered their mind. As far as they were concerned, your death would have been another tragic accident."

"Why the pressure, then, to sell?"

"Judd was just plain greedy. He was going to make a very healthy commission from the sale. I had Jonah convinced Elly was senile. The fool was trying to protect her. He pushed her to sell because he was concerned about her living alone in the house. After her death, he became convinced the house was dangerous. Judd's rants about the condition of the house only reinforced his belief. Then you showed up. Jonah thought you would give up and sell if he threw up enough roadblocks. He believed it would be in your best interest to get rid of the place."

"What about David?"

Another snort erupted. "David never believed Elly was senile. He refused to contest the will, even though it meant he would inherit. I suspect he had a fondness for the old lady."

Odd, a sense of relief overlaid the pain and fear. David hadn't tried to kill her. A feeling she'd sort out later, that is, if she got the chance.

"How did you get in the house?"

"A tunnel. Elly's mother wrote about it in the diary. You should have seen Elly's face when I told her I'd been sneaking in and out of the house for months. She was so certain no one knew about it."

"Then you did kill her!"

Sam chortled. "Another fortuitous encounter since she already suspected I'd been siphoning money from the estate."

Tori twisted, moving her legs. He stepped closer, and the light swung. She could see more of the room.

"You're just like her. You had to go nosing around. Linc told Jonah you were looking at Elly's bank statements and the checkbooks. When Jonah told me, I had to move fast before you told someone."

"Why didn't you toss me down the stairs like you did Elly?"

"Someone drove in and was snooping around the garage. I didn't have time to kill you and make it look like an accident. Instead, I had to haul you down here. As it was, I barely managed to close the door to the secret room before the man walked into the house."

Parker. He'd be looking for her, though the thought didn't spark any hope. No one knew about the tunnel.

"Since you hadn't found the treasure, why would selling the house help you? Whoever bought the house would own it."

"You still don't get it, do you? I'm the one buying the property. No one knew, including Judd and Jonah. I'll make millions on the deal. Of course, I'll miraculously discover a fortune in lost jewels and artwork. With you out of the way, nothing can stop me."

A low, demonic chortle echoed. It made her skin crawl. Sam was insane, making him all the more dangerous.

"What are you going to do with me?"

"Poof. You disappear, at least for a while. After all, Jonah can't petition the court to make David the heir without your body. An anonymous phone call and the cops will find you in some remote field in the county. Another legend in Granbury history will be born. What happened to that poor woman who inherited the Leichter estate?" Another scornful laugh erupted.

"In the meantime, Jonah will put me back in charge of the estate. I'll be able to add to my bank account from Elly's estate before I file the final tax return. Of course, by then, I will have doctored the books. No one will ever know."

Sam stepped closer. His feet were inches from her. "For now, consider this your home, fitting in a way, since it was built by your great-grandfather. Well, my dear, as much as I have enjoyed our little tête-à-tête, I must return to the house and join the search. Oh, how regretful I'll be. So distressed by your unwarranted actions toward me. What a strain you must have been under."

He leaned down, grabbed a handful of hair and jerked her forward to look at her hands. When Sam shoved her, her head slammed against the wall. "Very good. You won't be going anywhere."

Bile rose in her throat as searing pain sliced through her.

Another laugh echoed. Sam's voice faded. "It won't do you any good to scream. No one will hear you."

Chapter 25

The door closed, and darkness encased her. Hot needles stabbed her head. Blood seeped down her neck. Tori had never felt such intense pain. Everything was spinning. She couldn't pass out. Breathe, slow, even breaths, she kept telling herself. Shifting to ease the pressure on her head, something poked her butt. Still dizzy, it took a moment to realize it was the phone. Tucked in a back pocket of her jeans, the oversized sweatshirt had covered it.

But it wouldn't do her any good, or would it? Hope flared. Was it possible? At least she had learned something useful when Sam flashed his light around. He used tape.

It took some maneuvering, twisting and turning her body before she could get her fingers around the edge of the phone. Tori tugged. It slipped from her grasp. Frantic, her hands scraped the floor until she found it.

She fingered it to make sure it was screen-side up before sliding over it. The screen's glow let her keep track of it as she scooted until the phone was at the back of her heels. Tori lifted her legs and slammed her feet down. She missed, and the phone slid.

She repositioned and tried again. The heel of her boot struck the glass. Off-balance, she fell back. Her head hit the floor. This time she couldn't stop the slide into darkness.

When Tori came to, her sweatshirt clung to her back. How much blood had she lost? Getting upright again was a torturous struggle. Her strength waning, she sucked in a deep breath before groping for a piece of glass. There had to be one large enough. The movements intensified the pain, excruciating and deep, that pounded in her head.

A sense of urgency drove her. If she didn't get out of this room fast, Sam wouldn't have to kill her. Minutes passed. Desperation built as each piece was too little. Then one stabbed her finger. Barely large enough, it might work. Thumb braced on one side, her fingers formed a claw. A shock rippled through her. She couldn't reach the edge of the tape because of how her hands were tied.

No matter how she twisted them, it was hopeless. Her shoulders slumped in despair. She had to rest, even if it meant leaning her head against the wall, while her mind raced to figure out a way to cut the tape. An idea erupted. Would it work?

Holding the glass in one hand, she slid the knuckles on the other across the floor, searching for a gap between the wood slats. When Tori found one, she maneuvered the glass into place, jamming it between the boards. With cautious movements to keep from jarring it, Tori squirmed until the edge of the tape was against the broken piece. Slowly, she sawed.

Unable to keep her fingers steady, they grew wet with blood from scraping the glass. Tori couldn't tell if she was even cutting the tape, but she had to keep going, even though the motions were steadily getting weaker.

At the slight give between her hands, adrenaline spiked. Tori twisted and tugged until the tape split. Her hands were free but numb. She shook her arms, rubbing her hands until the feeling returned. Wiping them on her sweatshirt, she picked at the tape around her feet. Unable to see, her fingers sore and trembling, she couldn't grasp the end.

She'd have to cut it with the glass. If it didn't work, she might be able to untie the boots and slip out of them. Tori sawed with the piece of glass, pushing deep with hard strokes. The tape tore, and she was able to grab the end, ripping it from her ankles.

Despite the nausea and lightheadedness, she pushed herself to her feet. In what she hoped was a straight line, Tori moved forward, her arms outstretched. She refused to give in to the fear the door could be locked. If it was, she was doomed.

Touching the wall, she moved sideways, only to discover she'd gone the wrong way. She collided with an end wall. For a moment, Tori rested her forehead against the wood before going back the other way. The doctor's words suddenly came to mind. "Nothing strenuous." *Right doc*, she thought.

Though her steps were slower, she kept moving until

her hand rubbed the edge of the door. Fumbling for the knob, she turned it. It opened, and she staggered out. Hanging onto the door, she felt for the wall before letting go. Her back against it, Tori's head moved from side to side. While she was out of the room, she still had no idea where she was. Woozy from the pain and loss of blood, it was hard to think.

Sam had mentioned a tunnel and the room Frankie built. She had to be somewhere close to the house. But which way? Tori didn't dare stray from the wall. It was her only point of reference in the total darkness. She couldn't even see her hand in front of her face. But in one direction, it didn't seem as intense.

Her hand on the wall, Tori shuffled, testing the ground in front of her before taking a step. It was dirt and could have holes or obstacles she couldn't see. It was slow going, and Tori was getting weaker. How much longer could she even stay on her feet?

Another step, then she lost contact with the wall. Tori stepped back, her arm flailing. Relief almost took her to her knees when the back of her hand smacked the wall. This time her hand inched forward. The tunnel turned. As Tori eased around it, she could see a faint glow ahead. Staggering, she kept moving forward. The glow turned into an outline of light above a ladder.

She grasped the rails, but her hands, wet with blood, slipped. Tori wiped them on her pants and tried again. Pulling on her remaining strength, she hauled herself up. With one hand wrapped around the rail to keep from falling, she pushed on the cover with the other. It wobbled and dropped back down. She muttered, "Just do it," and shoved with a last burst of energy. The cover flew back. Tori crawled out, collapsing on the ground. It was almost dark.

In the distance, she heard voices. She wanted to cry out, but where was Sam? He said he was joining the search. If he reached her before the others, she'd be dead.

As the voices drew nearer, it was David and Parker. Tori tried to stand but couldn't. Before she could scream, she heard Sam's voice. Frightened, she huddled in the weeds, barely breathing.

"I've already looked in this area," Sam said. "We should move to the other side of the property."

Parker said, "I'll head that way. Cantrell, come with me. You know this place better than I do."

"I'll circle around this side," David said, "and meet you there."

Persistent, Sam said, "I still think we are wasting time here."

David said, "Maybe so, but I want to take another look at that old well. I'm not taking a chance."

Footsteps came closer. Whose were they?

When David came into view, she cried, "David."

He shouted, "I've found her," dropping to his knees beside her. "She's hurt. Get an ambulance."

As he scooped her off the ground, Tori, her voice faint, said, "Sam tried to kill me."

"Tori?" When she didn't answer, his heart pounding from the fear ripping his insides, he picked up his pace. Parker and Sam ran toward him.

"She's unconscious." For now, David couldn't do anything about Sam except keep him away from Tori.

Striding alongside him, Sam said, "Why don't you let me take her. You and Parker can go ahead and get help."

So you can kill her, he thought. "No! I don't want to move her any more than necessary. I don't know how bad she's hurt. Sam, you go ahead and let the others know."

He hesitated but finally turned and trotted away.

David softly whispered, "Parker, stay with him. Tori said he tried to kill her."

Without a word, Parker took off, running to catch up with Sam.

As David climbed the steps, Mia stood by the open door. When she got a good look at Tori, covered with blood, she gasped, "How bad?" as he brushed by her.

"I don't know. Did someone call an ambulance?"

"I did. I was watching from the back porch and heard you shout. Put her on the couch. I've already got it ready."

David gently laid her down, easing her head against the pillow. His gaze swept over her. Blood matted her hair. It streaked down her face and neck, staining her sweatshirt and jeans.

Beside him, Mia held a wet towel. She cried out, "David! Her hands."

Cut and bloody, pieces of tape adhered to her wrists. An indescribable rage built in him at the sight. David glanced around the room. Where was Sam? Had he escaped? Cantrell had better hope the cops got to him first.

At the sound of a ruckus by the door, David looked over his shoulder. Two cops dragged Sam into the room, his clothes dirty and his face bruised. Parker trailed behind them just as dirty and disheveled, with blood oozing from a cut over his eye.

"Let me go. I didn't do anything. I'll sue you for assault and false arrest," Sam screamed.

The officers shoved him into a chair. He stared at Tori with a malevolent expression.

David turned his attention back to Tori and saw her eyes blink.

It was the warmth of a wet cloth on her forehead that Tori felt as her mind began to clear. David's face came into view as he bent over her.

She panicked. Her hand clutched David's arm. She whispered, "Where's Sam?"

David leaned closer. "Don't worry. You're safe."

A medic raced in, followed by a second one pulling a stretcher.

David and Mia stepped to the side.

The first one knelt next to the couch. "I told you we had to stop meeting this way."

While the medic examined the wound on Tori's head, a

police officer knelt beside the couch. "Can you tell me what happened?"

Her voice weak, Tori said, "Sam Cantrell tried to kill me."

Sam leaped to his feet, only to be pushed back into the chair by one of the cops. He screamed, "She's lying. I never touched her. And you can't prove I did."

Her voice faint but determined, Tori said, "Look at his shoes. They've got my blood on them." The room was spinning, and she knew she was going under again.

The medic exclaimed, "That's enough. Let's get her to the hospital. Anything else will have to wait."

When Tori woke, voices murmured. She was in a hospital bed. David and Parker stood in the corner, and Mia was in a chair. She lifted a hand to find it was bandaged.

Alerted by her movement, Mia jumped up. "She's awake." She rushed to the side of the bed. David and Parker stepped alongside her.

Her face pale with worry, Mia asked, "How do you feel?"

"Warm and fuzzy." Her words slightly slurred, she added, "Hey, with the drugs that are probably racing in my system, I just hope I make sense. How bad?"

Mia said, "Not as bad as you looked when David carried you into the house. The doc sewed up your head and the cuts on your hands and replaced the blood you lost."

"Parker, what happened to you?" Tori eyed the bandage on his forehead.

David answered for him. "Sam tried to get away, and Parker stopped him."

Her body tensed. "Sam?"

Parker said, "Don't worry. He's in jail and not going anywhere."

Relaxing, she asked, "When can I go home?"

"Maybe tomorrow. You have a concussion," Mia said.

"If you feel up to it, the police want to talk to you," Parker told her.

She nodded. Parker stepped to the door, and a few minutes later, a man in plain clothes walked in.

"Ms. Winters, I'm Detective Grayson. I have a few questions. If you get tired, let me know. I'll be recording our conversation." He placed a small tape recorder on the table. "I'll need everyone to leave."

"No," Tori said. "Please. I'd like for them to stay."

"All right, with the understanding that nothing Ms. Winters says is to be repeated other than among yourselves." After identifying himself and the individuals in the room, he said, "Tell me what happened."

It took a while, but she told him everything except about the room she'd found. It would have to wait. Once she had answered Grayson's questions, he picked up the recorder and left, followed by Mia, who had tears streaming down her face.

Grim-faced by Tori's revelations, Parker and David stepped beside the bed.

David's hand lightly touched her arm. "You are an amazing woman."

A warm sensation seeped through her, something else she'd have to think about later.

Parker asked, "Did you know there was a tunnel?"

"I didn't until Sam dumped me there."

"Seems no one else did either. We backtracked from where David found you and located the room."

Parker wasn't about to tell her how devastating the crime scene was. Bloodstains on the wall and floor, bloody pieces of tape and glass, and bloody handprints all along the walls inside and outside the room. The bloodstains on the floor sealed Cantrell's fate. He didn't know that he had stepped in the blood. Not only was the blood on his shoes, but he'd left bloody footprints. If Cantrell hadn't already been in police custody, Parker didn't know if he could have stopped David from killing the man. The police had obtained a search warrant and were searching Cantrell's house. Parker expected they'd find more evidence.

The door opened. Mia walked in, followed by Heidi, Tina, and Cammie.

Since he knew the doctor had limited the number of visitors, Parker said, "Didn't the nurse try to stop you?"

Mia said, "I know someone."

Tori chuckled. "Of course, you do."

Heidi said, "We're staying long enough to see how you are doing."

The four women formed a line at the end of the bed.

Mia said, "Okay, here's the deal. If they let you out tomorrow, I'll be here to take you home. You are to follow orders when we get there." She looked at the three women beside her. "No arguments. If you don't, we'll make sure you do."

Tori smiled. "Yes, ma'am."

Seeing the strain on Tori's face, Mia said, "Time for everyone to leave."

With tears in their eyes, Heidi, Cammie, and Tina kissed her cheek before walking out.

Mia sniffed. "You scared the hell out of us when you disappeared. I don't want to ever feel like that again." Unable to grasp Tori's bandaged hands, Mia touched the back of her hand against Tori's face, then turned and walked out.

David leaned over her. His eyes gleamed with a warm light as his fingertips brushed her lips. At the startled look in her eyes, he smiled. "I'll ... see you tomorrow."

Parker gave her a small salute as he followed David.

Once the room cleared, a nurse turned down the lights. As she drifted off to sleep, Ethel's words came to mind. She was right when she said, "The house and its secrets killed Elly." And the secrets had come close to killing her.

Chapter 26

A week later

Her hands and wrists still bandaged, Tori pecked at the keyboard with two fingers. Layton had called. Ready to release her jewelry, he needed an address. Tori didn't have to fess up. He'd seen the news story and learned she was in Texas. She'd become an overnight sensation. A real rags to riches kind of story, mixed with murder, a missing treasure, and Texas-sized skullduggery, one reporter had written.

Tori glanced at her watch. She still had some time before the appointment with another contractor.

She leaned back, and as was the case whenever she relaxed, her thoughts spun back to that horrific day. A nightmare she couldn't stop reliving. But it wasn't the first time it had happened. Like Springfield, she knew it would take time to leave it in the past.

Sam's plan might have worked if it hadn't been for Parker and Mia. No one would have known she was missing until the next day, giving Sam ample time to kill her and dump her body in some field.

Parker had found the house and garage unlocked. Then Mia showed up, concerned when Tori didn't answer the phone. The man assigned to watch the house said she was inside. When she wasn't, Parker called out the troops, first the cops, then Dan, who in turn called Jonah. Jonah and Linc showed up with David close behind. Mia called her team, and they rushed over.

With a search underway, Sam was stuck. He had to wait to get rid of her, though he showed up to keep an eye on the search. Parker said Sam had strutted around, proclaiming his concern.

Parker had already decided to watch all the suspects. In his books, Sam was at the top of the list. He never let the man out of his sight. After David found her, Sam tried to leave, but Parker stopped him, albeit not without a struggle.

Once she was on the way to the hospital, the men backtracked and found the entrance to the tunnel near the old well house. It led to the door underneath the attic staircase.

The day she was released from the hospital, she called Parker, David, Jonah, and Linc, despite Mia's very vocal objections, and asked them to come to the house. When she showed them the room and contents, it jumpstarted an intense discussion. What to do with the paintings and jewelry? Parker finally called his friend with the FBI, triggering a full-scale investigation.

The two artists, Langford and Sewell, were not well-known. Nevertheless, their paintings were extremely valuable. Before the paintings could be moved, experts had to be consulted. It took three days before the paintings were transported to the Kimball Art Museum in Fort Worth to be authenticated. An FBI agent showed up, took pictures of the room and safe, then confiscated the jewelry. She still didn't know whether the paintings or the jewelry had been stolen. Parker had told her it would take a few weeks.

David came by one evening. They talked, though Mia limited the visit. It turned out David suspected Elly had been murdered and initiated his own investigation. It's why he was 'johnny on the spot' the night she chased Sam out of the house. And, there wasn't a poker game that night. He'd been keeping an eye on the place. He told her that he thought he saw a flicker of light on several occasions when the house was empty. But when he searched, he didn't find anyone.

When Tori had the first car accident, his concern deepened, but all he had was conjecture, though Linc was his prime suspect. Linc had sounded him out about contesting the will. It's what caused the rift between David and the Greers. David wasn't willing to declare Elly incompetent. While Tori felt they had more to say, it had to wait. Between the concussion and loss of blood, she quickly tired.

Her grandmother's book, the one Sam stole, had been found in his house. Ironically, Tori had proof of the embezzlement in the small notebook she'd found in Elly's purse. It seems she had another connection to Elly—to-do lists. Her grandmother had written several references about unauthorized payments and her activities to prove Sam had been stealing money.

Tori also discovered a false bottom in one of the drawers in the desk. Inside the compartment was a stack of Elly's notepads. There were also boxes in the secret room that contained more of her grandmother's journals. One day, when everything had settled, she'd take time to read them.

The revelations about Sam's embezzlements and attempts to kill Tori set off a flood of rumors and conjectures. During a visit, Jonah and Linc admitted their actions were prompted by Sam's recommendations to sell the house. They had believed him when he said Elly was senile. After all, as Elly's financial advisor and administrator, Sam had more contact with her than they did.

Jonah, who looked like he'd aged ten years, said he thought he was acting in Tori's best interest in how he handled the whole affair. He would understand if she decided to fire him. She didn't, nor did she tell him that both he and his son had become her prime suspects. Nothing was to be gained by adding fuel to what was already a painful subject.

As for the poker chips, she hoped there would be a clue about them in Elly's journals. If not, she had to figure it was Elly's way of pointing her to the treasure. It certainly worked. She had some ideas about what she could do with them, but that was down the line.

"What do you think you're doing?"

Startled, Tori looked up.

Mia glared at her from the doorway. "Until your hands are healed, the Doc told you to not break open those cuts. You don't need to be typing."

Mia and her crew had become absolutely militant in

watching her every move. Tori grumbled, "I'm being careful, but I've got to do something. I can't sit around. I've been working on the wine cellar inventory. This is an old list. Jonah said it wasn't updated for the probate, which is something I need to do."

"Not yet, you don't."

A wry chuckle erupted. "I know. Not until my hands are healed."

"Yep. Not a good patient, are you?"

Tori grinned. "No, I'm not."

"Well, this should brighten your day. You've got visitors."

She perked up. "Who?" Mia and her team had zealously guarded the front door. No one got in without Mia's approval. Daily, it seemed, the doorbell rang, and it was another reporter.

With an evil grin, Mia said, "Myra and Carly."

"Oh … you didn't."

"Yes, I did. They are in the living room."

Tori rose, and as she passed Mia, she hissed, "I'll get even."

The two women, perched on the edge of the couch, turned as she entered.

Myra's eyes dropped to Tori's bandaged hands. The only evidence of embarrassment was the tinge of red that blossomed on her cheeks.

"Hello, Myra, Carly."

"Oh, my dear. How *are* you doing? Such a dreadful experience, though I must say the outcome has been nothing short of spectacular."

Obviously, Myra was going to ignore that her husband had also been sucked into Cantrell's plot. Unlike Jonah and Linc, he wasn't fessing up to anything.

Carly gave her a patronizing nod. Tori gritted her teeth.

"Please, do sit down. I'll get a crick in my neck if I have to keep looking up at you," Myra told her.

Tori figured the fastest way to get rid of them was to find out what they wanted. They didn't drop by out of any concern for her well-being. She sat.

"The reason we are here is ... well, of course, we wanted to see how you were doing, but also to find out your plans for the jewels and paintings."

"I don't have any until the investigation is complete."

Myra waved a hand as if shooing a fly. "Mere bagatelle. Jonah informs me it's routine in cases like this. I have a suggestion."

Of course, you do, Tori thought, though her expression remained mildly interested.

"You need to sponsor a charity event and have the paintings and jewelry on display. I expect it would be a sell-out. Of course, we," her hand motioned toward Carly, "would host it since I'm certain you've never had any experience with such a large-scale event. The country club has several available dates in the near future."

Carly piped up. "I spoke to *David* about it. He's quite excited over the idea and has promised to help."

"How nice." *In a pig's eye,* she thought. "It's a wonderful thought, Myra."

The woman's lips pursed into a pompous smile.

"However, I can't commit to any, as you say, large-scale events in the near future. Perhaps down the line, I'll reconsider."

Maybe she would forgive Mia for letting them into the house. Seeing Myra's face collapse was worth it.

Tori rose. "Thank you for stopping by since I know *you* have a busy schedule."

With no choice, they stood. After the front door closed behind them, Tori turned. "All right, where are you?"

Mia stuck her head around the door to the music room. Laughter bubbled from her. "Sorry, I couldn't resist. What a pair those two are. What's the old saying, birds of a feather?"

The doorbell rang again. Still thinking about Myra, she frowned as she opened it.

A tall, broad-shouldered man dressed in pressed blue jeans and a white long-sleeved shirt with pearl snaps stood on her front porch. Grey eyes twinkled with humor in a tanned, rough-hewn face. A dark scruff of beard covered a determined jaw. From the black felt cowboy hat, to the belt with the oversized buckle, to the alligator boots, he was the epitome of a Texas cowboy. The only discordant note was the briefcase dangling from one hand.

"Ma'am, I'm Colter McLean. I have an appointment with Tori Winters." His face concerned, he asked, "I hope I didn't come at a bad time."

Jolted out of her stupor, she laughed. "No, and I'm Tori Winters. Please come in."

He removed his hat as he stepped into the entryway, gazing about him, studying the staircase, then looking up at the chandelier. He drawled in a slow, mild tone, "I've seen some mighty fine old houses in my time, but this is about as fine a one as I've ever seen. She just needs to be prettied up."

Mia strolled out of the music room, heading toward them.

Colter, seeing her, nodded his head.

"Mr. McLean, this is the head of my team, Mia O'Brien."

"Nice to meet you, ma'am. It's Colter. Actually, most people call me Colt. Mr. McLean is my father."

Her eyes lit up with interest. Mia said, "You're the contractor?"

"Yes, I am."

Tori asked, "Would you like something to drink? Coffee, tea, soda. We have most anything."

"Not right yet. Before we get down to the brass tacks, would you please give me a tour? I need an idea of what is involved. And, even if you don't hire me, I'd like to see this house."

"Okay, let's start with the library."

"Nice to meet you, Colt. Tori, I'll be in the kitchen if you need anything," Mia said.

Inside the library, the hat and briefcase were laid on a table as his gaze swept the room. "You said your team?"

Impressed that he'd picked up on the introduction, she said, "Yes, four extraordinary women. If you come on board, you'll get to know them quite well."

From inside the briefcase, he pulled out a computer notepad and stylus. As they moved from room to room, Tori outlined her vision for the inn. Colt took copious notes and pictures. He had an eye for detail and didn't miss much. And he didn't hesitate to disagree when an idea didn't work, even explaining why in layman's terms. The other two contractors she'd interviewed placated her by agreeing to any suggestion.

It wasn't long before Tori began to eye his notepad with interest, surprised the use of one had never occurred to her. Handy, and so much easier than carrying paper notepads and pen. She made a mental note to purchase one.

Before heading upstairs, she showed him the wine cellar.

Colt said, "This is truly impressive."

With a smug smile, she said, "Yes, and I have some ideas I'd like to discuss with you."

Next, they headed upstairs. At the sound of their voices, Heidi, Tina, and Cammie, already alerted by Mia, popped out of the rooms. She introduced each as a member of her team, but as with Mia, the comment went right over their heads. She suppressed the excitement about the grand announcement she planned to make later.

In the master bedroom, she activated the switch to open the door to the secret room, then switched on the light.

"I read about this in the paper," Colt said as he looked around. "What do you have in mind for the room?"

"I'm not sure. Any suggestions?"

"Let me think about it."

After he finished examining the attic, she showed him

the door concealed underneath the staircase. As she slid it open, the wood creaked and scraped the floor, the mysterious sound she'd never been able to identify.

"Now, if that don't beat all, " he commented. "Where does it lead?"

"A small room at the bottom of the stairs. I think it's next to the wine cellar under the kitchen. It has a door that opens into the tunnel."

Colt followed her down the stairs. From a table, Tori grabbed a flashlight, then opened the door.

Her voice echoed in the dark, dank tunnel. "I don't know if you are aware of the history of this house. My great-grandfather Frankie Leichter, a notorious crime lord in the 1930s and 40s, built it. I'm not certain, but I think these rooms were used to store liquor and guns." The door to the one where Cantrell dumped her was closed, and she didn't open it. Tori didn't want to answer questions about the blood inside the room, though she shuddered as she walked by it.

At the end, they climbed out.

Colt eyed the wooden structure. "What is this?"

"The old well house. It needs to be torn down."

He turned to look back at the entrance to the tunnel. "I didn't believe I could ever be astonished by a feature of a house, but you have proved me wrong. Do you have any plans for the tunnel?"

"Not yet. Still thinking about it." They stopped to survey the guesthouse and garage on their way back to the house.

Colt gazed around the property. "The potential is

amazing."

With a satisfied smile, she said, "Yes. I think so. Let's go see about those brass tacks." As they passed through the kitchen, Tori poured two cups of coffee.

What followed was an intense couple of hours discussing the renovations. At the end, Colt asked, "Do you want me to draw up a contract?"

"Yes, I do. I'll need two copies. One I'll forward to my attorney, Daniel Foote."

With an expression of approval, he said, "I've worked with Dan in the past. A good man."

As he stood, she reached across the desk, extending her hand, stitches and all. He gingerly shook it as she said, "Welcome to my team. This is going to be an adventure."

Colt smiled. "Yes, ma'am. I believe it will be."

After he left, Mia marched into her office and plopped in the chair. Fanning herself with her hand, she said, "Be still my heart. Tell me you hired him. Please, please tell me you did."

Tori danced around the desk. "I did, yes, I did. All that's left is to sign the contract. Where is everyone?"

"Upstairs, why?"

"Tell them they are done for the day. I'd like to talk to them."

Puzzled, Mia said, "Be right back."

When everyone was in the office, she asked, "Does anyone have any earthshaking plans tonight?"

Mystified, the women shook their heads.

"Well, now you do. It's party time, and we're going to

celebrate. I do believe I've got some dang fancy champagne in the cellar. I'd go, but Mia will start nagging about my hands. Who wants to volunteer? We need to get it on ice."

Heidi said, "I'll get it. How many bottles?"

"Oh, at least four or five. Pizza okay with everyone?"

On her new cellphone, Tori called and ordered the pizza. Mia went with Heidi to get the champagne. Tina made a run to get ice. Cammie set the table. Once the ice arrived, bottles of champagne were placed in the large sink in the utility room and ice dumped around them. All the while, they chattered. The main topic was Colt McLean.

When the doorbell rang, Cammie said, "I'll get it," expecting it would be the delivery man. Instead, David walked in.

Mia rolled her eyes at Tori, who gave her a narrow-eyed look before turning to say hello. Ever since David's dramatic entry as he carried her in his arms, she'd been the brunt of many jokes, even references to Rhett Butler and Scarlett O'Hara in *Gone With the Wind.*

"What's going on?" he asked, looking at the preparations.

"A party. I hired a contractor."

"Colter?"

"Okay, how'd you know?" Tori asked.

"He's a friend. We play poker together."

"You do? Why didn't Mia know him? She knows everyone." Tori glowered at him.

"He just moved here from Houston. We were roommates at Texas A&M. What's the big deal?"

"Just for once, I'd like to do something before everyone else knows I'm going to do it."

All four women laughed. The doorbell rang again.

Heidi said, "That has to be the pizza."

"You really are having a party? Can I get an invite?"

Tori looked at everyone. "Should we take pity on him?"

"After the way, he carried you into this house, I'd say it's the least you could do," Mia said with a knowing smile.

The bell rang again. "While you ladies argue about it, I'll get the pizza."

When he returned, his arms loaded with boxes, he said, "My god, this is enough to feed an army."

Tori asked, "Do you think the champagne is cold?"

"I don't know. Let's check." Mia said, walking into the utility room with Tori and David behind her.

David's eyes widened. "Champagne?" He threw back his head as laughter erupted at the sight of the bottles in the sink.

Tori and Mia glared at him.

When he was finally able to talk, he said, "Really! In the sink? Do you realize that you have over a thousand dollars sitting in ice in the *sink*?"

Tori said, "It doesn't matter. We plan to drink every drop of it."

"Okay, grab a couple of bottles. I'll open them, otherwise, you'll spray the stuff all over the kitchen."

When they were seated with the Waterford glasses filled with the amber liquid and plates piled with slices of pizza, Tori stood.

She raised her glass. "A toast … to Elly."

Everyone cheered, clinking their glasses. "To Elly."

David said, "I wonder what she'd think if she saw this."

Tori's face glowed. "I think she would approve."

For a moment, her gaze scanned the faces of the four women who had become her family. She tapped her glass with a fork. "And now, I have another announcement."

Once all eyes were on her, she said, "You have been with me from the start. This house isn't just about me. It's about us. So, I've made a decision. The future of this house belongs to all of us." She motioned with her glass to each woman. "Mia, Heidi, Cammie, Tina. I want you to be my team. Let's turn this place into the finest bed and breakfast inn that Granbury … no … Texas has ever seen."

Mia gasped. "Oh, my god! That's what you meant when you introduced me to Colt as the head of your team. Jeez, it went right over my head. How in heaven's name did I miss it?"

With a knowing grin, Tori said, "All of you missed it. I suspect you had something, or should I say, someone else on your minds. How about it, ladies? Are you in?"

All four gave a resounding yes.

Tori lifted her glass. "A toast. To my team and the future of the new Red Door Inn."

As they cheered, David stood. He waited until he had their attention.

"My turn." His eyes gleamed as he lifted his glass. "To Tori, an amazing woman, who won't give up."

The Story Behind the Fiction

Dallas Crime Lord

While Frankie Leichter is fictional, the character is grounded in fact. Benny Binion was born in 1904 in Pilot Grove, Texas, a small town north of Dallas. Binion's career started in the prohibition era, moonshining. His criminal history included thefts, weapons charges, and murder convictions.

In the late 1920s, Binion branched into the numbers game. By the 1930s, he had gained control of most of the gambling syndicate in Dallas and soon became the kingpin, the mob boss of Dallas.

Many casinos were located in hotels, the main one in the Strickland Hotel. It became known as the Southland Syndicate.

Binion was ruthless, and his enforcers didn't hesitate to use deadly force to eliminate the competition. Witnesses had a way of disappearing. Nicknamed "The Cowboy" for killing a rum-runner, cowboy style, Binion was convicted of the murder.

In the 1940s, Binion tried to expand his illegal gambling operation into Fort Worth. He bought his way into the operation of the fancy and popular Top O' Hill Terrace in Arlington when the owner couldn't pay his gambling debts.

While the restaurant was a legitimate business, the basement housed the crap, poker, blackjack, slot machines and roulette wheels.

Guards and dogs protected the area, and a locked gate provided ample warning of a raid. The gambling equipment could be quickly moved behind wood-paneled walls, and a tunnel allowed guests to escape into the woods or to the tea garden.

The Top O' Hill Terrace still exists and is now a museum. During the facility's renovation, an "RM" poker chip was found and is believed to have been used in Binion's casino.

When the Dallas political climate changed, Benny Binion fled to Las Vegas, where he opened the Horseshoe Casino.

Additional information on the Top O' Hill Terrace Museum can be found at: https://www.topohillterrace.com/

Granbury, Texas

Selecting a location for my novels is always a fun-filled endeavor, an adventure. This time, I needed a place that provided a wide variety of interests for a new series, the Tori Winters Mysteries.

Located southwest of Fort Worth, Granbury's rich culture and history was the perfect setting. The historic square, unique shops, the fabulous courthouse with the clock tower, the historic and still operational Opera House, wineries, Lake Granbury, historic houses, a trolley, drive-in movie theater, and even a ghost tour provide a plethora of backdrops for not only my first book, *Deadly Keepsakes*, but also the books to follow.

A few I have already used in this book. One of which was the Granbury Opera House. I'm certain my words didn't do justice to this historic site's breathtaking beauty and elegance.

There is a beach, and the Bulls on the Beach, bull riding, is an actual event. There is even an attorney's office with a herd of cattle painted on the side. Of course, something similar became the office for Jonah Greer.

I am looking forward to the next book in the series and the unique activities and culture of Granbury I can use to bring my characters and scenery to life.

For more information about this quaint town, please visit:

https://www.visitgranbury.com/

About the Author

Anita Dickason is a twenty-two-year veteran of the Dallas Police Department, where she served as a patrol officer, undercover narcotics detective, advanced accident investigator, and Dallas SWAT tactical officer and first female sniper.

Her law enforcement experience and knowledge provide an endless source of inspiration for her characters and plots.

Please leave a review at your favorite retail outlet if you enjoyed the book.

Additional information can be found at:
anitadickason.com

https://www.facebook.com/AnitaDickasonAuthor
https://twitter.com/anita_dickason
https://www.pinterest.com/anitadickason
https://www.linkedin.com/in/anita-dickason-7b6b6650
https://vimeo.com/anitadickason

An Author's World YouTube
https://www.youtube.com/channel/UCyR63cX0YBdIGnu6DTSGztQ

Book Chatter & More YouTube
https://www.youtube.com/channel/UCkntQMs-GMOhS184NRDW8pqw